Nirali's New Series

CONCISE STUDY SERIES

(50 Marks)

ELECTRICAL MEASUREMENTS AND INSTRUMENTATION

Sem - I

S.E ELECTRICAL ENGINEERING

As per New Revised Syllabus of University of Pune

(Pattern 2012)

Mrs. Leena N. Suranglikar
M. E. (Electrical)
Pune.

ELECTRICAL MEASUREMENTS & INSTRUMENTATION (SE ELECTRICAL)

First Edition : June 2014

© : Author

The text of this publication, or any part thereof, should not be reproduced or transmitted in any form or stored in any computer storage system or device for distribution including photocopy, recording, taping or information retrieval system or reproduced on any disc, tape, perforated media or other information storage device etc., without the written permission of Authors with whom the rights are reserved. Breach of this condition is liable for legal action.

Every effort has been made to avoid errors or omissions in this publication. In spite of this, errors may have crept in. Any mistake, error or discrepancy so noted and shall be brought to our notice shall be taken care of in the next edition. It is notified that neither the publisher nor the authors or seller shall be responsible for any damage or loss of action to any one, of any kind, in any manner, therefrom.

Published By :
NIRALI PRAKASHAN
Abhyudaya Pragati, 1312, Shivaji Nagar,
Off J.M. Road, PUNE – 411005
Tel - (020) 25512336/37/39, Fax - (020) 25511379
Email : niralipune@pragationline.com

DISTRIBUTION CENTRES
PUNE

Nirali Prakashan
119, Budhwar Peth, Jogeshwari Mandir Lane
Pune 411002, Maharashtra
Tel : (020) 2445 2044, 66022708, Fax : (020) 2445 1538
Email : bookorder@pragationline.com

Nirali Prakashan
S. No. 28/25, Dhyari,
Near Pari Company, Pune 411041
Tel : (022) 24690204 Fax : (020) 24690316
Email : dhyari@pragationline.com
bookorder@pragationline.com

MUMBAI
Nirali Prakashan
385, S.V.P. Road, Rasdhara Co-op. Hsg. Society Ltd.,
Girgaum, Mumbai 400004, Maharashtra
Tel : (022) 2385 6339 / 2386 9976, Fax : (022) 2386 9976
Email : niralimumbai@pragationline.com

DISTRIBUTION BRANCHES

NAGPUR
Pratibha Book Distributors
Above Maratha Mandir, Shop No. 3, First Floor,
Rani Jhanshi Square, Sitabuldi, Nagpur 440012,
Maharashtra, Tel : (0712) 254 7129

JALGAON
Nirali Prakashan
34, V. V. Golani Market, Navi Peth, Jalgaon 425001,
Maharashtra, Tel : (0257) 222 0395
Mob : 94234 91860

BENGALURU
Pragati Book House
House No. 1, Sanjeevappa Lane, Avenue Road Cross,
Opp. Rice Church, Bengaluru – 560002.
Tel : (080) 64513344, 64513355,
Mob : 9880582331, 9845021552
Email:bharatsavla@yahoo.com

KOLHAPUR
Nirali Prakashan
New Mahadvar Road,
Kedar Plaza, 1st Floor Opp. IDBI Bank
Kolhapur 416 012, Maharashtra. Mob : 9855046155

CHENNAI
Pragati Books
9/1, Montieth Road, Behind Taas Mahal, Egmore,
Chennai 600008 Tamil Nadu, Tel : (044) 6518 3535,
Mob : 94440 01782 / 98450 21552 / 98805 82331, Email : bharatsavla@yahoo.com

RETAIL OUTLETS
PUNE

Pragati Book Centre
157, Budhwar Peth, Opp. Ratan Talkies,
Pune 411002, Maharashtra
Tel : (020) 2445 8887 / 6602 2707, Fax : (020) 2445 8887

Pragati Book Centre
676/B, Budhwar Peth, Opp. Jogeshwari Mandir,
Pune 411002, Maharashtra
Tel : (020) 6601 7784 / 6602 0855

Pragati Book Centre
Amber Chamber, 28/A, Budhwar Peth,
Appa Balwant Chowk, Pune : 411002, Maharashtra,
Tel : (020) 20240335 / 66281669
Email : pbcpune@pragationline.com

PBC Book Sellers & Stationers
152, Budhwar Peth, Pune 411002, Maharashtra
Tel : (020) 2445 2254 / 6609 2463

MUMBAI
Pragati Book Corner
Indira Niwas, 111 - A, Bhavani Shankar Road, Dadar (W), Mumbai 400028, Maharashtra
Tel : (022) 2422 3526 / 6662 5254, Email : pbcmumbai@pragationline.com

www.pragationline.com   info@pragationline.com

Dear Students,

It gives us great pleasure to introduce a New Series **"Concise Study Series"** for Second Year Engineering students. These **"CSS"** books are written by Experienced and Eminent Professors of respective subjects.

The specialty of this new Series **"CSS"** is that it:

- Covers full syllabus of University of Pune.
- Contains Matter written in Simple and Lucid language.
- Includes "To the Point" Topics and well arranged articles.
- Includes Most Likely Questions.
- Includes Previous Years University Question Papers.
- Available in all leading stores at Affordable Price.

Happy Studying and Best of Luck!!!

Nirali Prakashan

SYLLABUS

Unit 1 (A) Classification of Measuring Instruments

Characteristics of measuring instruments: Static and dynamic, accuracy, linearity, speed of response, dead zone, repeatability, resolution, span, reproducibility, drifts. Necessity of calibration, Absolute and secondary instruments, types of secondary instruments: indicating, integrating, and recording, analog / digital. Ammeter and Voltmeter theory: Essentials of indicating instruments deflecting, controlling and damping systems. Construction, working principle, torque equation, advantages and disadvantages of Moving Iron (MI) (attraction and repulsion), and Permanent Magnet Moving Coil (PMMC). *-

(B) Range Extension : PMMC ammeters and voltmeters using shunts, multipliers. Universal shunt, Universal multiplier. Instrument Transformers: Construction, connection of CT & PT in the circuit, advantages of CT / PT over shunt and multipliers for range extension of MI Instruments, transformation ratio, turns ratio, nominal ratio, burden, ratio and phase angle error.(Descriptive treatment only)

Unit 2 (A) Measurement of Resistance

Measurement of low, medium and high resistance. Wheatstone bridge, Kelvin's Double Bridge, Ammeter-Voltmeter method, Megger, Earth tester for earth resistance measurement.

(B) Measurement of Inductance : Introduction, sources and detectors for a.c. bridge, general equation for bridge at balance. Measurement of Inductance: Maxwell's Inductance & Maxwell's Inductance – Capacitance Bridge, Anderson's Bridge.

Unit 3 : Measurement of Power

Construction, working principle, torque equation, errors and their compensation, advantages/disadvantages of dynamometer type wattmeter, low power factor wattmeter, poly-phase wattmeter. Active & reactive power measurement in three phase system for balanced and unbalanced load using three wattmeter method, two wattmeter method & one wattmeter method. Power analyzer, TOD meter, multi meter.

Unit 4 : Measurement of Energy

Construction, working principle, torque equation, errors and adjustments of single phase conventional (induction type) energy meter, Calibration of energy meter. Block diagram and operation of electronic energy meter. Three phase energy meters.

Unit 5 : (A) Oscilloscope

Introduction, various parts, front panel controls, use of CRO for measurement of voltage, current, period, frequency, phase angle & frequency by lissajous pattern & Numerical.

(B) Transducers : Introduction, classification, basic requirements for transducers. Pressure measurement: Introduction, classification of pressure as low / medium / high, absolute / gauge / vacuum, static / dynamic & head pressure. High pressure measurement using electric methods, low pressure measurement by McLeod gauge and pirani gauge, capacitive pressure transducer.

Unit 6 (A) Level Measurement

Introduction and importance of level measurement, level measurement methods: mechanical, hydraulic, pneumatic, electrical, nucleonic and ultrasonic.

(B) Displacement measurement : LVDT & RVDT – construction, working, application, null voltage, specifications, advantages / disadvantages, effect of frequency on performance. Strain Gauge : Introduction, definition of strain, types of strain gauge: Wire strain gauge, foil strain gauge, semiconductor strain gauge etc; their construction, working, advantages and disadvantages.

CONTENTS

Unit - I

1. Classification of Measuring   1.1-1.22

1.1 Introduction   1.1
1.2 Evolution of instruments   1.1
1.3 Block diagram of electronic measurement system   1.2
1.4 Performance characteristics   1.2
    1.4.1 Static Characteristics   1.3
    1.4.2 Dynamic Characteristics   1.6
1.5 Classification of instruments   1.7
    1.5.1 Absolute Measuring Instruments   1.7
    1.5.2 Secondary Measuring Instruments   1.7
    1.5.3 Deflection Type Instruments   1.12
    1.5.4 Null Type Instruments   1.12
    1.5.5 Difference between Active and Passive Instrument   1.13
    1.5.6 Difference between Deflection Type and Null Type Instrument   1.13
    1.5.7 Difference between Analog and Digital Instruments   1.13
1.6 Moving Iron Instrument   1.14
    1.6.1 Construction of Moving Iron Instrument   1.14
    1.6.2 Errors in Moving Iron Instruments   1.16
1.7 Permanent Magnet Moving Coil Instrument   1.16
    1.7.1 Principle of Operation   1.17
    1.7.2 Controlling Torque   1.17
    1.7.3 Errors in Permanent Magnet Moving Coil Instruments   1.18
    1.7.4 Advantages of Permanent Magnet Moving Coil Instruments   1.18
    1.7.5 Disadvantages of Permanent Magnet Moving Coil Instruments   1.18
1.8 Error   1.18
    Numericals   1.19
    University Questions   1.21

2. Range Extension   2.1-2.18

2.1 Introduction   2.1
2.2 Basic ammeter circuit using PMMC meter   2.2
2.3 Multi-range ammeters   2.3

2.4	Multi-range voltmeter	2.4
2.5	Voltmeter sensitivity	2.5
2.6	Need of calibration	2.5
2.7	Universal shunt or Ayrton shunt	2.6
2.8	Voltmeter using multiplier	2.7
2.9	Instrument transformers	2.8
	2.9.1 Potential Transformer (P.T.)	2.8
	2.9.2 Current transformer	2.9
2.10	Construction of current transformer	2.10
2.11	Errors introduced by current transformer	2.12
2.12	Error in voltage transformer	2.13
2.13	Advantages of instrument transformers over shunts and multipliers	2.14
2.14	Difference between CT and PT	2.14
2.15	Burden of instrument transformer	2.15
2.16	Ratios of instrument transformers	2.15

Numericals — 2.16

University Questions — 2.18

Unit - II

3. Measurement of Resistance — 3.1-3.36

3.1	Introduction		3.1
3.2	Methods for measurement of low resistances		3.1
	3.2.1	Ammeter Voltmeter Method	3.1
	3.2.2	Potentiometer Method	3.2
	3.2.3	Kelvin's Double Bridge	3.2
3.3	Measurement of medium resistance		3.4
	3.3.1	Wheatstone's Bridge	3.4
	3.3.2	Sensitivity of Wheatstone's Bridge	3.5
	3.3.3	Limitations of Wheatstone's Bridge	3.8
	3.3.4	Galvanometer Current in Wheatstone's Bridge	3.8
	3.3.5	Errors in Measurement of Low, Medium and High Resistance using Wheatstone's Bridge Method	3.10
	3.3.6	Applications of Wheatstone's Bridge	3.10

3.4 Methods for measurement of high resistances ... 3.10
    3.4.1 Megger ... 3.11
3.5 Measurement of earth resistance by use of earth tester ... 3.13
    3.5.1 Earth Tester ... 3.13
3.6 A.C. bridges ... 3.15
    3.6.1 Sources and Detectors in A.C. Bridge ... 3.15
3.7 Bridge balance condition of four arm A.C. bridge ... 3.16
3.8 Maxwell's inductance bridge ... 3.17
3.9 Maxwell's inductance capacitance bridge ... 3.19
3.10 Anderson's Bridge ... 3.20
3.11 Schering Bridge ... 3.22
3.12 Hay's bridge for measurement of inductance ... 3.23
Numericals ... 3.24
University Questions ... 3.34

Unit - III

4 : Measurement of Power ... 4.1-4.26
4.1 Introduction ... 4.1
4.2 Dynamometer wattmeter ... 4.2
    4.2.1 Construction of Dynamometer Type Wattmeter ... 4.2
    4.2.2 Expression for the Deflection Torque ... 4.3
4.3 Types of Dynamometer wattmeter ... 4.4
    4.3.1 Suspended-Coil Torsion Wattmeters ... 4.4
    4.3.2 Pivoted-Coil Direct-Indicating Wattmeters ... 4.4
4.4 Advantages of dynamometer type wattmeter ... 4.5
4.5 Disadvantages of dynamometer type wattmeter ... 4.5
4.6 Measurement of power in a three phase circuit ... 4.5
    4.6.1 Three Wattmeter Method ... 4.5
    4.6.2 Two Wattmeter Method ... 4.6
    4.6.3 One Wattmeter Method for a Balanced Load ... 4.9
4.7 One wattmeter method for reactive power measurement ... 4.11
4.8 TOD meter ... 4.12
4.9 Wattmeter errors ... 4.12
4.9.1 Error Due to Inductance of Pressure Coil ... 4.12

4.9.2 Error Due to the Capacitance of Pressure Coil	4.13
4.9.3 Error Due to Eddy Current	4.14
4.9.4 Error Due to Method of Connection	4.14
4.10 Low power factor dynamometer wattmeter	4.15
4.11 Polyphase wattmeter	4.17
4.12 Electronic multimeter	4.18
Numericals	4.20
University Questions	4.25

Unit - IV

5. Measurement of Energy — 5.1-5.14

5.1 Introduction	5.1
5.2 Energy meter	5.1
5.2.1 Working Principle	5.2
5.3 Construction	5.2
5.4 Torque equation of single phase induction type energy meter	5.3
5.5 Errors of single phase conventional energy meter	5.5
5.6 Compensation of error	5.6
5.7 Calibration of energy meter	5.8
5.8 Electronic energy meter	5.8
5.9 Three phase energy meter	5.9
Numericals	5.11
University Questions	5.12

Unit - V

6. Oscilloscope — 6.1-6.18

6.1 Introduction	6.1
6.1.1 Analog Oscilloscopes	6.1
6.2 Basic Principle	6.2
6.3 Block diagram of CRO (Cathode Ray Oscilosope)	6.2
6.3.1 Functions of Various Parts of CRO	6.3
6.4 Parts of Cathode Ray Oscilloscope	6.4
6.5 Front panel controls of a CRO	6.7
6.6 Synchronization	6.11
6.7 Deflection sensitivity of CRO	6.12

6.8	Applications of cathode ray oscilloscope	6.12
6.9	CRO measurement	6.13
	6.9.1 Measurement of Voltage and Currents	6.13
	6.9.2 Measurement of Frequency	6.14

Numericals — 6.15

University Questions — 6.18

7. Transducers — 7.1-7.18

7.1	Introduction	7.1
	7.1.1 Block digram of transducers	7.1
7.2	Characteristics of transducers	7.2
7.3	Transducers selection factors	7.2
7.4	Classification of transducers	7.3
	7.4.1 Active Transducers	7.3
	7.4.2 Passive Transducers	7.4
	7.4.3 Primary and Secondary Transducers	7.5
	7.4.4 Classification according to Transduction Principle	7.5
	7.4.5 Analog and Digital Transducer	7.7
	7.4.6 Primary and Secondary Transducers	7.7
7.5	Pressure measurement	7.8
7.6	U-tube manometer	7.9
	7.6.1 Inclined Tube Manometer	7.10
7.7 Bourdon tube pressure gauge		7.11
7.8 Bellows		7.12
7.9 Pressure Sensor Types		7.13
7.10 low pressure measurement		7.15
	7.10.1 Pirani gauge	7.15
	7.10.2 McLeod gauge	7.16

University Questions — 7.17

Unit - VI

8. Level & Displacement Measurement — 8.1-8.26

8.1 Introduction	8.1
8.2 Methods of level measurement	8.1
8.3 Hydrostatic pressure methods of level measurement	8.3

Section	Page
8.4 Ultrasonic type detector or ultrasonic method of level measurement	8.5
8.5 Electrical methods for liquid level measurement	8.5
8.5.1 Resistive Method for Liquid Level Measurement	8.5
8.5.2 Inductive method for liquid level measurement	8.6
8.5.3 Capacitive Method for Liquid Level Measurement	8.7
8.6 Nucleonic method of level measurement	8.8
8.7 Introduction	8.9
8.8 Potentiometer	8.9
8.9 Linear Variable Differential transformer (LVDT)	8.10
8.9.1 Inductive Type Sensors	8.13
8.10 Rotary Variable Differential Transformer (RVDT)	8.13
8.11 Capacitance Sensors	8.14
8.12 Resistive Transducers	8.15
8.13 Strain	8.16
8.14 The Strain Gauge	8.16
8.15 Gauge factor	8.17
8.16 Derivation of gauge factor	8.18
8.17 Types of strain gauge based on mounting	8.20
8.18 Types of strain gauge based on construction	8.21
8.19 Types of strain gauges based on principle of working	8.22
8.19.1 Effect of Temperature	8.22
8.20 Foil strain-gauge	8.23
8.21 Rosette strain gauge	8.24
University Questions	8.26

•••

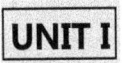

Chapter 1

CLASSIFICATION OF MEASURING INSTRUMENTS

1.1 INTRODUCTION

Measurement means to observe a process and using an instrument, express the parameter, quantity or a variable in terms of meaningful numbers. Measurement of a given parameter or quantity is the result of a quantitative comparison between a predefined standard and an unknown quantity to be measured.

Following are the basic requirements :
1. The comparison standard is accurately defined and commonly accepted.
2. The procedure and the instrument used for obtaining the comparison must be provable.

1.2 EVOLUTION OF INSTRUMENTS

1. **Mechanical :** These instruments are very reliable for static and stable conditions. But their drawback is that they are unable to respond rapidly to measurements of dynamic and transient condition.
2. **Electrical :** It is faster than mechanical instruments indicating the output. But it depends on the mechanical movement of meters. Response time is faster.
3. **Electronic :** It is more reliable than other systems. It uses semiconductor devices and weak signal can also be detected.
4. **Measuring Instrument :** It is defined as the device for determining the value or magnitude of a quantity or variable.

Advantages of electronic measurement :
- Electronic instrument are very sensitive to small change in deflection.
- Many measurements can be done simultaneously or in rapid succession.
- Low power consumption.
- Higher degree of reliability.
- They are light in weight.
- Higher sensitivity.
- An electrical or electronic signal can be amplified, filtered, multiplexed, sampled and measured.
- Most of the quantities can be converted by transducers into the electrical or by electronic signal.
- Electronic circuit can detect and amplify very weak signal and can measure the events of very short duration.

1.3 BLOCK DIAGRAM OF ELECTRONIC MEASUREMENT SYSTEM

Fig. 1.1 shows the block diagram of electronic measurement system. The various element of an electronic measurement system can be grouped as :

1. **Primary Sensing Element :** An element of an instrument which makes initial contact with the quantity to be measured. Transducers follows primary sensing element which converts the measured into corresponding electrical signal. Quantity to be measured is fed to the primary sensing element.
2. **Variable Conversion Element :** The output of the primary sensing element is in electrical form such as voltage, frequency. Such an output may not be suitable for actual measurement. So, variable conversion element is necessary. For e.g. if the measurement system is digital then the analog signal obtained from primary sensing element is not suitable for digital system.
3. **Variable Manipulation Element :** Thus, variable manipulation element manipulates the signal, preserving the original nature of the signal. This data is fed to the data transmission element.
4. **Data Transmission Element :** When the elements of system are physically separated, it is necessary to transmit the data from one stage to other. This is achieved by data transmission element.
5. **Data Presentation Element :** The data is monitored for analyzing purpose using data presentation element e.g. Visual display.
6. **Data storage :** Data from transmission element is fed to data storage element and is fed to the data presentation when required.

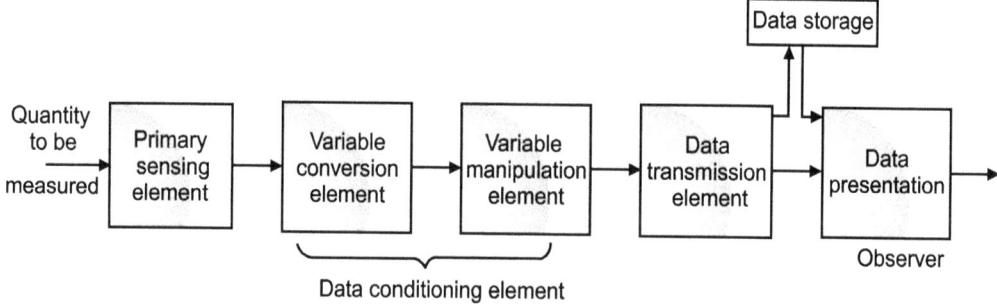

Fig. 1.1 : Block diagram of electronic measurement system

1.4 PERFORMANCE CHARACTERISTICS

Q. What is meant by static and dynamic characteristics of measuring instruments? Explain: Accuracy, resolution, drift.

Q. Give detailed classification of measuring instruments. Elaborate each type in brief.

1. **Static characteristics :** The set of criteria defined for the instruments which are used to measure the quantities which are slowly varying with time or mostly constant i.e. do not vary with time is called static characteristics.
2. **Dynamic characteristics :** When the quantity under measurement changes rapidly with time it is necessary to study the dynamic relations existing between input and output which is expressed as differential equation.

1.4.1 Static Characteristics

Static characteristics are :

1. Accuracy
2. Precision
3. Sensitivity
4. Linearity
5. Resolution
6. Threshold
7. Hysterisis
8. Dead zone

1. **Accuracy :** The accuracy of an instrument is a measure of how close the measured value of the instrument is to the true value.

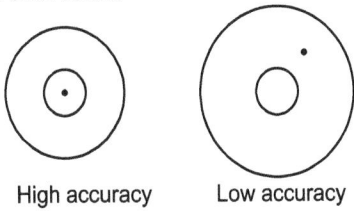

High accuracy   Low accuracy
Fig. 1.2

2. **Precision :** This is the ability of measuring instrument to give identical indications or responses for repeated applications of the same value of the measured quantity under same conditions of use.

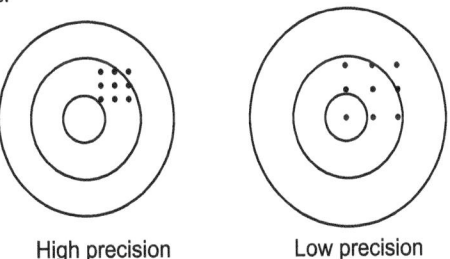

High precision   Low precision
Fig. 1.3

3. **Sensitivity :** This is a relationship between a change in the output reading for a given change of input. This relationship may be linear or non linear. An instrument with a large sensitivity will indicate a large movement of the indicator for a small input change.

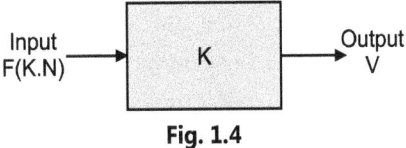

Fig. 1.4

Sensitivity, $K = \dfrac{5V}{KN}$

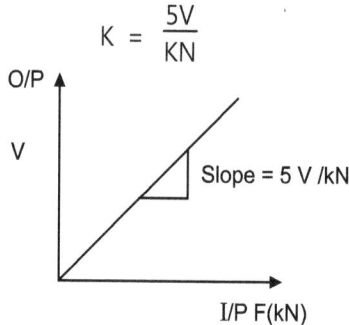

Fig. 1.5

Sensitivity is the ratio of O/P signal or response of the instrument to a change of input or measured variable.

$$\text{Sensitivity} = \dfrac{\text{Infinitesimal change in output}}{\text{Infinitesimal change in input}}$$

As shown in Fig 1.5 the sensitivity of the instrument is the slope of the curve. Sensitivity is always expressed by manufacturers as the ratio of the magnitude of quantity being measured to the magnitude of the response. Deflection factor is the reciprocal of the sensitivity. Units of sensitivity are millimeter per µA, mm/Ω, counts per volt etc. Sensitivity of the instrument should be as high as possible.

4. **Linearity :** Most instruments are specified to function over a particular range and the instruments can be said to be linear when incremental changes in the input and output are constant over the specified range. Fig. 1.6 shows the actual calibration curve which shows linearity curve between input and output.

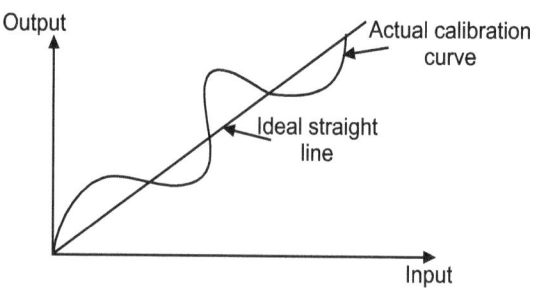

Fig. 1.6

5. **Resolution :** This is defined as the smallest input increment change that gives some small but definite numerical change in the output. If a non-zero input quantity is slowly increased, output reading will not increase until some minimum change in input occurs. This minimum change which causes change in the output is called resolution.

6. **Threshold :** If the instrument input is increased gradually from zero, there may be some minimum value below which no output change can be detected. This smallest measurable input value is called threshold.

7. **Hysterisis :** If the input to the instrument is increased from a negative value, the output also increases. This is curve 1. If the curve is decreased steadily, the output does not follow the same curve but lags by certain value. This is indicated by curve 2. Difference between two curves is called Hysterisis.

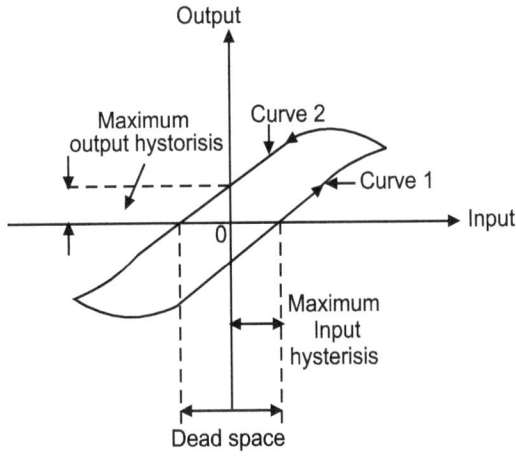

Fig. 1.7

8. **Dead space :** As shown in figure above, dead space is the range of input values where there is no change in output. Hysterisis is the non coincidence of loading and unloading curves. Fig. 1.8 shows the effect of loading and unloading which indicates hysterisis. Hysterisis is a phenomenon which depicts different output effects when loading and unloading.

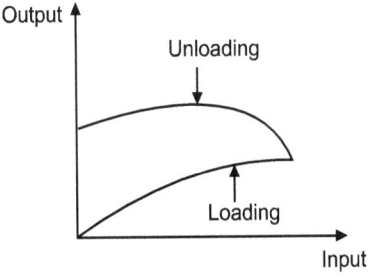

Fig. 1.8

1.4.2 Dynamic Characteristics

Instrument respond to the instantaneous change in the measured variables is slow due to mass, thermal capacitance and electrical capacities. These types of instruments are normally used for the measurement of quantities which fluctuate with time. The behaviour of a system where the input varies from instant to instant and output varies from instant to instant is called dynamic response of the system.

Dynamic characteristics are classified as :
(a) Speed of Response
(b) Fidelity
(c) Lag
(d) Dynamic Error

(a) **Speed of response :** The rapidity with which the system responds to the change in quantity to be measured is called speed of response. It indicates how fast the system reacts to the changes in the input.

(b) **Fidelity :** The degree to which a measurement system is capable of faithfully reproducing the changes in input, without any dynamic error is called as fidelity.

(c) **Measuring lag :** The retardation or delay in the response of a measurement system to changes in measured quantity is known as measuring lag.

Types of measuring Lag :
  (i) **Retardation type :** In this, the response of the measurement system begins immediately after a change in measured quantity has occurred.
  (ii) **Time delay type :** In this case the response of the system begins after a dead time after the application of the input.

(d) **Dynamic Error :** It is the difference between the true value of the variable to be measured, changing with time and the value indicated by the measurement system, assuming zero static error.

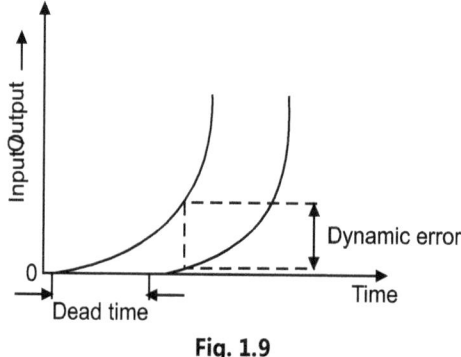

Fig. 1.9

1.5 CLASSIFICATION OF INSTRUMENTS

Q. Give Classification of instruments? [Dec. 11, 8 M]

- Absolute Measuring Instruments
- Secondary Measuring Instruments
- Analogue Instruments
- Digital Instruments
- Deflection Type Instruments
- Null Type Instruments
- Active Instruments
- Passive Instruments

1.5.1 Absolute Measuring Instruments

These instruments give output in terms of physical constant of the instruments. For example Rayleigh's current balance and Tangent galvanometer are absolute instruments.

1.5.2 Secondary Measuring Instruments

They are direct reading instruments. These instruments are constructed with the help of absolute instruments. Secondary instruments are calibrated by comparison with an absolute instrument. These are more frequently used in measurement of the quantities as compared to absolute instruments, as working with absolute instruments is time consuming. The value of quantity to be measured can be determined from the deflection of instrument. They are classified into following types:

1. Indicating Instruments
2. Integrating Instruments
3. Recording Instruments

1.5.2.1 Indicating Instruments

Indicating Instruments indicate the value of the electrical quantity to be measured generally by the deflection of the pointer on the calibrated scale. Eg : Wattmeter, Ammeter, Voltmeter.

Various forces/torques required in indicating instruments :

1. **Deflecting Torque/Force :** The defection of any instrument is determined by the combined effect of the deflecting torque/force, control torque/force and damping torque/force. The deflecting force can be produced by utilizing any of effect like magnetic, thermal, induction effect. The value of deflecting torque must depend on the electrical signal to be measured; this torque/force causes the instrument movement to

rotate from its zero position. Thus deflecting system of an instrument converts the electric current or potential into a mechanical force called deflecting force.

2. **Controlling Torque/Force :** This torque/force must act in the opposite sense to the deflecting torque/force, and the movement will take up an equilibrium or definite position when the deflecting and controlling torque are equal in magnitude. Spiral springs or gravity usually provides the controlling torque.

3. **Damping Torque/Force :** A damping force is required to act in a direction opposite to the movement of the moving system. This brings the moving system to rest at the deflected position rapidly without any oscillation or very small oscillation. This is provided by (i) air friction (ii) fluid friction (iii) eddy current. Any damping force shall not influence the steady state deflection produced by a given deflecting force or torque. Damping force increases with the angular velocity of the moving system. Its effect is greatest when the rotation is rapid and zero when the system rotation is zero.

All electrical indicating instruments require three essential system :

(a) **Deflecting or Operating System :** It is that part of the instrument mechanism which utilize some physical effect of electric current or voltage to produce mechanical force. A mechanical force produced by the current or voltage causes the pointer to deflect from its zero position. The magnitude of the deflection force depends on the value of the electrical quantity to be measured.

(b) **Controlling System :** This part of the instrument which brings into play a force called controlling force. The controlling force acts in opposition to the deflecting force and ensures that the deflection shown on the meter is always the same for a given measured quantity. It also prevents the pointer from going to the maximum deflection. There are two main types of controlling devices.
  (i) spring control
  (ii) gravity control

(i) **Spring Control :** In low resistance instruments, beryllium copper is used. It utilizes two spiral hair springs of non magnetic alloy such as phosphorous bronze or beryllium-copper. The springs are oppositely wound so when the moving system deflects, one spring winds up while the outer unwind thus the controlling torque is produce by the combines torsion of spring. The torsional torque is proportional to the angle of twist, the controlling torque is directly proportional to the angular deflection of pointer. Scale of spring control type instruments is uniform.

$$T_d \propto I,$$

Also, $\quad T_c \propto \theta$

At final deflection or steady state position :
$$T_c = T_d$$

Therefore, $\quad \theta \propto I$

(ii) **Gravity Control :** In this a small adjustable weight is attached to the moving system (pointer) in such a way that in deflection condition it produces a restoring or controlling torque. Weight W_1 provides the controlling torque, W_2 is for balancing the weight of the pointer. As shown in fig 1.11 the control weight is in vertical position and controlling torque is zero. So the pointer read zero.

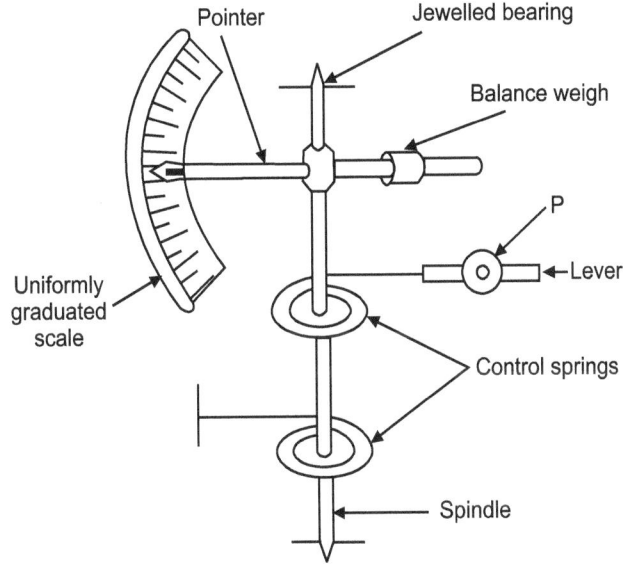

Fig. 1.10 : Spring control

$$T_c = W_1 \sin \theta \times L$$
$$= W_1 L \sin \theta$$

Thus, $\quad T_c \propto \sin \theta$

At steady state position deflection torque = controlling torque.

Thus, $\quad I \propto \sin \theta$

Thus, the scale of the gravity control type instruments is non-uniform as current is proportional to $\sin \theta$. It is cramped at lower end. Gravity control is cheap but it has disadvantage that it is not suitable for portable instruments.

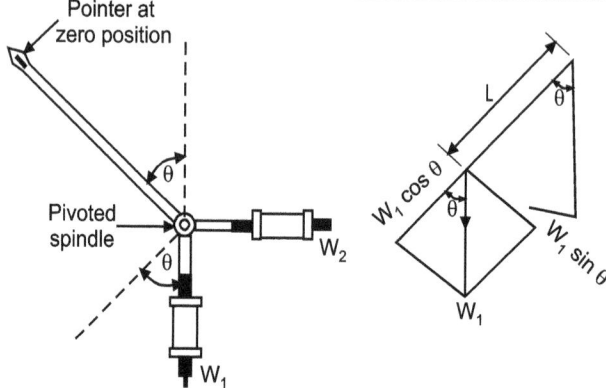

Fig. 1.11 : Gravity control

(c) **A Damping System :** The damping force ensures that the pointer comes to rest in its final position quickly and without undue oscillation. There are three main types of damping used :
   (i) Air-friction damping
   (ii) Eddy current damping
   (iii) Fluid friction damping

(i) **Air Friction or Pneumatic Damping :** In this system a light aluminium piston is attached to the spindles of the instrument which moves in a fix air chamber closed at one end. The cross-section of the chamber may be either circular or rectangular and the clearance between the piston and the side of the chamber is small and uniform. Compression and suction action of the piston on the air in the chamber damp the possible oscillations of moving system. The motion of the piston in either direction is oppose by the air.

In second type a thin aluminium vane, mounted on the spindle, moves with very small clearance in a sector shaped box. Any tendency of the moving system to oscillate is damped by the action of the air on vane.

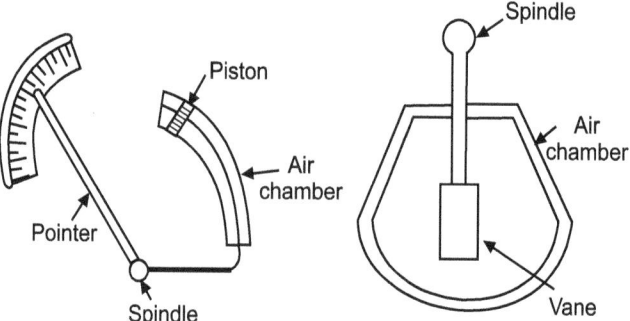

Fig. 1.12 : Air friction of pneumatic damping

(ii) **Eddy Current Damping :** It is the most efficient type of the damping. In this a thin disc usually of copper or aluminium is mounted on the spindle. When this disc moves in the magnetic field of permanent magnet, line of force are cut and eddy current are set up in it. The force that exists between these current and magnetic field is always in the direction opposing the motion and therefore, provide necessary damping. The magnitude of the induced current and therefore of the damping force which is dependent on it, is directly proportional to the velocity of moving system.

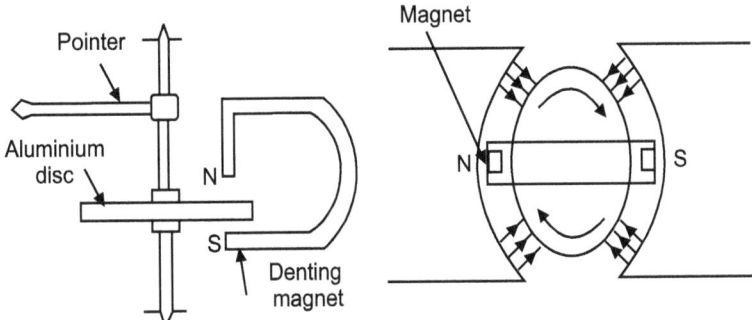

Fig. 1.13 : Eddy current damping

(iii) **Fluid Friction Damping :** Fig 1.14 shows two methods of fluid friction damping. In this method of damping, a light disc is attached to the spindle of the moving system and completely submerge in the damping oil in a pot. The motion of the disc is always opposed by a frictional drag on the disc. This frictional drag is zero when the disc is stationary and increases with the speed of the rotation of the disc. For increased damping, vanes in a vertical plane, carried on a spindle and immersed in oil are used. Fluid friction damping can only be used in the instruments which are used in the vertical position. Disadvantage of fluid friction damping is that the instruments must be kept in vertical position. It is also problematic to keep these instruments clean due to leakage of oil.

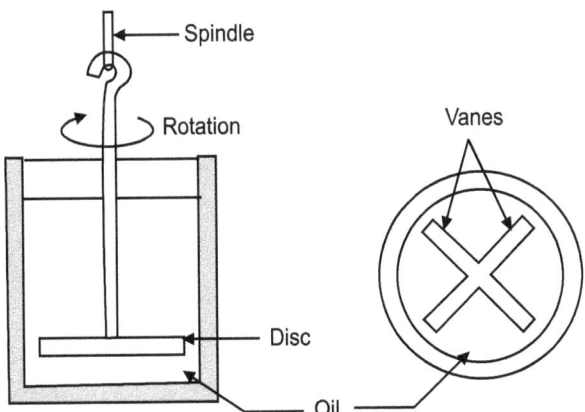

Fig. 1.14 : Fluid friction damping

1.5.2.2 Integrating Instruments

These instruments measure the total quantity of electricity delivered over the period of time. E.g. Energy meter.

1.5.2.3 Recording Instruments

These instruments give a continuous record of the given electrical quantity which is being measured over a specific period. E.g. Recorders, X-Y plotter.

1.5.3 Deflection Type Instruments

In deflection types of instruments, pointer of the electrical measuring instrument deflects to measure the quantity. The value of the quantity can be measured by measuring the net deflection of the pointer from its initial position. Consider deflection type permanent magnet moving coil ammeter which is shown in fig 1.15

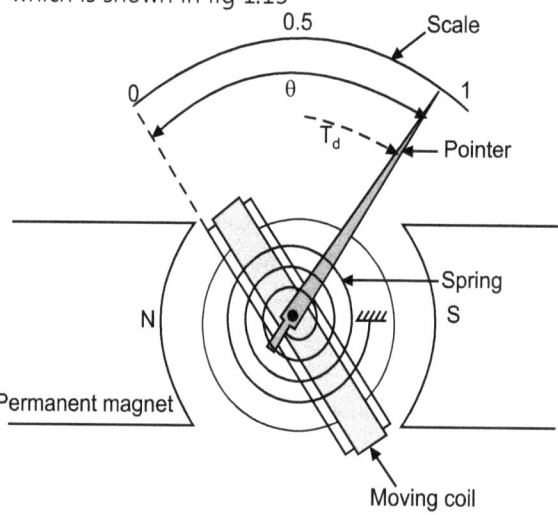

Fig. 1.15 : Deflection type Permanent Magnet Moving Coil Ammeter

Fig. 1.15 shows two permanent magnets which are called the stationary part of the instrument. The moving part is between the two permanent magnets which consist of pointer. The deflection of the moving coil is directly proportion to the current. Thus the torque is proportional to the current which is given by the expression $T_d = K.I$, where T_d is the deflecting torque. K is proportionality constant which depends upon the strength of the magnetic field and the number of turns in the coil. The pointer deflects between the two opposite forces produced by the spring and the magnets. The resulting direction of the pointer is in the direction of the resultant force. The value of current is measured by the deflection angle θ, and the value of K.

1.5.4 Null Type Instruments

In opposite to deflection type of instruments, the null or zero type electrical measuring instruments tend to maintain the position of pointer stationary. They maintain the position of the pointer stationary by producing opposing effect. Following steps are required for the operation of null type instruments:

1. Value of opposite effect should be known in order to calculate the value of unknown quantity.
2. Detector shows the balance and the unbalance condition accurately. The detector should also have the means for restoring force.

1.5.5 Difference between Active and Passive Instrument

Active instruments	Passive instrument
1. They are costly.	1. They are cheap.
2. They are complex to design.	2. They are simple to design.
3. The output produced by some external power input.	3. The output produced entirely by quantity being measured.
4. Resolution is high.	4. Resolution is less.
5. Eg. liquid level indicator.	5. Eg. voltmeter, ammeter.

1.5.6 Difference between Deflection Type and Null Type Instrument

Deflection type instrument	Null type instrument
1. They are more suitable for measurement under dynamic conditions.	1. They require manipulations before null conditions are obtained.
2. They are less sensitive.	2. It is highly sensitive.
3. Accuracy is less.	3. They have higher accuracy.
4. In these instruments the quantity to be measured produces the deflection of pointer against controlling torque.	4. It uses null detector.
5. Eg. Moving coil ammeter.	5. Eg. D.C. potentiometer.

1.5.7 Difference between Analog and Digital Instruments

Analog instruments	Digital instruments
1. In analog instrument the function varies continuously.	1. In digital instruments function does not varies continuously.
2. Programming is not possible.	2. Programming is possible.
3. Low input impedance.	3. Very high input impedance.
4. They are cheap.	4. They are costly.
5. Loading effect is present.	5. No loading effects.
6. Resolution is limited.	6. Resolution is high.
7. Less accuracy.	7. Accuracy is more.
8. Eg. voltmeter, ammeter.	8. Eg. multimeter, microprocessor based instruments.

1.6 MOVING IRON INSTRUMENT

This instrument is one of the most primitive forms of measuring and relay instrument. Moving iron type instruments are of mainly two types.
1. Attraction type instrument
2. Repulsion type instrument

1. **Attraction Type Instrument :** Whenever a piece of iron is placed near to a magnet it would be attracted by the magnet. The force of this attraction depends upon the strength of magnetic field. If the magnet is electromagnet then the magnetic field strength can easily be increased or decreased by increasing or decreasing electric current through its coil. Accordingly the attraction force acting on the piece of iron would also be increased and decreased. Depending upon this simple phenomenon attraction type moving iron instrument was developed.

2. **Repulsion Type Instrument :** Whenever two pieces of iron are kept side by side and a magnet is brought nearer to them the iron pieces will repulse each other. This repulsion force is induced in same sides the iron pieces due external magnetic field. This repulsion force increases if field strength of the magnet is increased. Like case if the magnet is electromagnet, then magnetic field strength can easily be controlled by controlling input current to the magnet. Hence if the electric current increases the repulsion force between the pieces of iron is increased and it the current decreases the repulsion force between them is decreased. Depending upon this phenomenon repulsion type moving iron instrument was constructed.

1.6.1 Construction of Moving Iron Instrument

Q. Explain with neat diagram Moving Iron Instruments?
Q. Describe moving Iron Instruments?
Q. Give advantages and disadvantages of moving iron instruments?
Q. State the errors in moving iron instruments?

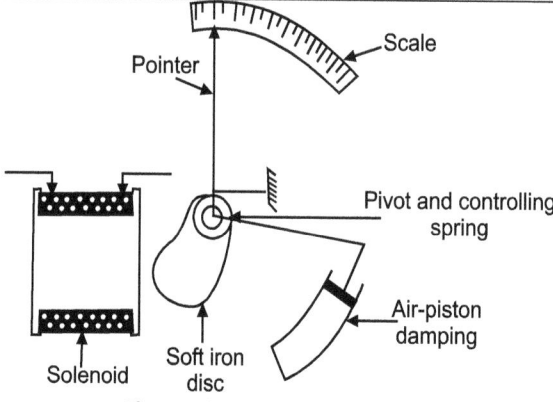

Fig. 1.16 (a) : Attraction Type

The basic construction of attraction type moving iron instrument is shown in Fig. 1.16 (a). A thin disc of soft iron is eccentrically pivoted in front of a coil. This iron tends to move inward that is from weaker magnetic field to stronger magnetic field, when current flowing through the coil. In attraction moving instrument gravity control method is replaced by spring control. By adjusting balance weight null deflection of the pointer is achieved. The required damping force is provided in this instrument by air friction. The Fig. 1.16 (a) shows a typical type of damping system provided in the instrument, where damping is achieved by a moving piston in an air syringe.

The repulsion type moving-iron instrument is shown in Fig. (b). Two pieces of iron are placed inside the solenoid, one being fixed, and the other attached to the spindle carrying the pointer. When current passes through the solenoid, the two pieces of iron are magnetized in the same direction and therefore repel each other. The pointer thus moves across the scale. The force moving the pointer is, in each type, proportional to I^2 and because of this the direction of current does not matter. The moving-iron instrument can be used on D.C. or A.C.; the scale, however, is non-linear.

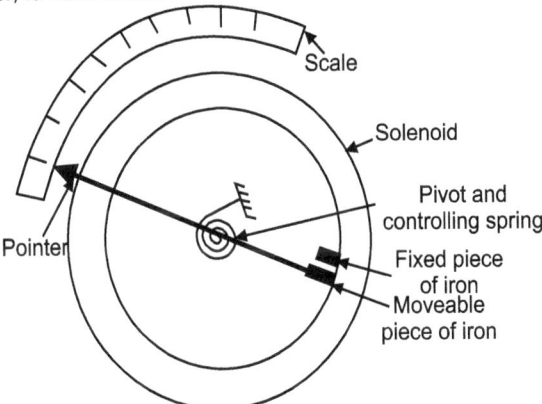

Fig. 1.16 (b) : Repulsion Type

Advantages of Moving Iron Instruments :
1. It can be used for A.C. as well as D.C. measurements.
2. These instruments are cheaper.
3. Rugged in construction.
4. Range of instruments can be extended.

Disadvantages of Moving Iron Instruments :
1. Scale is not uniform and hence accurate readings not possible.
2. Readings are affected due to increase in temperature.
3. Several errors due to hysteresis, frequency changes and stray magnetic field.
4. More power consumption.

1.6.2 Errors in Moving Iron Instruments

1. **Frequency Error :** The change in frequency affects the reactance of the working coil and also affects the magnitude of eddy currents.
2. **Eddy Current Error :** Eddy currents are produced in the iron parts of instruments when instrument is used for A.C. measurement. Eddy current are frequency dependants hence changing in frequency causes eddy currents.
3. **Hysteresis Error :** flux density for same current changes due to hysteresis effect. Meter reads higher for descending values of current or voltage. This can be removed by using small iron parts which can demagnetize quickly.
4. **Temperature Error :** Temperature error is caused due to self heating of the coil which changes the resistance of coil. This error is of the order of 0.02% per degree celcius change in temperature.

1.7 PERMANENT MAGNET MOVING COIL INSTRUMENT

The permanent magnet moving coil (PMMC) instrument uses two permanent magnets in order to create stationary magnetic field. These types of instruments are only used for measuring the dc quantities. It can measure the direct current very accurately. If we apply ac current to these types of instruments the direction of electric current will be reversed during negative half cycle and hence the direction of torque will also be reversed which gives average value of torque zero. The pointer will not deflect due to high frequency from its mean position showing zero reading. The construction of permanent magnet moving coil instruments is described below :

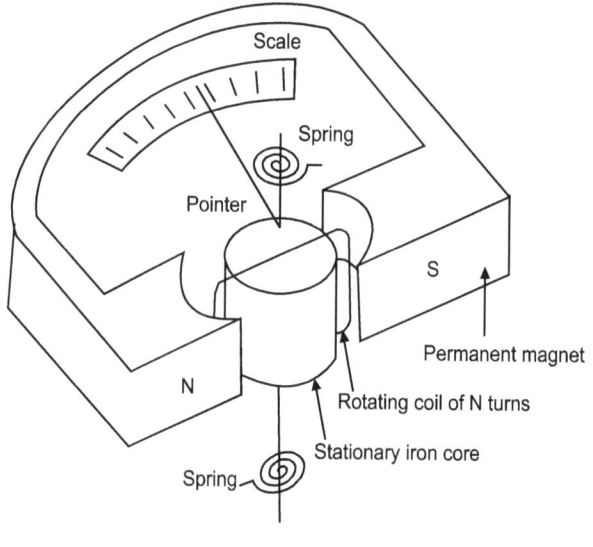

Fig. 1.17

1. **Stationary Part or Magnet System :** Magnets of high field intensities, high coercive force are used instead of using U shaped permanent magnet having soft iron pole pieces. The magnets are made up of materials like alcomax and alnico which provide high field strength.
2. **Moving Coil :** The moving coil can freely moves between the two permanent magnets as shown in the Fig. (1.17). The coil is wound with many turns of copper wire and is placed on rectangular aluminium which is pivoted on jeweled bearings.
3. **Control System :** The spring generally acts as control system for PMMC instruments. The spring also serves another important function by providing the path to lead current in and out of the coil.
4. **Damping System :** The damping force hence torque is provided by the movement of aluminium former in the magnetic field.
5. **Meter :** Meter of these instruments consists of light weight pointer and linear as well as uniform scale.

1.7.1 Principle of Operation

The interaction between the induced field and the field produced by the permanent magnet causes a deflecting torque, which results in rotation of the coil. For a moving coil instruments, deflecting torque should be proportional to current.

$$T_d = GI$$
$$G = NBdl$$
$$T_c = K\theta$$

where,

l = length of coil
d = Breadth of coil
N = Number of turns of coil
B = Flux density between two poles (Wb/m²)
I = Current flowing through coil (A)
K = Spring constant.

At steady state both the controlling and deflecting torques are equal.

∴ $$GI = K\theta$$

∴ $$\boxed{\theta \propto I}$$

Deflection is directly proportional to current flowing through coil.

1.7.2 Controlling Torque

The value of control torque depends on the mechanical design of the control device. For spiral springs and strip suspensions, the controlling torque is directly proportional to the angle of deflection of the coil.

Where, x = deflection angle in radians and k = spring constant.

T_c is controlling torque, on equating controlling torque with deflection torque

GI = K·x where, I is deflection current is given by $I = \frac{K}{G}x$. Since the deflection is directly proportional to the current therefore we need a uniform scale on the meter for measurement of current.

1.7.3 Errors in Permanent Magnet Moving Coil Instruments

There are three main types of errors :

(a) **Errors due to permanent magnets** : Due to temperature effects and aging of the magnets, the magnet may lose their magnetism to some extent. The magnets are generally aged by the heat and vibration treatment.

(b) **Error may appear in PMMC Instrument due to the aging of the spring** : However the error caused by the aging of the spring and the errors caused due to permanent magnet are opposite to each other, hence both the errors are compensated with each other.

(c) **Change in the resistance of the moving coil with the temperature** : Generally the temperature coefficients of the value of coefficient of copper wire in moving coil is 0.04 per degree celsius rise in temperature. Due to lower value of temperature coefficient the temperature rises at faster rate and hence the resistance increases. Due to this, significant amount of error is caused.

1.7.4 Advantages of Permanent Magnet Moving Coil Instruments

1. The scale is uniformly divided as the current is directly proportional to deflection of the pointer. Hence it is very easy to measure quantities from these instruments.
2. Power consumption is also very low in these types of instruments.
3. Higher value of torque to weight ratio.
4. Single instrument can be used for measuring various quantities by using different values of shunts and multipliers.

1.7.5 Disadvantages of Permanent Magnet Moving Coil Instruments

1. These instruments cannot measure ac quantities.
2. Cost of these instruments is high as compared to moving iron instruments.

1.8 ERROR

The algebraic difference between the indicated value and the true value of the quantity to be measured is called an error.

Absolute Error:

where,
$$e = A_t - A_m$$
e = error (or) absolute error
A_m = measured value of quantity
A_t = true value of quantity

Note : Instead of specifying absolute error, the relative or percentage of error is specified.

Relative error :

$$e_r = \frac{\text{Absolute error}}{\text{True value}}$$

$$e_r = \frac{A_t - A_m}{A_t}$$

Percentage relative error, $\quad \% e_r = \frac{A_t - A_m}{A_t} \times 10$

Accuracy, $\quad A = 1 - e_r$

$$= 1 - \left| \frac{A_t - A_m}{A_t} \right|$$

where, $\quad A$ = relative accuracy

Percentage accuracy, $\quad a = A \times 100\%$

Error as a % of full scale reading $= \dfrac{A_t - A_m}{\text{full scale deflection}} \times 100$

NUMERICALS

Q.1 A moving coil of a meter has 100 turns, its width is 2 cm and a depth of 3 cm. It is suspended in a uniform magnetic field of 60 Wb/m². Find the turning moment of a coil when it is carrying a current of 2 mA.

Sol. $T_d = N B I l d$
$N = 100$, $B = 60 \times 10^{-3}$ Wb, $I = 2 \times 10^{-3}$ A, $l = 3 \times 10^{-2}$ m, $d = 2 \times 10^{-2}$ m
$T_d = 100 \times 60 \times 10^{-3} \times 3 \times 10^{-2} \times 2 \times 10^{-2} \times 2 \times 10^{-3} = 7.2 \times 10^{-6}$ Nm

Q.2 Following is data given for moving coil instrument. Number of turns = 250, width = 25 mm, height = 30 cm, flux density in air gap = 0.1 Wb/m², moment of intertia of moving parts = 3×10^{-7} kg-m², torque produced by control spring = 10×10^{-6} Nm/rad. Find the current in the coil to produce a deflection of 100°.

Sol. For steady state deflection,
$$T_d = T_c$$
$$NBIld = 10 \times 10^{-6} \times \theta$$

$$250 \times 0.1 \times I \times 30 \times 10^{-12} \times 25 \times 10^{-2} = 10 \times 10^{-6} \times \left(100 \times \frac{\pi}{180}\right)$$

$$I = \frac{1.744 \times 10^{-6}}{18.750 \times 10^{-4}}$$

$$= 0.093 \times 10^{-2}$$

$$= 9.3 \text{ mA}$$

$$\therefore \quad I = 9.3 \text{ mA}$$

Q.3 PMMC instrument has a coil of dimensions 15 mm × 12 mm. The flux density in the air gap is 1.8×10^3 Wb/m² & spring constant is 0.14×10^{-6} Nm/rad. Determine the number of turns required to produce on angular deflection of 90° when a current of 5 mA is flowing through coil.

Sol. $L_d = 15 \times 12$ mm², $I = 5 \times 10^{-3}$ A, $B = 1.8 \times 10^{-3}$ Wb/m², $K = 0.14 \times 10^{-6}$ Nm/rad, $\theta = 90° = \frac{\pi}{2}$, $I = 5$ mA.

At steady state deflection,

$$T_d = T_c$$
$$NBLdI = k\theta$$
$$N = \frac{K\theta}{BLdI}$$

$$= \frac{0.14 \times 10^{-6} \times \pi/2}{1.8 \times 10^{-3} \times 15 \times 10^{-3} \times 12 \times 10^{-3} \times 5 \times 10^{-3}}$$

$$\boxed{N = 136}$$

Q.4 A PMMC voltmeter has following data. Resistance = 10 kΩ, coil dimensions = 3 cm × 3 cm, coil turns = 100, flux density = 0.08 tesla, control constant of spring = 36×10^{-7} Nm/deg. Find the deflection in degrees when 250 V D.C. is applied across the voltmeter.

Sol. V = 250 V, Current = $I = \frac{250}{10000} = 0.025$ A.

At steady state position,

$$T_d = T_c$$
$$NBLdI = K\theta$$
$$100 \times 0.08 \times 9 \times 10^{-4} \times 0.025 = 36 \times 10^{-7} \times \theta$$
$$\boxed{\theta = 50°}$$

Q.5 A coil of moving coil voltmeter has 120 turns and it is 25 cm wide and 30 cm long. The resistance of the instrument is neglected but the control spring exerts a torque of 200×10^{-6} N when deflection is 100 div on full scale. If the air gaps flux density is 0.9 tesla. Calculate the series resistance to be placed with the coil to give 1 V/div.

Sol. Deflecting torque, T_d = (NBILd) Nm = $120 \times 0.9 \times I \times 0.03 \times 0.025$, $T_d = (0.081\ I)$ Nm

At steady state condition,
$$T_c = T_d$$
$$200 \times 10^{-6} = 0.081 \times I$$
$$I = 2.469 \times 10^{-3}\ A$$

Voltage across voltmeter = IR = 0.002469 R

$$\text{volt/div.} = \frac{0.002469\ R}{100}$$

To get 1 volt/div then,
$$\frac{0.002469\ R}{100} = 1$$

$$\boxed{R = 40502.22\ \Omega}$$

Q.6 A 60 cm scale has 60 uniform divisions. $1/10^{th}$ scale of a scale division can be estimated with a fair degree of certainty. Determine the resolution of the scale in mm.

Sol. 1 scale division = $\frac{\text{Full scale deflection}}{\text{Number of divisions}} = \frac{60}{60} = 1$ cm

Resolution = $\frac{1}{10} \times$ Scale division = $\frac{1}{10} \times (10\text{ mm}) = 1$ mm

UNIVERSITY QUESTIONS

Dec. 2010

Q.1 What is meant by static and dynamic characteristics of measuring instruments? Explain: Accuracy, resolution, drift. **(8 Marks)**

Q.2 Give detailed classification of measuring instruments. Elaborate each type in brief. **(8 Marks)**

Q.3 With a neat sketch, explain construction and working of moving iron instrument. What are the advantages of this instrument? **(6 Marks)**

May 2011

Q.4 Explain the term Linearity, Drifts, Reproducibility, Resolution, Speed of Response. **(8 Marks)**

Q.5 Compare the following:
  (i) Absolute and secondary instruments. **(8 Marks)**

Dec. 2011

Q.6 Explain in detail the classification of the measuring instruments. **(8 Marks)**

Q.7 Which three forces are required for satisfactory operation of an analog indicating instrument? State the function of each force. **(6 Marks)**

May 2012

Q.8 Explain the following terms : **(8 Marks)**
   (i)   Static and dynamic accuracy
   (ii) Speed of response
   (iii) Repeatability
   (iv) Reproducibility

Dec. 2012

Q.9 Compare giving example : **(6 Marks)**
   (i)   Repeatability and reproducibility
   (ii) Reliability and maintainability
   (iii) Scale range and scale span

Q.10 The inductance of a certain moving iron ammeter is $\left(8 + 40\theta - \frac{1}{2}\theta^2\right)$ µH, where θ is the deflection in radians from zero position. Calculate the scale position in radians for a current of 10 A if the deflection for a current of 5 A is π/6 rad. Also determine the spring constant. **(6 Marks)**

Q.11 Classify different types of standards used in measurement with their scope of applications. **(6 Marks)**

Q.12 State and explain the causes of errors occurring in moving iron instruments with both DC and AC measurements. **(6 Marks)**

UNIT I

CHAPTER 2

RANGE EXTENSION

2.1 INTRODUCTION

Moving coil instruments, which are used as ammeters and voltmeters are designed to carry maximum current of 50mA and withstand a voltage of 50mV. Hence, to measure larger currents and voltages, the ranges of these meters have to be extended. The following methods are employed to increase the ranges of ammeters and voltmeters

- By using shunts the range of dc ammeters is extended
- By using multipliers, the range of dc voltmeter is extended
- By using current transformers the range of ac ammeter is extended
- By using potential transformer the range of ac voltmeter

2.2 BASIC AMMETER CIRCUIT USING PMMC METER

Q.1 Explain basic ammeter circuit using PMMC meter.   [Dec. 10,11, May. 11, 10 M]

The basic movement of a D.C. ammeter is a PMMC d' Arsonval galvanometer. The coil winding of a basic movement is small and light and it can carry very small currents. When heavy currents are to be measured, the major part of the current is by passed through a low resistance called a 'shunt'. Fig. 2.1 below shows basic ammeter circuit.

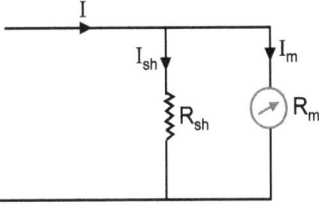

Fig. 2.1

R_m = Internal resistance of movement
R_{sh} = Resistance of shunt
I_m = Full scale deflection current of movement in A
I_{sh} = Shunt current
I = Current to be measured
Voltage drop across shunt = Voltage drop across movement

As the shunt resistance is in parallel with the meter movement.

$$I_{sh}R_{sh} = I_m R_m$$

$$\therefore \quad R_{sh} = \frac{I_m R_m}{I_{sh}}$$

But,

$$I_{sh} = I - I_m$$

$$\therefore \quad R_{sh} = \frac{I_m R_m}{I - I_m}$$

$$\therefore \quad R_{sh} = \frac{R_m}{m - 1}$$

where,

$$m = \frac{I}{I_m}$$

m = multiplying power of the shunt. It is defined as the ratio of total current to the current through the coil.

$$\boxed{m = \frac{I}{I_m} = 1 + \frac{R_m}{R_{sh}}}$$

To increase the range of ammeter 'm' times the shunt resistance required is $\frac{1}{(m-1)}$ times the basic meter resistance. This is called as extension ranges of an ammeter.

2.3 MULTI-RANGE AMMETERS

An ammeter is required to measure the current in a circuit and connected in series with the components carrying the current. If the ammeter resistance is not very much smaller than the load resistance, the load current can be substantially altered by the inclusion of the ammeter in the circuit. To operate a moving coil instrument of current around 50mA, weight of the coil that would be required would be bulky. So, it is necessary to extend the meter-range shunts in case of ammeters.

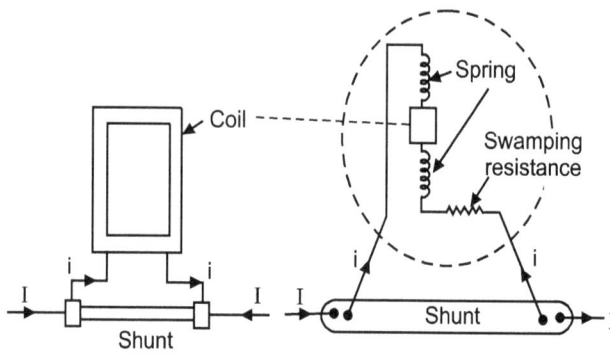

Fig 2.2

For higher range ammeters a low resistance made up of manganin is connected in parallel to the moving coil as shown in fig 2.2 and instrument may be calibrated to read directly to the total current. They are called shunts. The movement of PMMC instrument may be temperature-compensated by the appropriate use of series and shunt resistors of copper and manganin. The magnetic field strength and spring-tension, decrease with an increase in temperature. The coil resistance increases with an increase in temperature. These changes lead to make the pointer read low for a given current with respect to magnetic field strength and coil resistance. Use of manganin resistance also known as swamping resistance, in series with the coil resistance can reduce the error due to the variation of resistance of the moving coil. A multi range ammeter can be constructed by employing several values of shunt resistances, with a rotary switch to select the desired range. Fig. 2.3 shows the circuit arrangement.

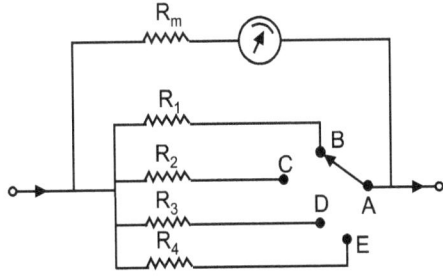

Fig 2.3

When an instrument is used then care must be taken to ensure shunt does not become open-circuited, even for a very short moment. When the switch is moved from position 'B' to 'C' or moved to any positions, the shunt resistance will remain open-circuited for a fraction of time, resulting in a very large current may flow through the ammeter and damage the instrument. To avoid such situation, one may use the make-before-break switch as shown in Fig. 2.4.

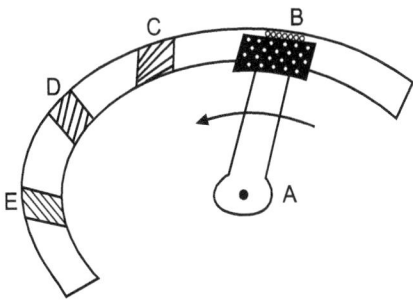

Fig 2.4

The wide-ended moving contact connected to the next terminal to which it is being moved before it loses contact with the previous terminals. Thus, during the switching time there are two resistances in parallel with the instrument and finally the required shunt only will come in parallel to the instrument.

2.4 MULTIRANGE VOLTMETER

Fig. 2.5 (a) and 2.5 (b) shows two different circuits of multirange voltmeter. In Fig. 2.5 (a), a tap changing switch with resistances R_1, R_2, R_3 and R_4 is used for voltage ranges V_1, V_2, V_3 and V_4 respectively. For each range a separate multiplier has been used. The values of resistances R_1, R_2, R_3 and R_4 can be calculated by using equation.

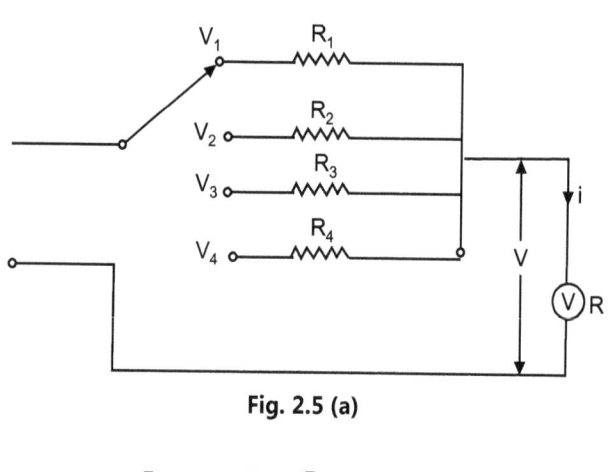

Fig. 2.5 (a)

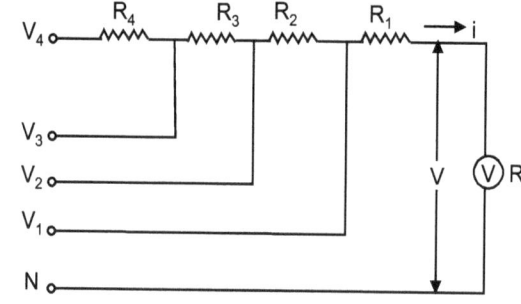

Fig. 2.5 (b)

$$R_s = \left(\frac{V}{i} - R\right)$$

$$= R\left(\frac{V}{v} - 1\right)$$

$$= R(N-1)$$

V = Voltage to be measured
R = Voltmeter resistance

R_s = Series resistance

v = Voltage drop across the instrument for full scale deflection

$N = \dfrac{V}{v}$ = Multiplying power

Fig. 2.5 (b) shows multirange voltmeter circuit. In this type the connection are made at the junction of resistance R_1, R_2, R_3 and R_4 in series to obtain the ranges V_1, V_2, V_3 and V_4. Series resistances R_1, R_2, R_3, R_4 can be calculated as given below.

$$R_1 = \dfrac{V_1}{i} - R$$

$$R_2 = \dfrac{V_2}{i} - R - R_1$$

$$R_3 = \dfrac{V_3}{i} - R - R_1 - R_2$$

$$R_4 = \dfrac{V_4}{i} - R - R_1 - R_2 - R_3$$

where, $V_4 > V_3 > V_2 > V_1$

2.5 VOLTMETER SENSITIVITY

The sensitivity of a voltmeter is given in ohms per volt. Sensitivity is expressed as follows:

$$\text{sensitivity} = \dfrac{R_m + R_s}{E}$$

$$\text{sensitivity} = \dfrac{\text{ohms}}{\text{volt}} = \dfrac{1}{\text{ampere}}$$

2.6 NEED OF CALIBRATION

Calibration defines the accuracy and quality of measurements recorded using a piece of equipment. The need of calibration is to minimize any measurement uncertainty by ensuring the accuracy of test equipment. Calibration quantifies and controls errors or uncertainties within measurement processes to an acceptable level.

Main reasons for having instruments calibrated are :

- To ensure readings from an instrument are consistent with other measurements.
- To determine the accuracy of the instrument readings.
- To establish the reliability of the instrument.

Calibration is the process of configuring an instrument to provide a result for a sample within an acceptable range. Instrument calibration is one of the primary processes used to maintain instrument accuracy. Calibration process generally involves using instrument to test samples of one or more known values called calibrators. Calibrations are performed using only a few calibrators to establish the correlation at specific points within the instrument operating range.

2.7 UNIVERSAL SHUNT OR AYRTON SHUNT

Q. Write note on shunt?

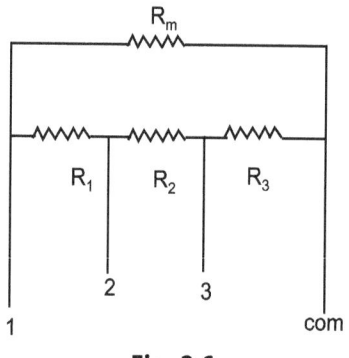

Fig. 2.6

Consider the circuit shown above. The shunt resistors R_1, R_2, R_3 are all in series and collectively in parallel to the meter movement. Ayrton shunt eliminates the possibility of having a meter without a shunt. Selector switch selects the shunt required to change the range of the meter. When the resistance R_1 is in parallel with R_2, R_3 and R_m the current through the shunt is more than the current through the meter and the basic meter is protected by this. In the position 3, resisitances R_1, R_2 and R_3 in series and acts as the shunt. In this position, the maximum current flows through the meter. Voltage drop across two parallel branches is always same.

∴ $$I_{sh}R_{sh} = I_m R_m$$

In position 1, R_1 in parallel with $R_2 + R_3 + R_m$

∴ $$I_1 R_1 = I_m [R_2 + R_3 + R_m]$$

In position 2, $R_1 + R_2$ is in parallel with $R_3 + R_m$

∴ $$I_2 (R_1 + R_2) = I_m (R_3 + R_m)$$

In position 3, $R_1 + R_2 + R_3$ is in parallel with R_m

∴ $$I_3 (R_1 + R_2 + R_3) = I_m R_m$$

I_1 is maximum and I_3 is minimum current.

2.8 VOLTMETER USING MULTIPLIER

A permanent magnet moving coil basic meter [d' Arsonval Meter] is converted into a voltmeter by connecting a series resistance with it. This series resistance is known as multiplier. The combination of meter movement and the multiplier is put across the circuit whose voltage is to be measured.

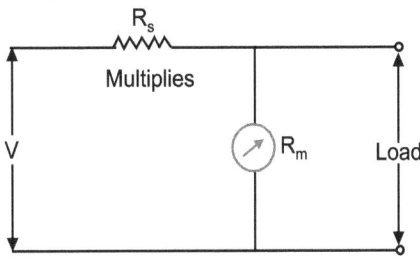

Fig. 2.7

R_m = Internal resistance of meter movement
R_s = Multiplier resistance
V = Full range voltage of instrument
I_m = Full scale deflection current

$$V = I_m (R_m + R_s)$$
$$V = I_m R_m + I_m R_s$$
$$R_s = \frac{V - I_m R_m}{I_m}$$

$$\boxed{R_s = \frac{V - R_m}{I_m}}$$

Multiplying factor for multiplier,

$$m = \frac{\text{Full range voltage of instrument}}{\text{Voltage drop across basic meter}}$$

$$= \frac{I_m (R_m + R_s)}{I_m R_m}$$

$$m = 1 + \frac{R_s}{R_m}$$

Resistance of multiplier $R_s = (m - 1) R_m$.

Hence, for the measurement of voltage 'm' times the voltage range of instrument, the series multiplying resistance should be (m – 1) times the meter resistance.

Requirements of Multiplier :
- Materials used for construction of multiplier are manganin and constant.
- Resistance should not change with time.
- Change in resistance value with temperature should be small.

2.9 INSTRUMENT TRANSFORMERS

The name instrument transformer is a general classification applied to current and voltage devices used to change currents and voltages from one magnitude to another or to isolate the utilization current or voltage from the supply voltage for safety to both the operator and the end device in use. Instrument transformers are designed specifically for use with electrical equipment falling into the broad category of devices commonly called instruments such as voltmeters, ammeters, watt meters, watt-hour meters, protection relays, etc.

Instrument transformers are divided into two types

(1) Current transformers

(2) Potential transformers

Advantages of Instrument transformers are:

1. Single range instrument can be used for measurement of current or voltages of various ranges by using a multi range current or voltage transformer.

2. When measurement is to be done on a high tension circuit, the instrument can be located at some distance from the circuit. This gives safety to the observer.

3. Measuring Instrument is isolated from high tension circuit. So it is not insulated for high voltage.

4. Current in a heavy current bus bar can be measured with the help of a current transformer without breaking the current circuit.

2.9.1 Potential Transformer(P.T.)

P.T. is used to measure a large voltage using a low range voltmeter.

Potential transformers consist of two separate windings on a common magnetic steel core. One winding consists of fewer turns of heavier wire on the steel core and is called the secondary winding. The primary winding consists of a relatively large number of turns of fine wire, wound on top of the secondary. The primary is connected across high voltage line while secondary is connected to low range voltmeter coil. The high voltage V_p being measured is given by, $V_p = nV_s$ Where, $n = N_p/N_s$ = turns ratio. A typical connection is as follows:

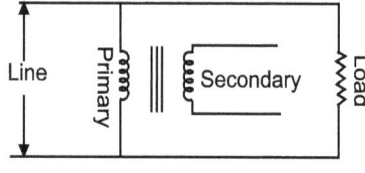

Fig. 2.8

The primary is connected across high voltage line while secondary is connected to low range voltmeter coil. Potential transformers are normally connected across two lines of the circuit in which the voltage is to be measured. Normally they will be connected L-L (line-to-line) or L-G (line-to-ground). In a voltmeter which operates on the magnitude of the voltage, there is no need to observe the polarity of the transformer. However, in watthour meter applications, polarity must always be observed.

The high voltage Vp being measured is given by,

$$Vp = nVs \text{ Where, } n = Np/Ns = \text{turns ratio}$$

2.9.2 Current transformer

CT is the one which is to be measure a large current in circuit using low range ammeter.

Current transformers are constructed in various ways. One method is similar to that of the potential transformer. There are two separate windings on a magnetic steel core. But the primary winding consists of a few turns of heavy wire capable of carrying the full load current while the secondary winding consist of many turns of smaller wire with a current carrying capacity of between 5/20 amperes, dependent on the design. This is called the wound type due to its wound primary coil.

Another type of construction is called as "window," "through" or donut type current transformer in which the core has an opening through which the conductor carrying the primary load current is passed. This primary conductor constitutes the primary winding of the CT which pass through the "window" represents a one turn primary, and must be large enough in cross section to carry the maximum current of the load.

CT with wound primary have their primary windings connected in series with the line and the load and their secondary windings connected to the burden as shown below

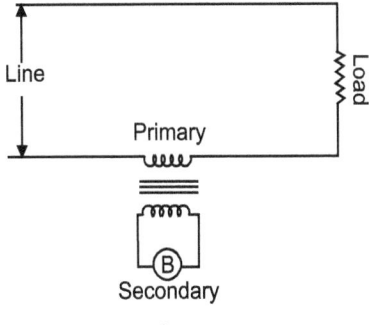

Fig. 2.9

Current transformers having a center tapped secondary are referred to as a dual ratio CT. They are used in applications where it is necessary to have available two ratios of primary to secondary current from the same secondary winding of the CT. This may be accomplished by adding a tap in the secondary winding to get a second ratio. The ratio obtained by the tap is usually one-half the ratio obtained by the full secondary winding.

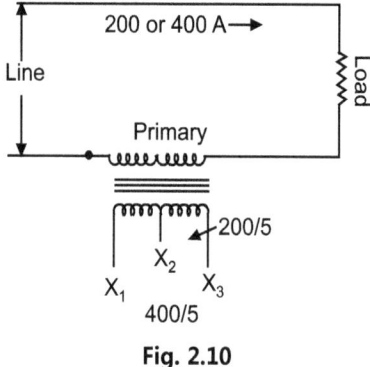

Fig. 2.10

It is not recommended to reconnect while the unit is energized The secondary terminals must be short circuited so as not to induce high voltage in the secondary circuit when the circuit is opened. On a dual ratio tapped secondary CT, both the full winding and the tapped winding cannot be operated simultaneously. The unused terminal must be left open to avoid short circuiting a portion of the secondary winding.

It is very important that secondary of C.T. should not be kept open. If it is left open, then current through secondary becomes zero. Hence, the ampere turns produced by secondary which generally oppose primary ampere turns becomes zero. As there is no counter m.m.f., unopposed primary mmf produces high flux in the core. This produce excessive core loss, heating the core beyond limits. Similarly heavy emf's will be induced on the primary and secondary side. This may damage the insulation of winding. Never open secondary winding circuit of a CT, while its primary winding is energized.

2.10 CONSTRUCTION OF CURRENT TRANSFORMER

Some of the common features of current transformer are :

1. **Primary Ampere Turns :** The core material used for the transformer must have high permeability and low loss. Mumetal, a nickel iron alloy containing copper, is most widely used for current transformers. With Mumetal core a bar-primary transformer of primary current as low as 100 A can be constructed with a reasonable good performance. Stalloy is used for primary current of about 500 A. Mumetal is a costly material used for precision current transformers.

2. **Core :** The core must have low reluctance and so the core material must have high permeability. To reduce the core reluctance, the length of magnetic path should be as

small as consistent with good mechanical construction and with insulation. Three commonly used types of cores are :

(a) Core type
(b) Shell type
(c) Ring type

Core type, built up of L shaped punching has the winding placed on one of its shorter limbs with the primary winding usually wound over the secondary. It has advantage of ample space for insulation and is used for high voltage work. In shell type, windings are placed on the central limb. This is difficult to build up. The ring type, made up of ring stampings is used when primary current is large. Primary winding is a single bar surrounded by the ring on which the secondary winding is uniformly distributed. The advantage of ring type is robust construction, jointless core and very small leakage reactance.

3. **Windings :** Primary and secondary winding should be close together in order to reduce the secondary leakage reactance which tends to increase the ratio error.

4. **Insulation :** For lower line voltages, the windings are separately wound and are insulated by impregnated tape and varnish. For higher voltages of 7 kV and above transformers are filled with solid insulating compound or are oil immersed. Primary may be insulated by bakellite, fibre or porcelain tube. A porcelain bushing and oil filling are used for very high voltages.

Types of current transformer are :

- **Window Type :** One or more turns of a flexible conductor is passed through the core and secondary winding as the primary winding. The core is of stadium, rectangular or circular shape.

- **Wound Primary Type :** These are low current transformers. To obtain sufficient ampere turns, more than one turn are wound on the core.

- **Bar Primary Type :** Insulated bar carrying the primary current is an integral part of the transformer and is used as primary conductor. For a very high current rating a single turn is enough to give required ampere turns.

- **Bushing Type :** These are actually window type transformers specially designed to fit on the bushing of power transformers, circuit breakers.

- **Split Core Type :** These are special type of window type transformers with hinged core. The core opens so it can be clamped around the conductor carrying the current to be measured, avoiding the necessity of opening the load circuits.

2.11 ERRORS INTRODUCED BY CURRENT TRANSFORMER

Q. Explain error introduced by current transformer?
Q. How to reduce error in current transformer?

I_p, primary current in CT is not exactly equal to the secondary current multiplied by turn's ratio i.e. $K_p I_s$. The difference is due to the primary current and is contributed by the core excitation current. The error in current transformer introduced due to this difference is called current error of CT or sometimes ratio error in current transformer.

$$\text{Ratio error} = \frac{\text{Nominal ratio} - \text{Actual ratio}}{\text{Actual ratio}}$$

$$= \frac{K_n - K}{K}$$

where,

K_n = Nominal ratio

Actual ratio = $K = n + \dfrac{I_m \sin\delta + I_c \cos\delta}{I_s}$

I_m = Magnetising component of no load current $I_o = I_o \sin\phi$
I_c = Core loss component of no load current $I_o = I_o \cos\phi_o$
I_s = Secondary current
δ = Phase angle of total impedance of secondary

$$\delta = \tan^{-1}\left(\frac{X_s + X_e}{r_s + r_e}\right)$$

δ is +ve → Lagging p.f. load
δ is −ve → Leading p.f. load

As loads are inductive, δ is very small.

$$\sin\delta \to 0 \text{ and } \cos\delta \approx 1$$

∴ $\quad R = n + \dfrac{I_c}{I_s} \quad$ where, $n = \dfrac{I_p}{I_s}$

∴ $\quad R = n + \dfrac{n I_c}{I_p}$

Phase angle error : For an ideal CT the angle between the primary and reversed secondary current vector is zero. But for an actual CT there is always a difference in phase between two due to the fact that primary current has to supply the component of the exciting current. The angle between the above two phases is termed as phase angle error in current transformer. It is denoted by angle θ.

Phase angle error is given by :

$$\theta = \frac{180}{\pi}\left[\frac{I_m \cos\delta - I_c \sin\delta}{n I_s}\right] \text{ degrees}$$

In practice δ is very small and positive.

∴ $\cos\delta \approx 1$ and $\sin\delta \approx 0$

∴ $R = n + \dfrac{I_c}{I_s}$

$\theta = \dfrac{180}{\pi}\left[\dfrac{I_m}{n I_s}\right]$

∴ $\boxed{\theta = \dfrac{180}{\pi}\left[\dfrac{I_m}{I_p}\right] \text{ degrees}}$ $\left[\because n = \dfrac{I_p}{I_s}\right]$

Following are the methods to reduce error in current transformer :
- By decreasing the secondary terminal impedance
- By keeping the rated burden near to the value of the actual burden
- By using a core of high permeability and low hysterisis loss magnetic materials

2.12 ERROR IN VOLTAGE TRANSFORMER

Ratio error and phase angle error are the errors in voltage transformer. For the measurement of voltage, only ratio error is important while for measurement of power both ratio error and phase angle errors are responsible for wrong measurement. Both the errors depend on the reactances and resistances of the transformer windings as well as upon the value of exciting current of the transformer.

$$\% \text{ Ratio error} = \dfrac{K_n - R}{R} \times 100$$

where, $R = \text{Actual ratio} = \dfrac{V_p}{V_s}$

$R = n + \dfrac{nI_s[R_{2e}\cos\Delta + X_{2e}\sin\Delta] + I_c r_p + I_m X_p}{V_s}$

where,
- I_c = Core loss component of I_o.
- I_m = Magnetising component of I_o.
- V_p = Primary voltage.
- V_s = Secondary voltage
- r_p = Resistance of primary winding
- X_p = Reactance of primary winding
- R_{2e} = Equivalent resistance referred to secondary
- X_{2e} = Equivalent reactance referred to secondary

$$\Delta = \text{Phase angle of secondary load current} = \tan^{-1}\left(\frac{X_e}{r_e}\right)$$

Phase angle error : Angle θ between primary system voltage and reverse secondary voltage is the phase error.

$$\theta = \frac{I_s}{V_s}[X_{2e}\cos\Delta - R_{2e}\sin\Delta] + \frac{I_c X_p - I_{mr_p}}{nV_s} \text{ radians.}$$

2.13 ADVANTAGES OF INSTRUMENT TRANSFORMERS OVER SHUNTS AND MULTIPLIERS

They may be listed as follows :
- When the measurement is to be done on a high tension circuit, the instrument can be located at some distance from the circuit, giving safety to the observer.
- As the measuring instrument is isolated from high tension circuit, it need not be insulated for high voltage.
- A single range instrument can be used for the measurement of current or voltages of various ranges by using a multirange current or voltage transformer or several single range transformers.
- They can be used for operating of protective devices like relays.
- Power output is very small as loads are light and hence heating is not severs.

2.14 DIFFERENCE BETWEEN CT AND PT

Q. Compare current transformer (CT) with potential transformer (PT).

- CT is also known as series transformer. The secondary of CT is virtually under short circuit conditions when the primary of CT is energized. The PT is also known as parallel transformer. The secondary of PT can be left open circuited without any damage either to transformer or to the operator.
- The current in the primary of CT is independent of secondary winding conditions whereas current in the primary of PT depends on the secondary circuit burden.
- Primary winding of PT is connected across full line voltage where as CT is connected in series with one of the lines and therefore a small voltage exists across its terminal. However the current transformer carries full line current.
- Line voltage of PT is constant near normal conditions. The flux density and the exciting current of a PT varies between small range whereas primary current and excitation of a CT varies over a wide range under normal working conditions.

2.15 BURDEN OF INSTRUMENT TRANSFORMER

> Q. Explain the meaning of term burden in an instrument transformer?
> Q Define the following terms associated with instrument transformer :
> (i)   Transformation ratio
> (ii) Turns ratio
> (iii) Nominal ratio

The rated burden of instrument transformer is the volt ampere loading which is permissible without errors exceeding the limits. Burden across the secondary of an instrument transformer is also defined as the ratio of secondary voltage to secondary current.

$$Z_L = \frac{\text{Secondary voltage}}{\text{Secondary current}} = \frac{V}{I}$$

Unit of burden is ohms.

Secondary winding burden due to load
= (Secondary winding current)^2 × (Impedance of load on secondary)

The nominal ratio of an instrument transformer varies as the load on secondary changes. It changes due to the effect of secondary current, power factor etc. and this causes errors in measurement. For particular class of transformers the specific loading at rated secondary winding voltage is such that errors do not exceed the limit. This permissible load is called burden of an instrument transformer.

2.16 RATIOS OF INSTRUMENT TRANSFORMERS

The ratios defined for instrument transformers are

1. Actual ratio: It is the ratio of the magnitude of actual primary phasor to the corresponding magnitude of actual secondary phasor.

C.T. Ratio = magnitude of actual primary current / magnitude of actual sec. current

P.T. Ratio = magnitude of actual primary voltage / magnitude of actual secondary voltage.

2. Nominal ratio (Kn) The nominal ratio is defined as the ratio of rated primary quantity to rated secondary quantity, either current or voltage

For C.T.
$$K_n = \text{rated primary current / rated sec. current}$$

For P.T.
$$K_n = \text{rated primary voltage/ rated sec. voltage}$$

3. Turns ratio(n)

C.T. n = no. of turns of sec. winding / no. of turns of primary winding

P.T. n = no. of turns of primary winding / no. of turns of sec. winding

NUMERICALS

Q.1 The deflection obtained on a standard 220V voltmeter is a full scale deflection when its primary is connected across the supply. If the turns ratio of P.T. is 30 : 1. Find the magnitude of supply voltage.

Sol.
$$\frac{T_p}{T_s} = \frac{V_p}{V_s} = \text{Turns ratio} = 30$$

$$\frac{V_p}{220} = 30$$

$$\therefore V_p = 6600 \text{ V}$$

Q.2 For a 200/5 A current transformer, with secondary burden of 10 VA at the rated load current. Find the value of load impedance on the secondary side.

Sol. For secondary burden of 10 VA, secondary potential difference at the terminals of C.T.

$$= \frac{10 \text{ VA}}{5 \text{ A}} = 2 \text{ volts}$$

$$\text{Load impedance} = \frac{\text{Secondary P.D.}}{\text{Secondary current}} = \frac{2}{5} = 0.4 \, \Omega$$

Q.3 A moving coil instrument gives max deflection for a current of 10 mA. It has a resistance of 10 Ω. Calculate the value of shunt resistance required to make it read upto 20 A.

Sol.
$$\text{Multiplying power} = \frac{\text{Current to be measured}}{\text{Current through ammeter}}$$

$$= \frac{20}{10 \times 10^{-3}}$$

$$M = 2000$$

$$\text{Resistance of shunt} = \frac{\text{Ammeter resistance}}{M - 1} = \frac{10}{2000 - 1}$$

$$\therefore R_s = 0.005$$

Q.4 A moving coil instrument gives a full scale deflection of 10 mA when the potential difference across its terminals is 100 mV. Calculate shunt resistance for a full scale deflection corresponding to 100 A.

Sol.
$$I_m = 10 \text{ mA}$$

$$R_m = \text{Meter resistance} = \frac{100}{10} = 10 \, \Omega$$

$$\text{Shunt multiplying factor} = m = \frac{I}{I_m} = \frac{100}{10 \times 10^{-3}} = 10000$$

$$\text{Shunt resistance} = R_{sh} = \frac{R_m}{m - 1} = \frac{10}{10000 - 1}$$

$$\therefore R_{sh} = 0.001 \, \Omega$$

Q.5 A moving coil instrument gives a full scale deflection of 24 mA when P.D. across its terminals is 72 mV. Calculate (a) Shunt resistance for a full scale deflection of 120 A, (b) Series resistance for full scale deflection of 600 V.

Sol. Meter current, I_m = 24 mA

Meter resistance, $R_m = \dfrac{72}{24} = 3\,\Omega$

Shunt multiplying factor, $m = \dfrac{I}{I_m} = \dfrac{120}{24 \times 10^{-3}} = 5000$

Shunt resistance = $R_{sh} = \dfrac{R_m}{m-1} = \dfrac{3}{5000-1} = 0.6\,m\Omega$

when, V = 600 V

Voltage multiplying factor = $\dfrac{V}{V_m} = \dfrac{600}{72 \times 10^{-3}} = 8333.33$

Multiplying resistance = $(m-1)\,R_m = (8333.33 - 1) \times 3 = 2.496\,\Omega$

Power dissipation = $V\,I_m = 600 \times 24 \times 10^{-3} = 14.4$ W

Q.6 A moving coil instrument gives a full scale deflection for a current of 20 mA with a potential difference 200 mV across it. Calculate the multiplier required to use it as a voltmeter of range 0 – 500 V.

Sol. V = 500 V

$R_s = \dfrac{V}{I_m} - R_m$

$= \dfrac{500}{20 \times 10^{-3}} - \left(\dfrac{200}{20}\right)$

= 24.99 KΩ

Q.7 The ammeter has a resistance of 7.5 Ω and a shunt of 0.005 Ω. Calculate the current through a milliameter if it is connected in a circuit carrying a current of 15 A.

Sol. Multiplying power of shunt = $1 + \dfrac{R}{R_s}$

$= 1 + \dfrac{7.5}{0.005}$

M = 1501

$M = \dfrac{I}{i}$

$i = \dfrac{I}{M}$

$= \dfrac{15}{1501}$

= 9.98 mA

Q.8 A moving coil instrument having a resistance of 5Ω gives a full scale deflection when a current of 2×10^{-3} A is passed through it. Calculate the value of resistance to be connected in parallel with an instrument to be used to measure current upto 1 A.

Sol.
$$M = \frac{I}{I_m} = \frac{1}{2 \times 10^{-3}} = 500$$

$$M = 500$$

$$R_s = \frac{R_m}{(m-1)}$$

$$= \frac{5}{(500-1)} = 0.01 \, \Omega$$

UNIVERSITY QUESTIONS

Dec. 2010

Q.1 Describe construction and working of PMMC instrument with suitable diagram Derive its torque equation with usual notations. **(10 Marks)**

Q.2 Define the following terms associated with instrument transformer : **(6 Marks)**
(i) Transformation ratio
(ii) Turns ratio
(iii) Nominal ratio

May 2011

Q.3 Draw and explain the construction and working of PMMC instrument. Derive its torque equation. **(10 Marks)**

Q.4 State the purpose of instrument Transformers in measurement of electrical quantity. Draw neat connection diagram for measuring high voltage and high current with the help of C.T. and P.T. **(8 Marks)**

Q.5 State difference between power transformer and instrument transformer. **(5 Marks)**

Dec. 2011

Q.6 With a neat sketch describe construction and working of PMMC instrument. Derive the torque equation for this instrument. Comment on shape of scale. **(10 Marks)**

Q.7 Explain advantages and disadvantages of MI and PMMC instrument. **(8 Marks)**

Q.8 Compare current transformer (CT) with potential transformer (PT). **(6 Marks)**

Q.9 Explain the meaning of term burden in an instrument transformer. **(4 Marks)**

Chapter 3

MEASUREMENT OF RESISTANCE

3.1 INTRODUCTION

Q. Explain types of resistance.

The value of resistance to be measured is an important factor for the choice of a suitable method of measurement of resistance. Other factors may be the accuracy of measurement, working conditions etc. The classification of resistances from the point of view of measurement is as follows :

1. **Low resistances :** All the resistances of the order of 1 Ω and lower values come under this class of resistances e.g. Armature series winding resistances of large machines, resistances of ammeter shunts.
2. **Medium resistances :** All the resistances of value between 1 Ω and 100 KΩ come under this class of resistances e.g. most of the electrical apparatus used in practice.
3. **High resistances :** Resistances of 100 kΩ and above are termed as high resistances e.g. insulation resistance of cables, resistances of dielectrics etc.

3.2 METHODS FOR MEASUREMENT OF LOW RESISTANCES

Following are the methods for the measurement of low resistance :
1. Ammeter Voltmeter method
2. Potentiometer method
3. Kelvin double bridge method

3.2.1 Ammeter Voltmeter Method

This method of measuring resistances is the simplest of all methods. It is used for the accuracy required is of the order of 1 per cent. The circuit diagram of this method is shown below.

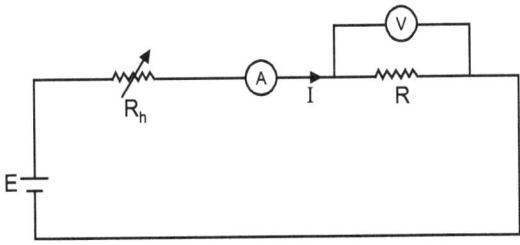

Fig. 3.1: Ammeter voltmeter method

R is the unknown resistance to be measured, V is the high resistance voltmeter of resistance R_v, A is an ammeter connected in series with a regulating rheostat R_h. We assume that the current through the voltmeter is negligibly small and hence the value of unknown resistance is :

$$R_m = \frac{\text{Voltmeter reading}}{\text{Ammeter reading}}$$

$$R_m = \frac{V}{I}$$

Practically the voltmeter reading is the true voltage across the resistance to be measured but the ammeter carries the total current which is sum of the current through resistance and the current through voltmeter. Current through unknown resistance R is

$$I' = \frac{R_v}{R_v + R} I$$

$\therefore \quad V = \frac{R R_v}{R_v + R} I$ ... (1)

$R_m = \frac{V}{I}$ ... (2)

$\therefore \quad R_m = \frac{R R_v}{R + R_v}$ ... From (1) and (2)

$$R = \frac{R_m R_v}{R_v - R_m}$$

$$R = K R_m$$

$\therefore \quad K = \text{Correction factor} = \frac{R_v}{R_v - R_m}$

Accuracy of measurement is limited by the accuracy of ammeter and voltmeter. It is desirable to use highly accurate type of ammeter and voltmeter.

3.2.2 Potentiometer Method

Advantages of this method are its high accuracy and no power consumption from the circuit when it is balanced.

3.2.3 Kelvin's Double Bridge

This bridge is best available for the measurement of low resistance. It eliminates the errors due to contact and lead resistances. Kelvin's double bridge has another set of ratio arms. The first set of ratio arm is P and Q and second set of ratio arm is p and q which is used to connect the galvanometer to point 'c'. It uses four terminal resistors for the low resistance arms. The ratio p/q is made equal to P/Q. Standard resistance is 'S' and known resistance is

'R'. Under balance condition there is no current through the galvanometer. The voltage drop between 'a' and 'd' is E_{ad} is equal to voltage drop between 'a' and 'c' i.e. E_{amc}.

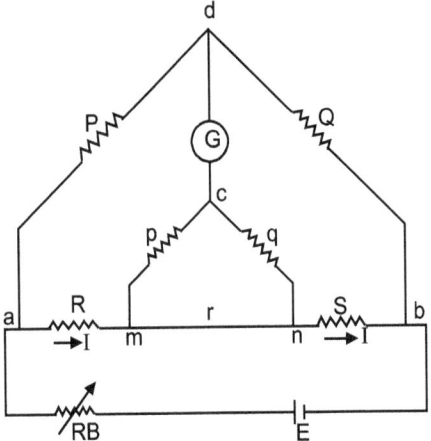

Fig. 3.2 : Kelvin double bridge

$$E_{ad} = \frac{P}{P+Q} E_{ab}$$

$$E_{ab} = I\left[R + S + \frac{(p+q)r}{p+q+r}\right]$$

$$E_{amc} = I\left\{R + \frac{p}{(p+q)}\left[\frac{(p+q)r}{p+q+r}\right]\right\}$$

$$= I\left(R + \frac{pr}{p+q+r}\right)$$

For null deflection of galvanometer,

$$E_{ad} = E_{amc}$$

∴ $$\frac{P}{P+Q} I\left[R + S + \frac{(p+q)r}{p+q+r}\right]$$

$$= I\left(R + \frac{pr}{p+q+r}\right)$$

∴ $$R = \frac{P}{Q} \cdot S + \frac{qr}{p+q+r}\left[\frac{P}{Q} - \frac{p}{q}\right]$$

when, $\frac{P}{Q} = \frac{p}{q}$ then, $R = \frac{P}{Q} \cdot S$

The resistance of connecting lead 'r' has no effect on measurement when two set of ratio arms have equal ratios. With battery connections reversed and by making another measurement, the effect of thermoelectric e.m.fs can be eliminated.

3.3 MEASUREMENT OF MEDIUM RESISTANCE

Q. List the methods for measurement of medium resistance.
Q. Draw the circuit of Wheatstone's bridge and derive the condition of balance.

Measurement of medium resistance can be done using following methods.
- Ammeter voltmeter method
- Ohmmeter method
- Substitution method
- Wheatstone's bridge method

1. **Ammeter Voltmeter Method :** This is already discussed in 3.2.1
2. **Ohmmeter Method :** Using this method the value of resistance can be measured directly. It is simple and easy to use but accuracy is moderate.
3. **Substitution Method :** It involves comparison. Though this method is simple, it has many causes of errors as
   (i) Battery may not supply a constant current during test.
   (ii) The resistance of the circuit other than unknown resistance to be measured and known variable resistance may change due to heating. For this reason the variable resistance and unknown resistance should be large compared to that of the circuit resistance.
4. **Wheatstone's Bridge Method :** This is commonly used method for medium resistances. It is most accurate and reliable method.

3.3.1 Wheatstone's Bridge

The basic circuit of Wheatstone bridge is shown in Fig. 3.3.

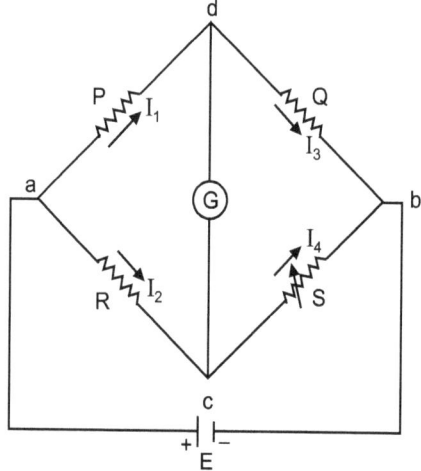

Fig. 3.3 : Wheatstone's bridge

Wheatstone's bridge is used for the measurement of medium resistances. The bridge consists of four resistive arms together with a source of e.m.f and a null detector. The null detector is usually a galvanometer G. The current through the galvanometer depends on the potential difference between points c and d. The arms consisting of resistances P and Q are called ratio arms. The arms consisting of known resistance 'S' is called standard arm. The arm containing resistance R is the unknown resistance.

Balance Condition : The current through the galvanometer depends on the potential difference between points c and d. The bridge is balanced when there is no current through the galvanometer or the potential difference across the galvanometer is zero. Balance condition is achieved when the voltage from point 'a' to point 'd' equals the voltage from point 'a' to 'c'. Balance condition can also be achieved when voltage from point 'd' to 'b' equal to the voltage from 'c' to 'b'

∴
$$E_{ad} = E_{ac}$$
$$I_1 P = I_2 R \qquad \ldots (1)$$

As galvanometer current is zero, $I_1 = I_3$ and $I_2 = I_4$

Considering battery path under balanced condition

$$I_1 = I_3 = \frac{E}{P + Q} \qquad \ldots (2)$$

and,
$$I_2 = I_4 = \frac{E}{R + S} \qquad \ldots (3)$$

where E is the e.m.f of battery.

Using equation (1), (2) and (3),

$$\frac{E}{P + Q} P = \frac{E}{R + S} R$$

∴ $$\frac{P}{P + Q} = \frac{R}{R + S}$$

∴ $$QR = PS$$

∴ $$\boxed{R = \frac{PS}{Q}} \qquad \ldots (4)$$

Equation (4) is the required balance condition of Wheatstone's bridge.

3.3.2 Sensitivity of Wheatstone's Bridge

> Q. Explain the sensitivity of Wheatstone's bridge and give the expression for it.
> Q. Derive the expression required for the sensitivity of Wheatstone bridge and also state its limitations.

It is desirable to know the sensitivity of the bridge which depends on the sensitivity of galvanometer. When the bridge is balanced, the current through the galvanometer is zero. The amount of deflection depends on the sensitivity of the galvanometer. Expression for sensitivity is given as

$$\text{Sensitivity (S)} = \frac{\text{Deflection}}{\text{Current}}$$

$$\boxed{S = \frac{D}{I}}$$

Where, D = deflection and I = current. Unit of sensitivity is mm/µA, radians/µA or degrees/µA.

For the same amount of current, sensitivity is directly proportional to deflection.

Bridge sensitivity is defined as the deflection of the galvanometer per unit fractional change in the unknown resistance.

$$S_B = \frac{\text{Deflection of galvanometer}}{\text{Unit fractional change in unknown resistance}}$$

∴ $$\boxed{S_B = \frac{\theta}{\Delta_{R/R}}}$$

Sensitivity to unbalance can be determined by solving the bridge circuit for small unbalance. This is done by converting the Wheatstone bridge into Thevenin's equivalent circuit. When the branch resistances are P, Q, R and S the bridge is balanced.

∴ PS = QR

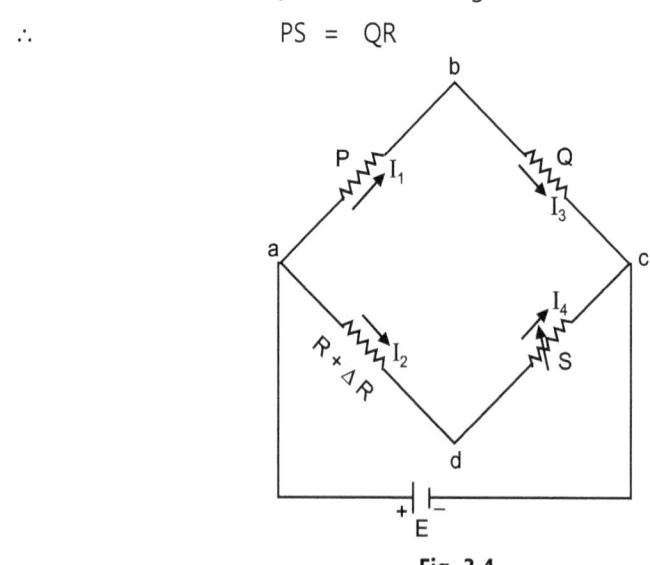

Fig. 3.4

Now consider resistance R is changed to R + Δ_R creating unbalance. This will generate e.m.f 'e' across the galvanometer branch. With the galvanometer branch open, the voltage drop across point a and b is

$$E_{ab} = I_1 P = \frac{EP}{P + Q}$$

$$E_{ad} = I_2(R + \Delta_R)$$
$$= \frac{E(R + \Delta_R)}{R + \Delta_R + S}$$

∴ Voltage difference between b and d is

$$e = E_{ad} - E_{ab}$$
$$= E\left(\frac{R + \Delta_R}{R + \Delta_R + S} - \frac{P}{P + Q}\right)$$

Under balance condition,

$$\frac{P}{P + Q} = \frac{R}{R + S}$$

∴ $$e = E\left(\frac{R + \Delta_R}{R + \Delta_R + S} - \frac{R}{R + S}\right)$$

$$e = \frac{E S \Delta_R}{(R + S)^2 + \Delta_R(R + S)}$$

$$e \approx \frac{E S \Delta_R}{(R + S)^2} \qquad \text{[Neglecting } \Delta_R(R+S)\text{]}$$

Let, S_v be the voltage sensitivity of galvanometer.

∴ Deflection galvanometer $= \theta = \frac{E S \Delta_R}{(R + S)^2} \cdot S_v$

Bridge sensitivity $S_B = \dfrac{\theta}{\Delta_{R/R}}$

∴ $$S_B = \frac{E S \Delta_R \times R}{\Delta_R (R + S)^2}$$

$$= \frac{S_v E S R}{(R + S)^2}$$

∴ $$\boxed{S_B = \frac{S_v E S R}{(R + S)^2}} \qquad \ldots (A)$$

Equation (A) is the equation for bridge sensitivity which depends on bridge voltage, bridge parameters and the voltage sensitivity of the galvanometer.

It can be expressed as, $S_B = \dfrac{S_v E}{(R + S)^2 / SR}$

$$= \frac{S_v E}{\frac{R^2}{SR} + \frac{2RS}{SR} + \frac{S^2}{SR}}$$

$$S_B = \frac{S_v E}{\frac{R}{S} + 2 + \frac{S}{R}}$$

$$S_B = \frac{S_v E}{\frac{P}{Q} + 2 + \frac{Q}{P}}$$

Maximum sensitivity occurs when $\frac{R}{S} = 1$. For higher or lower values of R and S, the sensitivity decreases.

When arm resistances are equal then bridge sensitivity,

$$S_B = \frac{S_v E}{4}$$

The reduction in sensitivity causes reduction of accuracy with which a bridge can be balanced.

3.3.3 Limitations of Wheatstone's Bridge

1. When measuring very high resistances, leakage over insulation of the bridge arms is introduced this makes inaccuracy of bridge.
2. Heating effect due to large current may generate heat which may cause the permanent change in the resistance.
3. The effect of lead resistance and contact resistance is very much significant while measuring low resistances.

3.3.4 Galvanometer Current in Wheatstone's Bridge

Q. Write the expression for galvanometer current in Wheatstone's Bridge.
Q. List various errors encountered while using Wheatstone's Bridge.
Q. Give the applications of Wheatstone's Bridge.
Q. Derive the expression for current through galvanometer.
Q. Derive the expression to justify following statement.

The current through the galvanometer can be calculated using Thevenin equivalent circuit. Thevenin voltage appearing between terminals 'b' and 'd' with galvanometer circuit open circuited is

$$E_o = E_{ad} - E_{ac}$$
$$= I_2(R + \Delta_R) - I_1 P$$
$$= \frac{E(R + \Delta_R)}{R + \Delta_R + S} - \frac{EP}{P + Q}$$
$$= \frac{E(R + \Delta_R)}{R + \Delta_R + S} - \frac{P}{P + Q}$$

when, $R = S = P = Q$,

then, $$E_o = E\left(\frac{R + \Delta_R}{R + \Delta_R + R} - \frac{R}{R + R}\right)$$

$$E_o = E\left(\frac{R + \Delta_R}{\Delta_R + 2R} - \frac{1}{2}\right)$$

$$E_o = E\left(\frac{\Delta_R}{4R}\right) \qquad (\because \Delta R \ll R)$$

Thevenin equivalent circuit of Wheatstone's bridge is shown in Fig. 3.5 below.

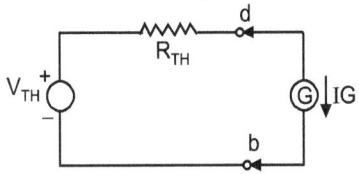

Fig. 3.5

Thevenin equivalent resistance is given as:

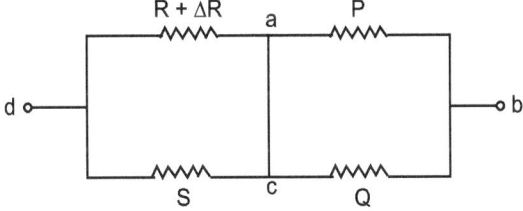

Fig. 3.6

$$R_{TH} = \frac{RS}{R + S} + \frac{PQ}{P + Q} \qquad (\because \Delta R \ll R)$$

when, $P = Q = R = S$

then, $R_{TH} = R$

Current in galvanometer is $I_G = \dfrac{V_{TH}}{R_{TH} + G}$

where, G = Resistance of galvanometer

when, $P = Q = R = S$

then, $$I_G = \frac{E(\Delta_{R/4R})}{(R+G)}$$

3.3.5 Errors in Measurement of Low, Medium and High Resistance using Wheatstone's Bridge Method

- In case of low resistance measurement, the resistance of contacts and leads are included in it. This causes errors in measurement. To avoid these errors the resistances are provided with four terminals.
- In the measurement of medium resistance by Wheatstone's bridge the errors are caused by -
  (a) Resistance of connecting leads.
  (b) Thermoelectric effects : Thermoelectric e.m.f are present in measuring circuit which affect the galvanometer deflection.
  (c) The errors caused by change of resistance due to change of temperature.
  (d) Contact resistance of switches may cause serious errors.
- Due to electrostatic effect stray changes can appear in measuring circuit causing errors.

3.3.6 Applications of Wheatstone's Bridge

- It is used to measure D.C. resistance of various types of wires.
- It is used to measure the resistance in the range of 1 Ω to few Mega ohm.
- It is used by telephone companies to locate cable faults.
- It is used to measure the resistance of motor winding, relay coils.

3.4 METHODS FOR MEASUREMENT OF HIGH RESISTANCES

Q. List the methods for measurement of high resistance.

1. **Direct Deflection Method :** In this method the unknown resistance is obtained according to the deflection of galvanometer. It is very costly method. Very sensitive galvanometer with high resistance is used in this method.

2. **Loss of Charge Method :** The resistance to be measured is connected in parallel with a capacitor c and a electrostatic voltmeter. The capacitor is charged to suitable voltage by means of battery having voltage V and it is then allowed to discharge through the resistance under test. Terminal voltages across the resistance are recorded for a considerable period of time during discharge. This is time consuming method. Results are less accurate because of the internal resistance of voltmeter and leakage resistance of capacitor.

3. **Mega Ohm Bridge :** Mega ohm bridge includes power supplies, bridge member amplifiers and indicating instruments. It has range from 0.1 MΩ to 10^6 MΩ. The accuracy is within 3% for lower part of range to possible 10% above 10,000 MΩ.

4. **Megger :** It is used for measuring resistance in mega ohm i.e. insulation resistance. It is based on the principle of electromagnetic induction.

3.4.1 Megger

Insulation resistance quality of an electrical system degrades with time, environment condition i.e. temperature, humidity, moisture and dust particles. It also get impacted negatively due to the presence of electrical and mechanical stress, so it's become very necessary to check the Insulation resistance of equipment at a constant regular interval to avoid any measure fatal or electrical shock. Megger enable us to measure electrical leakage in wire, results are very reliable as we shall be passing electric current through device while we are testing. The equipment basically use for verifying the electrical insulation level of any device such as motor, cable, generator winding, etc.

Types of Meggers :

This can be separated into mainly two categories :
1. Electronic Type (Battery Operated)
2. Manual Type (Hand Operated)

But there is another types of megger which is motor operated type which does not use battery to produce voltage it requires external source to rotate a electrical motor which in turn rotates the generator of the megger.

Construction of Megger :

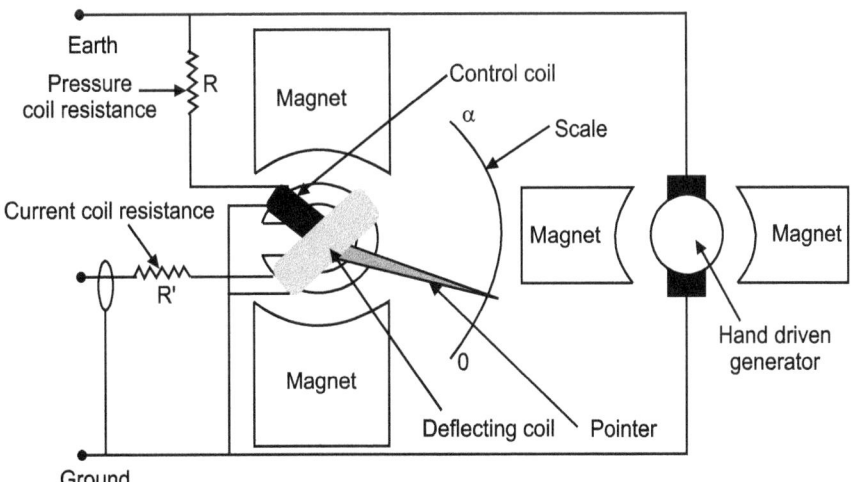

Fig. 3.7 : Megger

Circuit Construction features are as follows :
- Deflecting & Control coil is connected parallel to the generator, mounted at right angle to each other and maintain polarities in such a way to produced torque in opposite direction.
- Permanent Magnets produce magnetic field to deflect pointer with North-South pole magnet.
- One end of the pointer connected with coil another end deflects on scale from infinity to zero.
- A scale is provided in front-top of the Megger from range 'zero' to 'infinity', enable us to read the value.
- Testing voltage is produced by hand operated D.C. generator for manual operated Megger. Battery/electronic voltage charger is provided for automatic type Megger for same purpose.
- Pressure coil resistance and Current coil resistance is used to protect instrument from any damage because of low external electrical resistance under test.

Working of Megger : Deflecting coil or current coil connected in series and allows flowing the electric current taken by the circuit being tested. The control coil also known as pressure coil is connected across the circuit. Current limiting resistor (CCR & PCR) connected in series with control and deflecting coil to protect damage in case of very low resistance in external circuit. 500 Volt DC is sufficient for performing test on equipment range up to 440 Volts. In hand operated megger electromagnetic induction effect is used to produce the test voltage i.e. armature arranges to move in permanent magnetic field or vice-versa. Where as in electronic type megger, batteries are used to produce the testing voltage. As the voltage increases in external circuit the deflection of pointer increases and deflection of pointer decreases with a increases of current. Hence, resultant torque is directly proportional to voltage and inversely proportional to current. When electrical circuit being tested is open, torque due to voltage coil will be maximum and pointer shows 'infinity' means no shorting throughout the circuit and has maximum resistance within the circuit under test. If there is short circuit pointer shows 'zero', which means 'NO' resistance within circuit being tested. The deflection torque is produced with megger tester due to the magnetic field produced by voltage and current, similarly like 'Ohm's Law'. Torque of the megger varies in ratio with V/I, (Ohm's Law : $V = IR$ or $R = V/I$). Electrical resistance to be measured is connected across the generator and in series with deflecting coil. Produced torque shall be in opposite direction if current supplied to the coil.

- High resistance = No current. No current shall flow through deflecting coil, if resistance is very high i.e. infinity position of pointer.

- Small resistance = High current. If circuit measures small resistance allows a high electric current to pass through deflecting coil, i.e. produced torque make the pointer to set at 'ZERO'.
- Intermediate resistance = varied current. If measured resistance is intermediate, produced torques aligns or set the pointer between the range of 'ZERO to INIFINITY'.

3.5 MEASUREMENT OF EARTH RESISTANCE BY USE OF EARTH TESTER

Main factors on which the resistance of any earthing system depends are :
1. Shape and material of earth electrode or electrodes used.
2. Depth in the soil at which the electrodes are buried.
3. Specific resistance of soil surrounding and in the neighbourhood of electrodes.

   Specific resistance of the soil varies from one type of soil to another. The amount of moisture present in the soil affects its specific resistance. Hence the resistance of the earth electrode is not a constant factor but suffers seasonal variations. A periodic testing of earthing is required to ensure that the earthing system remains reasonably effective.

3.5.1 Earth Tester

- The resistance of earth is also measured with an earth tester, the constructional details of which are shown in Fig. 3.8. It consists of a hand cranked type generator; the magnet poles, crossed coils and flexible spirals. Each commutator has four fixed brushes in contact with it. It consists of a rotating current converter and a rectifier in addition to a ohm-meter. Both of these consist of commutator made up of 'L' shaped segments, mounted on the shaft of the generator and rotated at the same speed by the operating handle.
- As the armature rotates, one pair of each set is so positioned that they make contact alternately with one segment and then with other. The second pair of each set of brushes is positioned on the commutator, so that continuous contact is made with one segment, whatever be the position of the commutator.
- Considering the action of the 'current reverser' a unidirectional voltage is applied to the first pair of brushes from the generator so that as the shaft rotates each segment of the commutator makes alternate connections, first with the positive and then with the negative brush; the voltage on the segments thus reverses, giving an alternating voltage, as the commutator rotates which will appear across the second pair of brushes. In this way alternating voltage is produced across the terminals C_1 and C_2.

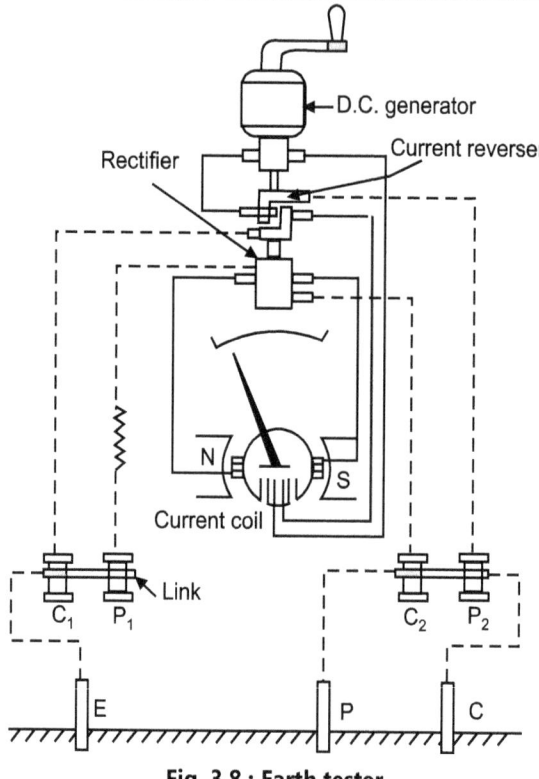

Fig. 3.8 : Earth tester

- With the rectifier commutator the action is the reverse of the above, the alternating voltage across P_1, P_2 being turned into a direct voltage which is then applied to the movement of the instrument. Since both commutators rotate at the same speed, the converting and rectifying actions are in step, i.e. they synchronize.

Principle of operation:

- It is connected to the earth whose resistance is to be measured and the other spikes P and C, as shown in Fig. (3.8), when handle is rotated (Generator), the direct current flows from the generator through the current coil of the movement to the current reverser, and alternating current from the reverser through the soil between the electrodes E and C.

- The alternating voltage drop between the electrodes P and E is rectified, by the rectifier and fed to the potential coil of the meter. As the indication of the meter depends upon the ratio of the potential across its potential coil, and current passing through its current coil; the deflection of its pointer will indicate directly the resistance in ohms of the earth under test.

- For measuring the earth resistance, the current electrode 'C' must be driven into the soil at a sufficient distance from the earth plate E. Also the potential electrode P must be driven in at a point which is outside the resistance area of both E and C. As a rough guide, the current electrode should be 25 m to 30 m away and potential electrode about half the distance from E. Take three readings of earth resistance with the potential electrode at different positions in turn; (a) Midway between E and C, (b) 3 m nearer E, (c) 3m nearer C. If the three readings agree substantially, take the mean of these as current value of earth resistance.

3.6 A.C. BRIDGES

Alternating current bridges are the most used method for the precise measurement of self and mutual inductances and capacitances. A.C bridge consists of 4 arms, a source of excitation and a balance detector. Each arm consists of an impedance. Supply is from an alternating current source. If supply is at normal commercial frequencies then a vibration galvanometer is used. At high frequencies, the electronic oscillators are used as the source. The balance detectors commonly used for A.C. bridges are head phones, tunable amplifier circuits or vibration galvanometer.

The alternating current bridge networks may be classified in the following three classes :

- Wheatstone impedance network without mutual inductance.
- Wheatstone networks in which there are mutual inductances between appropriate pair of branches.
- Network which are not of Wheatstone form and in which there are usually mutual inductances.

3.6.1 Sources and Detectors in A.C. Bridge

Q. Explain in detail sources and detectors in A.C. bridge.
Q. Write note on sources and detectors in A.C. bridge.

There are basically two types of sources used in A.C. bridges.

(a) For measurement at low frequency the power line may be used.

(b) For higher frequencies, electronic oscillators are universally used.

These oscillators have the advantage as frequency is constant, easily adjustable and determinable with accuracy. Waveform is close to sine wave and power output is sufficient for most bridge measurement. Typical oscillator has a frequency range of 40 Hz to 125 kHz with a power output of 7 W.

Detectors: Commonly used detectors for A.C. Bridge are given below.

- **Head phones :** Head phones are widely used as detectors at frequencies of 250 Hz and over upto 3 or 4 KHz.

- **Vibration galvanometer :** They are extremely useful for power and low audio frequency ranges. They work at various frequencies ranging from 5 Hz to 1000 Hz. They are commonly used below 200 Hz.
- **Tunable amplifier detector :** They the most versatile The transistor amplifier can be tuned electrically and thus can be made to respond to a narrow bandwidth at the bridge frequency. Output of the amplifier is fed to the indicating instrument. They can be used over a frequency of 10 Hz to 100 KHz.

3.7 BRIDGE BALANCE CONDITION OF FOUR ARM A.C. BRIDGE

Q. Discuss the bridge balance equation for four arm A.C. bridge.

The condition for balance of a bridge is that there should be no current through the detector. Fig. 3.9 shows a basic A.C. bridge network. Potential difference between points 'b' and 'd' should be zero. This is possible when the voltage drop from 'a' to 'b', equals to voltage drop from 'a' to 'd', both in magnitude as well as phase.

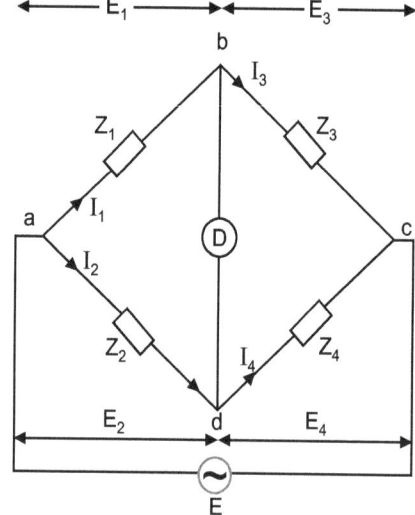

Fig. 3.9

∴ $E_1 = E_2$ ... (1)

$I_1 Z_1 = I_2 Z_2$ ... (2)

At balance

$$I_1 = I_3 = \frac{E}{Z_1 + Z_3}$$ ... (3)

$$I_2 = I_4 = \frac{E}{Z_2 + Z_4}$$ ... (4)

Put (3) and (4) in (2)

ELECT. MEASURE. & INSTRUS (S.E. ELECTRICAL)   MEASUREMENT OF RESISTANCE

$$\therefore \quad \frac{E}{Z_1 + Z_3} Z_1 = \frac{E}{Z_2 + Z_4} Z_2$$

$$\therefore \quad Z_1 Z_2 + Z_1 Z_4 = Z_1 Z_2 + Z_2 Z_3$$

$$\therefore \quad \boxed{Z_1 Z_4 = Z_2 Z_3} \quad \ldots (5)$$

Equation (5) is the basic equation of balance of an A.C. bridge. Equation (5) states that the product of impedance of one pair of opposite arm must equal to the product of impedance of other pair of opposite arms expressed in complex notation.

Polar form of impedance is $Z = Z \angle \theta$, where θ represents the phase angle of complex impedance and Z represents magnitude.

∴ Equation (5) becomes

$$(Z_1 \angle \theta_1)(Z_4 \angle \theta_4) = (Z_2 \angle \theta_2)(Z_3 \angle \theta_3)$$

$$Z_1 Z_4 \angle (\theta_1 + \theta_4) = Z_2 Z_3 \angle (\theta_2 + \theta_3)$$

Thus, while balancing following conditions must be satisfied.

(a) $\quad Z_1 Z_4 = Z_2 Z_3$

(b) $\quad \angle(\theta_1 + \theta_4) = \angle(\theta_2 + \theta_3)$

Phase angle are positive for an inductive impedance and negative for capacitive impedance.

3.8 MAXWELL'S INDUCTANCE BRIDGE

Maxwell's inductance bridges measure an inductance by comparison with a variable standard self inductance.

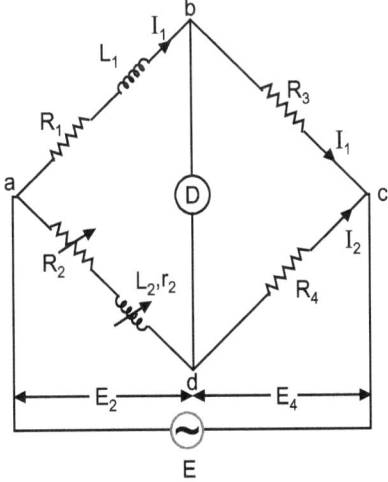

Fig. 3.10

L_2 = Variable inductance of fixed resistance r_2

R_2 = Variable resistance connected in series with inductance L_2

R_3, R_4 = Known non inductive resistance.

At balance,
$$Z_1 Z_4 = Z_2 Z_3$$

where
$$Z_1 = R_1 + j\omega L_1$$
$$Z_2 = R_2 + j\omega L_2 + r_2$$
$$Z_2 = R_3$$
$$Z_4 = R_4$$
$$R_4 (R_1 + j\omega L_1) = R_3 (R_2 + r_2 + j\omega L_2)$$
$$R_1 R_4 + R_4 j\omega L_1 = R_2 R_3 + r_2 R_3 + R_3 j\omega L_2$$
$$R_1 R_4 + R_4 j\omega L_1 = R_3 (R_2 + r_2) + R_3 j\omega L_2$$

$\therefore$
$$R_1 R_4 = R_3 (R_2 + r_2)$$

$$\boxed{R_1 = \frac{R_3}{R_4}(R_2 + r_2)}$$

$$R_4 j\omega L_1 = j\omega L_2 R_3$$
$$R_4 L_1 = L_2 R_3$$

$$\boxed{L_1 = \frac{L_2 R_3}{R_4}}$$

Phasor diagram is shown below.

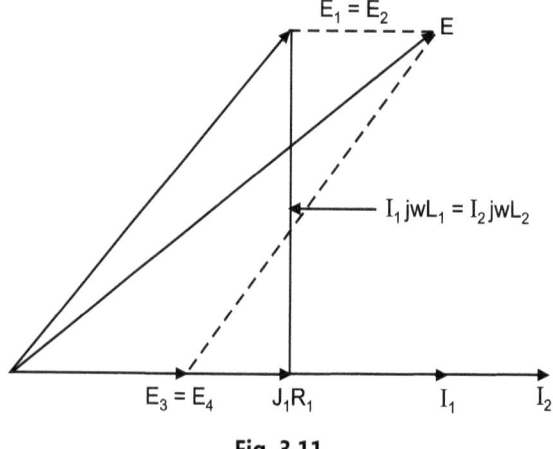

Fig. 3.11

3.9 MAXWELL'S INDUCTANCE CAPACITANCE BRIDGE

The connection for Maxwell's inductance capacitance bridge is shown in figure 3.12.

In Maxwell's inductance capacitance bridge the value of inductance is measured by the comparison with standard variable capacitance.

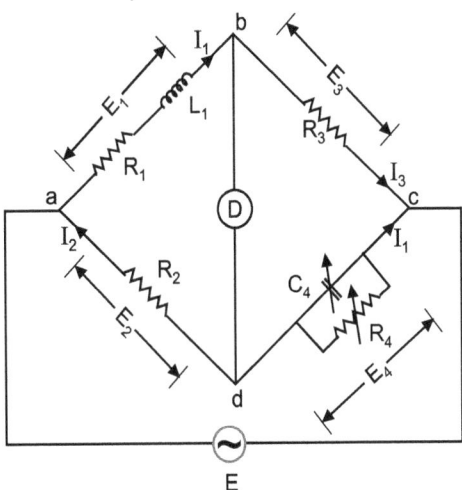

Fig. 3.12

Maxwell's inductance capacitance bridge for measurement of inductance

Let, R_2, R_3, R_4 = known non-inductive resistances

L_1 = unknown inductance

R_1 = effective resistance of inductor L_1

C_4 = variable standard capacitor

Under balance condition

$$(R_1 + j\omega L_1)\left(\frac{R_4}{1 + j\omega C_4 R_4}\right) = R_2 R_3$$

$$R_1 R_4 + j\omega L_1 R_4 = R_2 R_3 + j\omega R_2 R_3 C_4 R_4$$

Separating the real and imaginary terms,

$$R_1 = \frac{R_2 R_3}{R_4} \text{ and } L_1 = R_2 R_3 C_4$$

The expression for Q factor,

$$Q = \frac{\omega L_1}{R_1} = \omega C_4 R_4$$

Advantages of Maxwell's inductance capacitance bridge:

- The two balance equations are independent if we choose R_4 and C_4 as variable elements.
- The frequency does not appear in any of the two equations.

- This bridge yields simple expressions for L_1 and R_1 in terms of known bridge elements.

Disadvantages of Maxwell's inductance capacitance bridge :

This bridge requires a variable standard capacitor which may be very expensive if calibrated to the high degree of accuracy. Thus fixed standard capacitor is used, either because a variable capacitor is not available or because fixed capacitors have a higher degree of accuracy and are less expensive than the various ones. The balance adjustments are then done by :

1. Either varying R_2 and R_4 and since R_2 appears in both the balance equations, the balance adjustments become difficult; or
2. Putting an additional resistance in series with the inductance under measurement and then varying this resistance and R_4.

The bridge is limited to the measurement of low Q coils (1 < Q < 10). The measurement of high Q coils demands a large value of resistance R_4, of the order of 10^5 or 10^6 Ω. The resistance boxes of high values are very expensive. Thus for values of Q >10, the Maxwell's bridge is not suitable.

3.10 ANDERSON'S BRIDGE

Anderson's Bridge is the modification of the Maxwell's inductance-capacitance bridge. In Anderson's bridge a standard capacitor is used for the measurement of self inductance. This method can be used for the wide range of self inductance measurement. Figure 3.13 shows the Anderson's bridge for the balance conditions.

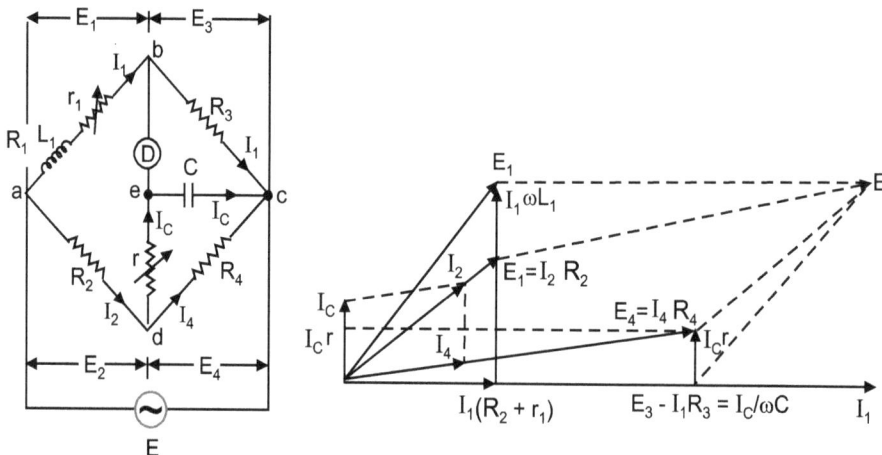

Fig. 3.13 : Anderson's Bridge

C = fixed standard capacitor.

L_1 = Self inductance to be measured,

R_1 = resistance of self-inductor,

r_1 = resistance connected in series with self-inductor,

At balance,

$$I_1 = I_3 \text{ and } I_2 = I_C + I_4$$

Now,
$$I_1 R_3 = I_C \times \frac{1}{j\omega C}$$

∴
$$I_C = I_1 j\omega C R_3$$

$$I_1(r_1 + R_1 + j\omega L_1) = I_2 R_2 + I_C r$$

$$I_C\left(r + \frac{1}{j\omega C}\right) = (I_2 - I_C) R_4$$

$$I_1(r_1 + R_1 + j\omega L_1) = I_2 R_2 + I_1 j\omega C R_3 r$$

$$I_1(r_1 + R_1 + j\omega L_1 - j\omega C R_3 r) = I_2 R_2 \qquad \ldots (1)$$

$$j\omega C R_3 I_1\left(r + \frac{1}{j\omega C}\right) = (I_2 - I_1 j\omega C R_3) R_4$$

$$I_1(j\omega C R_3 r + j\omega C R_3 R_4 + R_3) = I_2 R_4 \qquad \ldots (2)$$

From equation (1) and (2), we get,

$$I_1(r_1 + R_1 + j\omega L_1 - j\omega C R_3 r) = \left(I_1 \frac{R_2 R_3}{R_4} + \frac{j\omega C R_2 R_3 r}{R_4} + j\omega C R_3 R_2\right)$$

Equating real and imaginary parts,

$$\boxed{R_1 = \frac{R_2 R_3}{R_4} - r_1}$$

$$\boxed{L_1 = C \frac{R_3}{R_4}\left[r(R_4 + R_2) + R_2 R_4\right]}$$

Advantages of Anderson's Bridge:
- In Anderson's bridge it is very easy to obtain the balance point as compared to Maxwell's bridge.
- In this bridge a fixed standard capacitor is used therefore there is no need of costly variable capacitor.
- This method is very accurate for measurement of capacitance in terms of inductance.

Disadvantages of Anderson's Bridge:
- It has more parts and hence complex in set up and manipulate.
- An additional junction point increases the difficulty of shielding the bridge.

3.11 SCHERING BRIDGE

The connections and phasor diagram of the Schering bridge under balance conditions are shown in figure below.

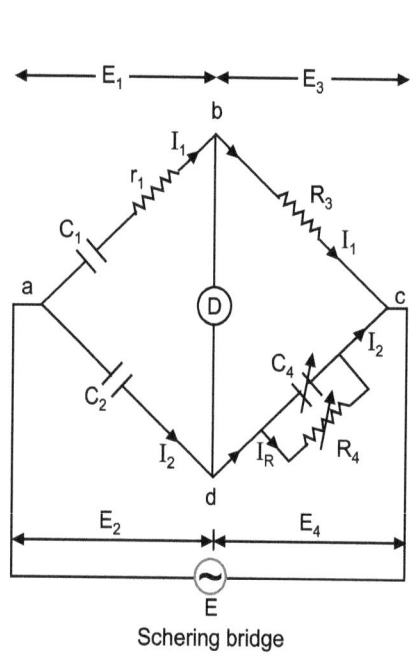

Fig. 3.14 : Schering Bridge Circuit   **Fig. 3.15 : Schering Bridge Phasor Diagram**

Let,

C_1 = capacitor whose capacitance is to be determined,
r_1 = series resistance representing the loss in the capacitor C_1
C_2 = standard capacitor
R_3 = non-inductive resistance
C_4 = variable capacitor
R_4 = variable non-inductive resistance in parallel with variable capacitor C_4

Now, when the Schering Bridge is balanced, then

$$\left[r_1 + \frac{1}{j\omega C_1}\right]\left[\frac{R_4}{1 + j\omega C_4 R_4}\right] = \frac{1}{j\omega C_2} \cdot R_3 \qquad \left[r_1 + \frac{1}{j\omega C_1}\right] R_4 = \frac{R_3}{j\omega C_2}(1 + j\omega C_4 R_4)$$

$$r_1 R_4 - \frac{jR_4}{\omega C_1} = -\frac{jR_3}{\omega C_2} + \frac{R_3 R_4 C_4}{C_2}$$

By equating real and imaginary part of the equation we get,

$$r_1 = \frac{R_3 C_4}{C_2} \text{ and, } C_1 \frac{C_2 R_4}{R_3}$$

Two independent balance equations are obtained if C_4 and R_4 are chosen as the variable elements. The dissipation factor is given by $D_1 = \tan \delta = \omega C_1 r_1$. The values of capacitance C_1 and its dissipation factor are obtained from the values of bridge elements at balance.

Advantages of Schering Bridge:
- The balance equation is independent of frequency.
- It is used for measuring the insulating properties of electrical cables and equipments.

3.12 HAY'S BRIDGE FOR MEASUREMENT OF INDUCTANCE

The Hay's bridge is modification of the Maxwell's bridge. The connection diagram of the Hay's bridge is shown in figure 3.16. Hay's bridge uses a resistor in series with a standard capacitor.

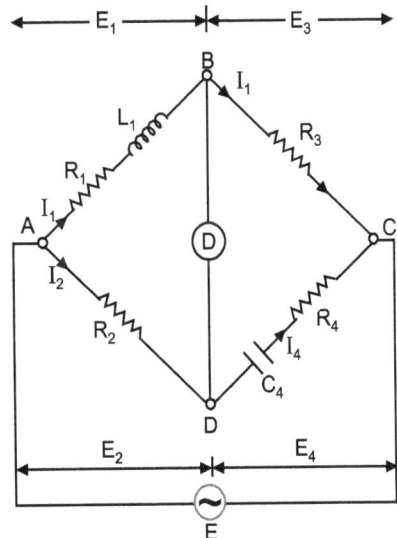

Fig. 3.16 : Hay's bridge for measurement of inductance

Let,
L_1 = unknown inducatnce having a resistance R_1,
R_2, R_3, R_4 = known non-inductive resistance,
C_4 = standard capacitor.

At balance,

$$(R_1 + j\omega L_1)\left(R_4 - \frac{j}{\omega C_4}\right) = R_2 R_3$$

$$R_1R_4 + \frac{L_1}{C_4} + j\omega L_1 R_4 - \frac{jR_1}{\omega C_4} = R_2 R_3$$

Separating real and imaginary parts

$$R_1R_4 + \frac{L_1}{C_4} = R_2R_3 \text{ and, } L_1 = \frac{R_1}{\omega^2 R_4 C_4}$$

Solving equations we have,

$$L_1 = \frac{R_2 R_3 C_4}{1 + \omega^2 C_4^2 R_4^2} \text{ and, } R_1 = \frac{\omega^2 R_2 R_3 R_4 C_4^2}{1 + \omega^2 C_4^2 R_4^2}$$

The Q factor of the coil is

$$Q = \frac{\omega L_1}{R_1} = \frac{1}{\omega C_4 R_4}$$

Advantages of the Hay's bridge :
- This bridge is suitable for coils having Q > 10.
- This bridge also gives the simple expression for Q factor.
- For high Q factor the value of resistance R_4 should be small.

Disadvantages of Hay's bridge :

- For inductors having Q values smaller than 10, the term $\left(\frac{1}{Q}\right)^2$ in the expression for inductance L_1 cannot be neglected. Hence this bridge is not suited for measurement of coils having Q less than 10 and for these applications a Maxwell's bridge is more suited.

NUMERICALS

Q.1 The values of resistance of various arms are P = 1 kΩ, Q = 100 Ω, R = 2.005 kΩ and S = 200 Ω. The battery e.m.f is 5 V with negligible internal resistance. The sensitivity of galvanometer is 10 mm/μA with 100 Ω internal resistance. Find the deflection of galvanometer and sensitivity of the bridge in terms of deflection per unit change in resistance.

Sol. P = 1 kΩ, Q = 100 Ω, R = 2.005 kΩ, S = 200 Ω, S_i = 10 mm/μA, E = 5 V, G = 100 Ω.

$$R = \frac{P}{Q} S$$

$$= \frac{1000}{100} \times 200$$

$$= 2000 \, \Omega$$

Deviation from balance is Δ_R = 2005 − 2000 = 5 Ω. Thevenin's voltage is given as :

$$V_{TH} = E\left[\frac{R}{R+S} - \frac{P}{P+Q}\right]$$

$$= 5\left[\frac{2005}{2005 + 200} - \frac{1000}{1000 + 100}\right]$$

$$= 1.0307 \times 10^{-3} \text{ V}$$

Internal resistance of bridge

$$R_{TH} = \frac{RS}{R + S} + \frac{PQ}{P + Q}$$

$$= \frac{2005 \times 200}{2005 + 200} + \frac{1000 \times 100}{1000 + 100}$$

$$= 272.7 \text{ }\Omega$$

Current through galvanometer

$$I_G = \frac{V_{TH}}{R_{TH} + G}$$

$$= \frac{1.0307 \times 10^{-3}}{272.7 + 100}$$

$$= 2.77 \text{ }\mu\text{A}$$

Deflection of galvanometer $= \theta = S_i I_G = 10 \times 2.77$

$$\boxed{\theta = 27.7 \text{ mm}}$$

Sensitivity of bridge $= \dfrac{\theta}{\Delta_R} = \dfrac{27.7}{5}$

$$\boxed{S_B = 5.54 \text{ mm}/\Omega}$$

Q.2 Calculate the value of unknown resistance assuming the bridge to be in balanced condition.

Sol. $P = 5\Omega$, $Q = ?$, $S = 10$ kΩ, $R = 2$ kΩ.

Under balanced condition,

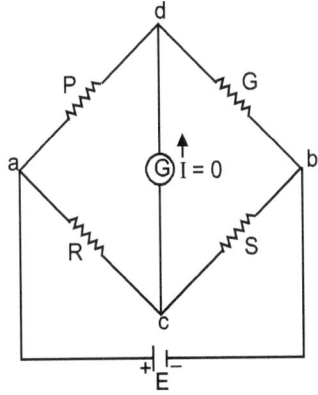

Fig. 3.17

$$Q = \frac{PS}{R} = \frac{10}{2} \times 5 = 25 \text{ k}\Omega$$

Therefore, Unknown resistance = 25 kΩ

Q.3 Three arms of Wheatstone's bridge have resistance of 100 Ω and fourth arm has resistance of 100.10 Ω. A galvanometer of 0.05 mm/μA sensitivity has resistance of 50 Ω. A battery e.m.f is 3 V is connected in series with a resistance of 200 Ω to other diagonal. What is the deflection in the galvanometer?

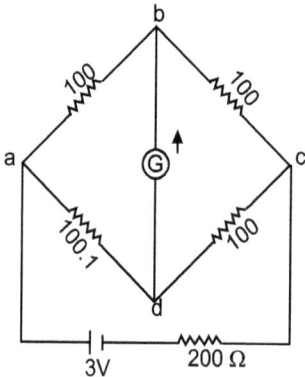

Fig. 3.18

Sol. P = Q = S = 100 Ω, E = 3 V, R = 100.1 Ω, R$_S$ = 200 Ω, G = 50 Ω.

For balance, the resistance of unknown resistor is

$$R = \frac{P}{Q} \cdot S = \frac{100}{100 \times 100} = 100 \, \Omega$$

$$\Delta R = 100.1 - 100 = 0.1$$

$$V_{TH} = E\left[\frac{R}{R+S} - \frac{P}{P+Q}\right]$$

$$= 3\left[\frac{100.1}{100.1 + 100} - \frac{100}{100 + 100}\right]$$

$$V_{TH} = 7.496 \times 10^{-4} \text{ V}$$

Internal resistance of bridge,

$$R_{TH} = \frac{RS}{R+S} + \frac{PQ}{P+Q}$$

$$= \frac{100.1 \times 100}{100.1 + 100} + \frac{100 \times 100}{100 + 100} = 100.02498 \, \Omega$$

$$I_G = \frac{E_o}{R_o + G}$$

$$= \frac{7.496 \times 10^{-4}}{100.02498 + 50}$$

$$= 4.9965 \times 10^{-6} \text{ A}$$

Deflection of galvanometer,

$$\theta = \frac{0.05 \times 10^{-3}}{10^{-6}} \times 4.9965 \times 10^{-6}$$

$$\theta = 0.249 \text{ mm}$$

Q.4 Kelvin's bridge is balanced with following values. Outer ratio arm = 100 Ω and 1000 Ω, Inner ratio arm = 99.92 Ω and 1000.6 Ω, Standard resistance = 0.00377 Ω. Find the value of unknown resistance P = 100 Ω, p = 99.92 Ω, r = 0.1 Ω, Q = 1000 Ω, q = 1000.6 Ω, S = 0.00377 Ω.

$$R = \frac{P}{Q} \cdot S + \frac{qr}{p+q+r}\left[\frac{P}{Q} - \frac{p}{q}\right]$$

$$= \frac{100}{1000} \times 0.00377 + \frac{1000.6 \times 0.1}{99.92 + 1000.6 + 0.1}\left[\frac{100}{1000} - \frac{99.92}{1000.6}\right]$$

$$\boxed{R = 3.89 \times 10^{-4} \text{ Ω}}$$

Q.5 The solution for unknown resistance for a Wheatstone's bridge is $R_n = \frac{R_1 R_2}{R_3}$.

Where $R_1 = 100 \pm 0.5\%$ Ω, $R_2 = 1000 \pm 0.5\%$ Ω, $R_3 = 842 \pm 0.5\%$ Ω. Calculate the magnitude of unknown resistance and limiting error.

Sol.

$$R_n = \frac{100 \times 1000}{842}$$

$$\boxed{R_n = 118.76 \text{ Ω}}$$

$$R_1 = 100 \pm 0.5\% \text{ Ω}$$

Relative limiting error of unknown resistance

$$\frac{\delta R_n}{R_n} = \pm\left[\frac{\delta R_2}{R_2} + \frac{\delta R_3}{R_3} + \frac{\delta R_1}{R_1}\right]$$

$$= \pm[0.5 + 0.5 + 0.5]$$

$$= \pm 1.5$$

Limiting error in Ω $= \pm \frac{1.5}{100} \times 118.76 = \pm 1.78$ Ω

Q.6 A four terminal resistor was measured by means of Kelvin's double bridge with following data.
(a) Standard resistor = 100.03×10^{-6} Ω
(b) Inner ratio arms = 100.31 Ω and 200 Ω
(c) Outer ratio arms = 100.24 Ω and 200 Ω

(d) Resistance of link connecting standard and unknown resistance = $700 \times 10^{-6}\,\Omega$.
Calculate the unknown resistance.

Sol. $S = 100.03 \times 10^{-6}\,\mu$
$Q = 200\,\Omega$
$q = 200\,\Omega$
$P = 100.24\,\Omega$
$p = 100.31\,\Omega$
$r = 700 \times 10^{-6}\,\Omega$

$$R = \frac{P}{Q} \cdot S + \frac{qr}{p+q+r}\left[\frac{P}{Q} - \frac{p}{q}\right]$$

$$= \frac{100.24}{200} \times 100.03 \times 10^{-6} + \frac{200 \times 700 \times 10^{-6}}{100.31 + 200 + 700 \times 10^{-6}}\left[\frac{100.24}{200} - \frac{100.31}{200}\right]$$

$R = 49.97 \times 10^{-6}\,\Omega$

Q.7 A Schering's bridge has following particulars as shown in Fig. Calculate the capacitance and loss angle at a frequency of 1 KHz.

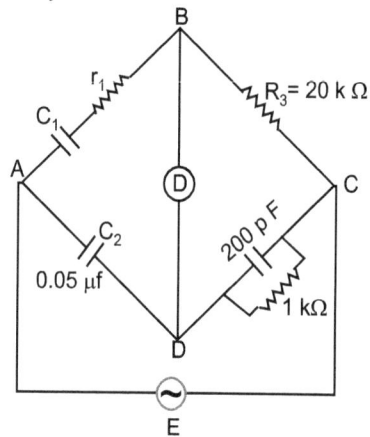

Fig. 3.19

Sol. At balance,

$$r_1 = \frac{C_4}{C_2} R_3$$

$$= \frac{200 \times 10^{-12}}{0.05 \times 10^{-6}} \times 20 \times 10^3$$

$r_1 = 80\,\Omega$

$$C_1 = \frac{R_4}{R_3} C_2$$

$$= \frac{1 \times 10^3}{20 \times 10^3} \times 0.05 \times 10^{-6}$$

$$= 2.5 \times 10^{-9} \text{ F}$$
$$C_1 = 2.5 \text{ nF}$$
$$\tan \delta = \omega C_1 r_1$$
$$= 2\pi \times 1 \times 10^3 \times 2.5 \times 10^{-9} \times 80$$
$$= 1.256 \times 10^{-3}$$
$$\boxed{\delta = 0.07196°}$$

Q.8 An A.C bridge has the following constants arm AB, R = 1000 Ω, in parallel with C = 0.159 μF. BC, R = 1000 Ω, CD – R = 500 Ω, DA – C = 0.636 μF in series with an unknown resistance. Find the frequency for which this bridge is in balance and determine the value of resistances in arm DA to produce this balance.

Sol.

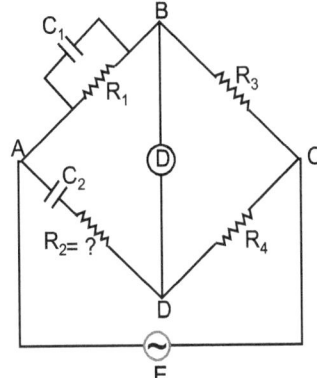

Fig. 3.20

$R_1 = 1000$ Ω, $C_1 = 0.159$ μF, $R_3 = 1000$ Ω,
$R_4 = 500$ Ω, $C_2 = 0.636$ μF.

At balance,

$$\frac{R_4}{R_3} = \frac{R_2}{R_1} + \frac{C_1}{C_2}$$

$$\frac{500}{1000} = \frac{R_2}{1000} + \frac{0.159 \times 10^{-6}}{0.636 \times 10^{-6}}$$

$$\boxed{R_2 = 250 \text{ Ω}}$$

$$F = \frac{1}{2\pi \sqrt{R_1 R_2 C_1 C_2}}$$

$$= \frac{1}{2\pi \sqrt{1000 \times 250 \times 0.159 \times 10^{-6} \times 0.636 \times 10^{-6}}}$$

$$\boxed{F = 1000.97 \text{ Hz}}$$

Q.9 Data for A.C. bridge is given as AB = Unknown capacitor in series with unknown resistance. BC = Standard capacitor of value of 10 µF, CD = Capacitor of value 5 nF in parallel with resistance of 100 kΩ. Derive the expression for unknown capacitance and unknown resistance and find out the values of unknown quantities.

Sol.

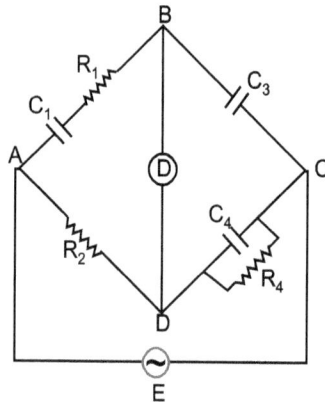

Fig. 3.21

$R_4 = 10\ k\Omega$, $C_4 = 5\ nF$, $R_2 = 100\ k\Omega$, $C_3 = 10\ \mu F$

At balance,

$$Z_1 Z_4 = Z_2 Z_3$$

$$\left(R_1 + \frac{1}{j\omega C_1}\right)\left(\frac{R_4}{1 + j\omega C_4 R_4}\right) = \frac{R_2}{j\omega C_3}$$

$$\left(R_1 + \frac{1}{j\omega C_1}\right) R_4 = \frac{R_2}{j\omega C_3}(1 + j\omega C_4 R_4)$$

$$R_1 R_4 - \frac{jR_4}{\omega C_1} = \frac{-jR_2}{\omega C_3} + \frac{R_2 C_4 R_4}{C_3}$$

$$R_1 = \frac{R_2 C_4}{C_3}$$

$$C_1 = \frac{R_4 C_3}{R_2}$$

$$R_1 = \frac{100 \times 10^3 \times 5 \times 10^{-9}}{10 \times 10^{-6}}$$

$$\boxed{R_1 = 50\ \Omega}$$

$$C_1 = \frac{10 \times 10^3 \times 10 \times 10^{-6}}{100 \times 10^3}$$

$$\boxed{C_1 = 1\ \mu F}$$

Q.10 A Schering bridge is used for measuring the power loss in dielectrics. The specimens are in the form of discs of 0.3 cm thickness and have dielectric constant of 2.3. The area of each electrode is 314 cm² and loss angle is known to be 9° for a frequency of 50 Hz. The fixed resistor of bridge has a value of 1 k and fixed capacitor of 50 µF. Determine values of variables R and C.

Sol. $D = 0.3$ cm, $A = 314$ cm², $F = 50$ Hz, $C_2 = 50 \times 10^{-6}$ F, $\delta = 9°$, $R_3 = 1$ kΩ, $\varepsilon_r = 2.3$, $\varepsilon_o = 8.854 \times 10^{-12}$ F/m, $C_1 = 2.131 \times 10^{-10}$ F

$$\tan \delta = \tan(9°) = 0.1584$$

$$\tan \delta = \frac{r_1}{X C_1}$$

$$r_1 = \tan\delta \cdot X$$

$$C_1 = \frac{0.1584}{\omega C_1}$$

$$= \frac{0.1584}{2\pi \times 50 \times 2.131 \times 10^{-10}}$$

$$r_1 = 2.366 \times 10^6 \, \Omega$$

$$C_1 = \frac{\varepsilon \varepsilon_r A}{d}$$

$$= \frac{8.854 \times 10^{-12} \times 2.3 \times 314 \times 10^{-4}}{0.3 \times 10^{-2}}$$

$$\boxed{C_1 = 2.131 \times 10^{-10} \, F}$$

At balance,

$$C_1 = \frac{R_4}{R_3} \cdot C_2$$

$$R_4 = \frac{C_1 R_3}{C_2}$$

$$= \frac{2.731 \times 10^{-10} \times 1000}{50 \times 10^{-6}}$$

$$R_4 = 4.262 \times 10^{-3} \, \Omega$$

$$C_4 = \frac{C_1 C_2}{R_3}$$

$$= \frac{2.366 \times 10^6 \times 50 \times 10^{-6}}{1000}$$

$$\boxed{C_4 = 118.3 \times 10^{-3} \, F}$$

Q.11 A sample of Bakelite is tested by the Schering Bridge at 25 KV, 50 Hz. The balance is obtained with a standard condenser of 106 µF a condenser of 0.4 µF in parallel with non-inductive resistor of 318 Ω and non-inductive resistor 120 Ω. Determine the capacitance, the equivalent series resistance and the dissipation factor of the specimen. Prove the relationship used in the bridge.

Sol. $R_3 = 120\ \Omega$, $C_2 = 106\ \mu F$, $C_4 = 0.4\ \mu F$, $R_4 = 318\ \Omega$, $F = 50\ Hz$, $E = 25\ kV$. Schering's A.C. bridge is shown below.

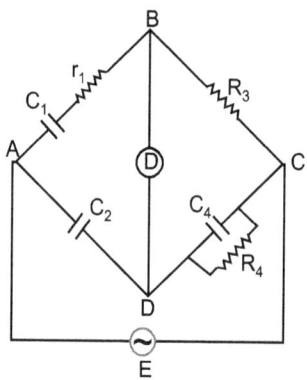

Fig. 3.22

At balance,

$$\left(r_1 + \frac{1}{j\omega C_1}\right)\left(\frac{R_4}{1 + j\omega C_4 R_4}\right) = \frac{R_3}{j\omega C_2}$$

$$r_1 R_4 + \frac{R_4}{j\omega C_1} = \frac{R_3}{j\omega C_2} + \frac{R_3 C_4 R_4}{C_2}$$

$$\therefore\quad r_1 R_4 = \frac{R_3 R_4 C_4}{C_2}$$

$$r_1 = \frac{C_4 R_3}{C_2}$$

$$r_1 = \frac{0.4 \times 10^{-6} \times 120}{106 \times 10^{-6}}$$

$$r_1 = 0.453\ \Omega$$

$$\frac{R_4}{j\omega C_1} = \frac{R_3}{j\omega C_2}$$

$$C_1 = \frac{R_4}{R_3} \cdot C_2$$

$$= \frac{318}{120} \times 106 \times 10^{-6} = 280.9 \times 10^{-6}\ F = 280.9\ \mu F$$

Dissipation factor $= D = \tan \delta = \omega C_1 r_1 = 2\pi \times 50 \times 280.9 \times 10^{-6} \times 0.453$

$$\boxed{D = 0.0399}$$

Q.12 A capacitance comparison bridge constants are $C_3 = 10\ \mu F$, $R_1 = 1.2\ k\Omega$, $R_2 = 100\ k\Omega$, $R_3 = 120\ k\Omega$. It is used at a frequency of 3 KHz. Calculate the values of series circuit of the unknown impedance.

Sol. Bridge balance equation $R_x = \dfrac{R_2 R_3}{R_1} = \dfrac{100 \times 10^3 \times 120 \times 10^3}{1.2 \times 10^3} = 10\ M\Omega$

$$C_x = \dfrac{R_1 C_3}{R_2} = \dfrac{1.2 \times 10^3 \times 10 \times 10^{-6}}{100 \times 10^3} = 0.12\ \mu F$$

Q.13 An inductance comparison bridge is used to measure inductive impedance at 1.5 KHz with bridge constants as $L_3 = 8\ mH$, $R_1 = 1\ k\Omega$, $R_2 = 25\ k\Omega$, $R_3 = 50\ k\Omega$. Find the equivalent series circuit of unknown impedance.

Sol. At balance condition $R_x = \dfrac{R_2 R_3}{R_1}$

$$= \dfrac{25 \times 10^3 \times 50 \times 10^3}{1 \times 10^3} = 1.25\ M\Omega$$

$$L_x = \dfrac{R_2 L_3}{R_1}$$

$$= \dfrac{25 \times 10^3 \times 8 \times 10^{-3}}{1 \times 10^3} = 200\ mH$$

Q.14 Anderson Bridge is shown in Fig below with bridge parameters shown in Fig. 3.22. Calculate R_x and L_x.

Sol.

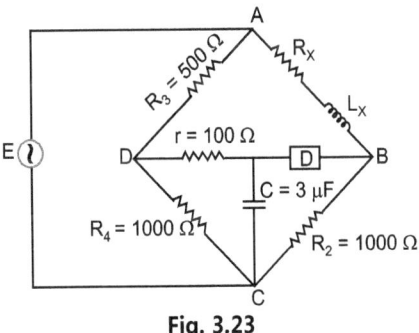

Fig. 3.23

$R_x = \dfrac{R_2 R_3}{R_4}$

$= \dfrac{1000 \times 500}{1000}$

$= 500\ \Omega$

$L_x = \dfrac{CR_2}{R_4}[R_3 r + R_4 r + R_3 R_4]$

$= \dfrac{3 \times 10^{-6} \times 1000}{1000}[500 \times 100 + 1000 \times 100 + 500 \times 1000]$

$= 1.95\ H$

UNIVERSITY QUESTIONS

Dec. 2010

Q.1 Give classifications of resistance. Give suitable method of measurement for each category. **(6 Marks)**

Q.2 What are the different detectors used in AC bridges? Elaborate each type in brief. Derive the general equation for bridge balance. **(6 Marks)**

Q.3 Draw circuit diagram of Kelvin's double bridge. Derive expression for unknown resistance with usual notations. **(6 Marks)**

Q.4 With a circuit diagram derive the equation for unknown capacitance measurement using Schering Bridge. **(6 Marks)**

Q.5 The arms of Anderson's bridge are as follows : **(4 Marks)**
(i) Arm AB : Unknown impedance with R_1, L_1 in series with variable resistor r_1.
(ii) Arm BC : Pure resistance $R_3 = 100\ \Omega$
(iii) Arm CD : Pure resistance $R_4 = 200\ \Omega$
(iv) Arm DA : Pure resistance $R_2 = 250\ \Omega$
(v) Arm DE : Variable pure resistance r
(vi) Arm EC : A loss free capacitor $C = 1\ \mu F$
(vii) Arm BE : A detector

AC supply is connected between terminal A and C. Calculate resistance and inductance R_1, L_1, if $r_1 = 43.1\ \Omega$ and $r = 229.7\ \Omega$ under balance condition.

May 2011

Q.6 Drive expression for insulation resistance with power ON. **(6 Marks)**

Q.7 Draw a circuit diagram if Maxwell's Induction Bridge. Also derive an expression for unknown inductance, resistance and Q-factor. **(10 Marks)**

Q.8 Draw a circuit diagram of Schering Bridge. Derive the expression for unknown capacitance. **(8 Marks)**

Q.9 Give classification of Resistance, State the methods suitable for measurement of low resistance. **(4 Marks)**

Q.10 In a Kelvin double bridge, there is error due to mismatch between the ratios of outer and inner arm resistances. The following data, relate to this bridge : **(4 Marks)**
(i) Standard resistance = $100.03\ \mu\Omega$
(ii) Inner ratio arms = $100.31\ \Omega$ and $200\ \Omega$
(iii) Outer ratio arms = $100.24\ \Omega$ and $200\ \Omega$
(iv) The resistance of connecting leads from standard to unknown resistor is $660\ \mu\Omega$. Calculate the unknown resistance.

Dec. 2011

Q.11 Draw circuit diagram of Kelvin's double bridge. Derive expression for unknown resistance with usual notations. **(8 Marks)**

Q.12 Write a short note on megger and earth tester. **(8 Marks)**

Q.13 Draw circuit diagram of Anderson's bridge. Derive the equation for unknown inductance and draw the phasor diagram. **(8 Marks)**

Q.14 In a Maxwell's inductance comparison bridge arm ab consists of a coil with inductance L_1 and resistance r_1 in series with a non-inductive resistance R. Arm be and cd are each a non-inductive resistance of 100 Ω. Arm ad consists of standard variable inductor L of resistance 32.7 Ω. Balance is obtained when L_2 = 47.8 mH and R = 1.36 Q. Find the resistance and inductance of the coil in the arm ab. **(4 Marks)**

May 2012

Q.15 Draw a circuit diagram of shearing bridge, derive its expression and draw phasor diagram. **(8 Marks)**

Q.16 Explain the construction and working principle of megger. **(8 Marks)**

Q.17 Draw a circuit diagram of Anderson's bridge. Derive the expression for unknown inductance and draw the phasor diagram. **(8 Marks)**

Q.18 A four terminal resistor was measured by means of a Kelvin double bridge having the following component resistances : **(8 Marks)**
(i) Standard resistor : 100.03 µΩ
(ii) Inner ratio arms : 100.31 Ω and 200 Ω
(iii) Outer ratio arms : 100.24 Ω and 200 Ω
(iv) Connecting resistance between four terminal resistor : 700 µΩ
(v) Calculate the unknown resistance to the nearest of 0.01 µΩ.

Dec. 2012

Q.19 Write notes on :
(i) Megger
(ii) Earth tester

Q.20 Draw the circuit diagram of Anderson Bridge and derive the equation for determining the unknown quantities. **(6 Marks)**

Q.21 In AC bridge is connected as follows :
Branchy AB is an inductive resistor; Branch BC, CD and DA are non-inductive resistors. A standard variable capacitor is connected across the variable resistor in branch CD. The supply is connected to A and C and the detector to B and D. Determine the resistance and inductance of branch AB by identifying the bridge. The resistances are as follows :

BC = 600 Ω, C = 1000 and C = 0.5 µF, DA = 400 Ω. **(6 Marks)**

Q.22 Classify the resistance into low, medium and high resistances. Explain the procedure of measuring a low resistance with the help of Kelvin's Double Bridge. **(6 Marks)**

Q.23 Describe how Schering Bridge is used for measurement of an unknown capacitance. Derive the condition of balance. Draw the phasor diagram of the bridge circuit under balance condition. **(6 Marks)**

Q.24 The arms of an AC bridge are arranged as follows : **(6 Marks)**

Arm AB : Z_1 = 50 ∠30° Ω, Arm BC : Z_2 = 100 ∠0° Ω

Arm CD : Z_4 = 100 ∠0° Ω, Arm BC : Z_3 = 200 ∠ –60° Ω

Determine whether it is possible to balance the bridge under above conditions.

UNIT III

Chapter 4

MEASUREMENT OF POWER

4.1 INTRODUCTION

The power measurements are made with the help of a wattmeter. Wattmeter is an indicating deflecting type of instrument used in laboratories for measurement of power in various ranges. A wattmeter consists of two coils as shown in the schematic representative figure 4.1.

Current Coil (CC) : It is connected in series with circuit and carries the load current. It is designed such that it is wound with few turns of thick wire and hence it has a very low resistance.

Voltage or Pressure or Potential Coil (PC) :

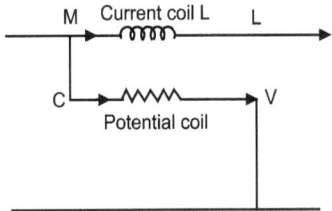

Fig. 4.1 : Wattmeter connections

It is connected across the load circuit and hence carries a current proportional to the load current. The total load voltage appears across the PC. It is designed such that it is wound with several turns of thin wire and hence it has a very high resistance. For power measurements in AC circuits, the wattmeter is widely adopted. In principle and construction, it is a combination of those applicable for an ammeter and a voltmeter.

Electrical Power can be of three forms:

- Real power or simply, the power is the power consumed by the resistive loads on the system. It is expressed in watts (W). This is also referred as true power, absolute power, average power, or wattage.
- Reactive power is the power consumed by the reactive loads on the system. It is expressed in reactive volt-amperes (VAr).
- Apparent power is the vector sum of the above two power components. It is expressed in volt-amperes (VA).

Thus, it is observed from the power triangle shown in Fig. 4.2, that more is the deviation of power factor from its unity value, more is the deviation of real power from the apparent power. Also, $VA^2 = W^2 + VAr^2$ and, Power factor, $\cos\phi$ = (Watts / VA).

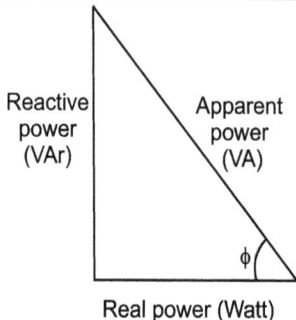

Fig. 4.2 : The Power triangle

4.2 DYNAMOMETER WATTMETER

Q. Explain in detail construction and working of a dynamometer type wattmeter.
[Dec. 10, 11]

Q. Draw and explain the construction, working of dynamometer type wattmeter. Also derive its torque equation.
[May. 11, 12]

4.2.1 Construction of Dynamometer Type Wattmeter

Fig. 4.3 shows the dynamometer wattmeter for measuring the power. An electrodynamometer wattmeter consists of two fixed coils, and a moving coil as shown in Fig. 4.3.

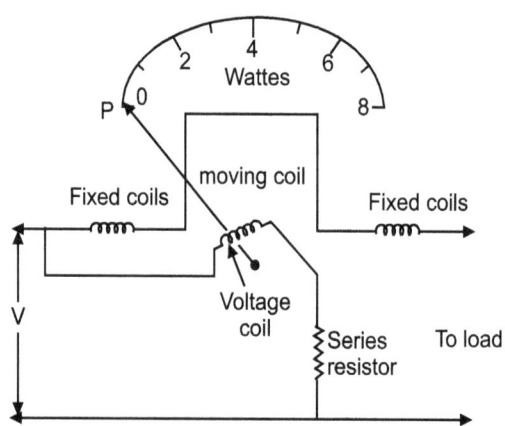

Fig. 4.3 : Dynamometer type wattmeter

The fixed coils are connected in series with the load and hence carry the load current. Fixed coils form the current coil of the wattmeter. The moving coil forms the potential coil of the wattmeter. The moving coil is connected across the load and hence carries a current proportional to the voltage across the load. A highly non-inductive resistance is put in series with the moving coil to limit the current to a small value. Spring control is used for movement and damping is by air. The deflecting torque is proportional to the product of the currents in the two coils. Theses wattmeters can be used for both DC and AC measurements. Since the deflection is proportional to the average power and the spring control torque is proportional to the deflection, the scale is uniform. The meter is free from waveform errors. However, they are more expensive.

4.2.2 Expression for the Deflection Torque

Let,

- i_c, i_p : Instantaneous values of Current in the fixed and moving coils respectively
- v : Instantaneous value of voltage
- M : Mutual inductance between the two coils
- θ : Steady final deflection of the instrument
- K : Spring constant
- V : RMS value of voltage
- I : RMS value of current
- R_p : Pressure coil resistance

Voltage across pressure coil, $v = \sqrt{2}\, V \sin wt$

Current in the pressure coil, $i_p = \sqrt{2}\, V/R_p \sin wt$

$\qquad\qquad\qquad\qquad\quad = \sqrt{2}\, I_p \sin wt$

Current in the current coil, $i_c = \sqrt{2}\, I \sin(wt - \phi)$

Instantaneous torque is given by $T_i = i_c\, i_p\, (dM/d\theta)$

$$T_i = [\sqrt{2}\, I \sin(wt - \phi)][\sqrt{2}\, I_p \sin wt]\,(dM/d\theta)$$

Average deflecting torque, $T_d = \left(\dfrac{1}{T}\right) \int_0^T T_i\, d\,wt$

$$= \left(\dfrac{1}{T}\right) \int_0^T I_p\, I\, [\cos\phi - \cos(2wt - \phi)]\,(dM/d\theta)\, d\,wt$$

$$= (VI/R_p)\cos\phi\,(dM/d\theta)$$

Controlling torque, $T_c = K\theta$

At balance, $T_d = T_c$

$\qquad\qquad\theta = [VI \cos\phi / (K R_p)]\,(dM/d\theta)$

$\qquad\qquad\quad = (K'\, dM/d\theta)\, P$

Where ($K' = K R_p$) and P is the power consumption.

Thus the deflection of the wattmeter is found to be the direct indication of the power being consumed in the load circuit.

4.3 TYPES OF DYNAMOMETER WATTMETER

Dynamometer wattmeters may be divided into two classes:
1. Suspended-coil torsion instruments.
2. Pivoted-coil, direct indicating instruments.

4.3.1 Suspended-Coil Torsion Wattmeters

These instruments are used largely as standard wattmeters.

- The moving, or voltage, coil is suspended from a torsion head by a metallic suspension which serves as a lead to the coil. This coil is situated entirely inside the current or fixed coils and the winding in such that the system is a static. Errors due to external magnetic fields are thus avoided.
- The torsion heads carries a scale, and when in use, the moving coil is bought back to the zero position by turning this head; the number of divisions turned through when multiplied by a constant for the instrument gives the power.
- Eddy currents are eliminated as far as possible by winding the current coils of standard wire and by using no metal parts within the region of the magnetic field of the instrument.
- The mutual inductance errors are completely eliminated by making zero position of the coil such that the angle between the planes of moving coil and fixed coil is 90 degree i.e. the mutual inductance between the fixed and moving coil is zero.
- The elimination of pivot friction makes possible the construction of extremely sensitive and accurate electrodynamic instruments of this pattern.

4.3.2 Pivoted-Coil Direct-Indicating Wattmeters

These instruments are commonly used as switchboard or portable instruments.

- In these instruments, the fixed coil is wound in two halves, which are placed in parallel to another at such a distance, that uniform field is obtained. The moving coil is wound of such a size and pivoted centrally so that it does not project outside the field coils at its maximum deflection position.
- The springs are pivoted for controlling the movement of the moving coil, which also serves as currents lead to the moving coil.
- The damping is provided by using the damping vane attached to the moving system and moving in a sector-shaped box.
- The reading is indicated directly by the pointer attached to the moving system and moving over the calibrated scale.
- The eddy current errors, within the region of the magnetic field of the instrument, are minimized by the use of non-metallic parts of high resistivity material.

4.4 ADVANTAGES OF DYNAMOMETER TYPE WATTMETER

- These instruments can be used on both A.C. as well as D.C
- High degree of accuracy can be obtained by careful design; hence these are used for calibration purposes
- Low power consumption
- Free from waveform errors
- Light in weight

4.5 DISADVANTAGES OF DYNAMOMETER TYPE WATTMETER

- The error due to the inductance of the pressure coil at low power factor is very serious.
- In dynamometer type wattmeter, stray field may affect the reading of the instrument. To decrease it, magnetic shielding is provided by enclosing the instrument in an iron case.
- These instruments are expensive.
- These instruments are very sensitive to overloads.

4.6 MEASUREMENT OF POWER IN A THREE PHASE CIRCUIT

Three phase systems may be of either four wires or three wires. As per Blondel's theorem, the number of wattmeters required to measure the power of a polyphase system is one less than the number of wires in the system, whether the system is balanced or unbalanced. Methods commonly used for measuring power in three phase system are

- Three Wattmeter method
- Two Wattmeter method
- One Wattmeter method

4.6.1 Three Wattmeter Method

The connection diagram for both star connected load and delta connected load shown in Fig. 4.4 (a) and 4.4 (b).

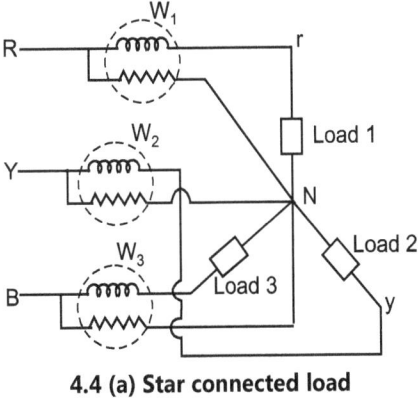
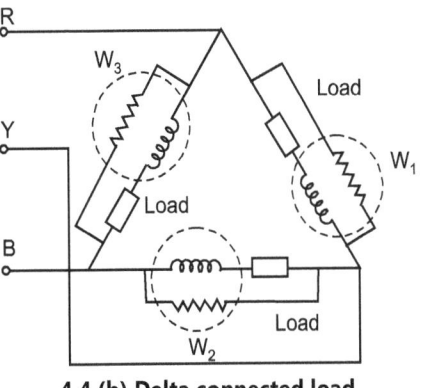

4.4 (a) Star connected load   4.4 (b) Delta connected load

W_1, W_2 and W_3 measure power in the load 1, load 2 and load 3 respectively. Total power is
$P = W_1 + W_2 + W_3$

Advantages of three wattmeter method
- This method is useful for both balanced as well as unbalanced loads.
- It indicates the contribution of each individual phase and it is used as a work test.

Disadvantages of three wattmeter method
- For star connected load, neutral point must be available for the connection of pressure coil.
- For delta connected load, it must be possible to open the closed delta for the insertion of wattmeter current coils.

For unbalanced load, $W_1 \neq W_2 \neq W_3$

∴ Total power = $W_1 + W_2 + W_3$

For balanced load $W_1 = W_2 = W_3$

Total power = $3W_1$ or $3W_2$ or $3W_3$

4.6.2 Two Wattmeter Method

This method is common for measurement of three phase power, when the load is unbalanced. It can be used for measuring power in three phase, three wire circuits with balanced load. The current coils of the two wattmeter are connected in any two of the lines and pressure coil of each wattmeter connected between its own current coil terminal and the line without a current coil.

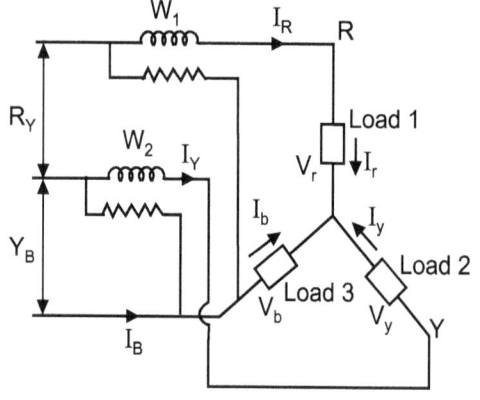

4.5 (a) Star connected load

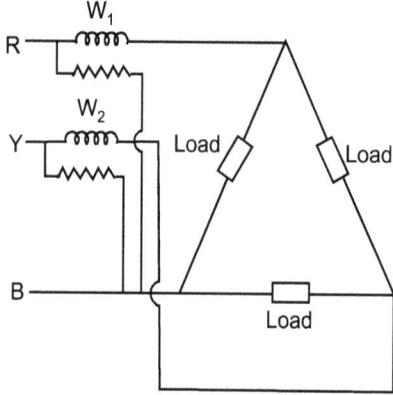

4.5 (b) Delta connected load

Fig. 4.5 (a) shows connection diagram for star connected load and Fig. 4.5 (b) shows connection diagram of two wattmeter method for delta connected load.

4.6.2.1 Measurement of power in three phase balanced loads (Star connected loads)

In Fig. 4.5 (a) W_1 and W_2 are measuring power taken by a balanced, 3ϕ, star connected load. Load is assumed as inductive in nature. V_r, V_y and V_b are the r.m.s values of phase voltages I_r, I_y, I_b are the r.m.s values of phase currents.

V_{RY}, V_{YB} and V_{BR} are r.m.s values of line voltages
- I_R, I_Y, I_B are r.m.s values of line currents
- I_R is the current through current coil of W_1
- V_{RB} is the voltage across pressure coil of W_1
- Fig. 4.5 (c) shows the phasor diagram of the two wattmeter star connected balanced load.
- Reading of $W_1 = V_{RB} I_R \cos(30° - \phi)$
- I_Y is current through current coil of W_2
- V_{YB} is voltage across pressure coil of W_2

$$\overline{V}_{YB} = \overline{V}_y - \overline{V}_b$$

- Reading of $W_2 = W_2 = V_{YB} I_Y \cos(30° + \phi)$

As the load is balanced,

$$I_R = I_Y = I_L$$
$$V_{RB} = V_{YB} = V_L$$
$$W_1 = V_L I_L \cos(30° - \phi)$$
$$W_2 = V_L I_L \cos(30° + \phi)$$

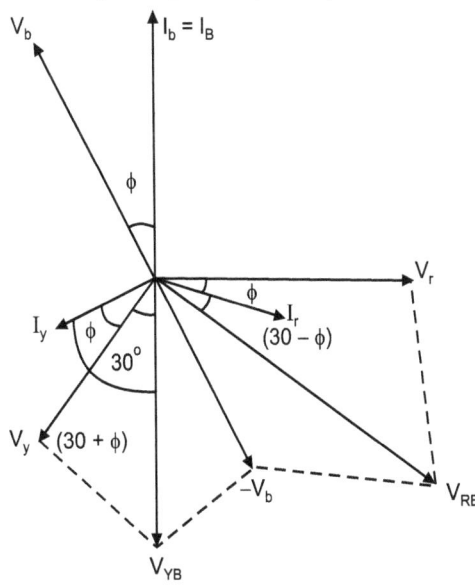

Fig. 4.5 (c)

$$W_1 + W_2 = V_L I_L \cos(30° - \phi) + V_L I_L \cos(30° + \phi)$$
$$= V_L I_L [\cos 30° \cdot \cos\phi + \sin 30° \cdot \sin\phi + \cos 30° \cdot \cos\phi - \sin 30° \cdot \sin\phi]$$
$$= 2V_L I_L \cos 30° \cos\phi$$
$$= 2 V_L I_L \times \frac{\sqrt{3}}{2} \cos\phi$$
$$W_1 + W_2 = \sqrt{3} V_L I_L \cos\phi$$

Phase sequence is assumed as R – Y – B. If the phase sequence is reversed then reading of wattmeter will interchange.

4.6.2.2 Power Factor for Balanced Load

For the balanced load, by using two wattmeter methods, power factor can be found from the wattmeter readings.

For a balanced 3ϕ load,

$$W_1 + W_2 = \sqrt{3} V_L I_L \cos\phi \quad \text{...(1)}$$
$$W_1 - W_2 = V_L I_L \cos(30° - \phi) - V_L I_L \cos(30° + \phi)$$
$$= 2V_L I_L \sin 30° \sin\phi$$
$$W_1 - W_2 = V_L I_L \sin\phi \quad \text{...(2)}$$

Divide (2) by (1),

$$\frac{W_1 - W_2}{W_1 + W_2} = \frac{V_L I_L \sin\phi}{\sqrt{3} V_L I_L \cos\phi}$$

$$\tan\phi = \sqrt{3}\left(\frac{W_1 - W_2}{W_1 + W_2}\right)$$

$$\cos\phi = \frac{1}{\sqrt{(1+\tan^2\phi)}}$$

$$\cos\phi = \frac{1}{\sqrt{1+3\left(\frac{W_1 - W_2}{W_1 + W_2}\right)^2}}$$

4.6.2.3 Effects of Power Factor on the Reading of Wattmeter

(i) With $\quad\quad \phi = 0°, \cos\phi = 1$

then, $\quad W_1 = W_2 = V_L I_L \cos 30° = \frac{\sqrt{3}}{2} V_L I_L$

Readings of both wattmeters are equal.

(ii) When $\quad\quad \phi = 30°, \cos\phi = 0.87$

$$W_1 = V_L I_L \cos(30° - 30°) = V_L I_L$$
$$W_2 = V_L I_L \cos(30° + 30°) = \frac{1}{2} V_L I_L$$

$$W_2 = \frac{1}{2}W_1$$

(iii) $\phi = 60°$ and Power factor = 0.5

$$W_1 = V_L I_L \cos(30° - 60°) = \frac{\sqrt{3}}{2} V_L I_L$$

$$W_2 = V_L I_L \cos(30° + 60°) = V_L I_L \cos 90° = 0$$

W_2 is zero and readings of W_1 gives total power.

(iv) If $\phi > 60°$ then $\cos\phi < 0.5$

Reading of W_2 is negative.

$$\text{Total power} = W_1 - W_2$$

(v) If $\phi = 90°$ and $\cos\phi = 0$

$$W_1 = V_L I_L \cos(30° - 90°)$$
$$= -V_L I_L \sin 30°$$
$$= -\frac{1}{2} V_L I_L$$

Disadvantages of two Wattmeter Method

- This method is not useful for 3ϕ, four wire system.
- Care is needed about signs of two wattmeter readings.

4.6.3 One Wattmeter Method for a Balanced Load

One wattmeter is applicable only for balanced loads. Fig. 4.6(a) shows the connection for measuring power by a balanced, three phase, and star connected load by one wattmeter method. Current coil of wattmeter is connected in any one line.

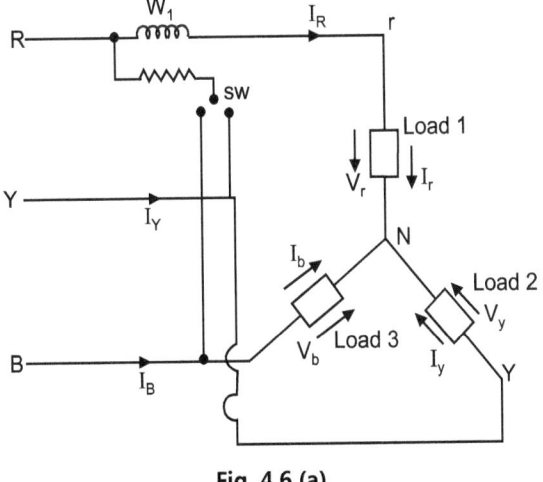

Fig. 4.6 (a)

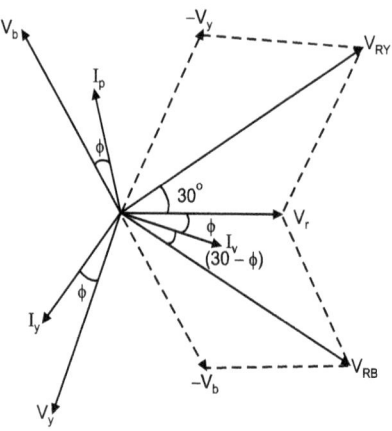

Fig. 4.6 (b)

Fig. 4.6 (b) shows the phasor diagram of circuit shown in Fig. 4.6 (a).

When switch is in position (1)

$$I_R = \text{Current through current coil}$$
$$V_{RB} = \text{Voltage across pressure coil}$$
$$\overline{V}_{RB} = \overline{V}_r - \overline{V}_b$$

$\angle$ between $\overline{V}_{RB}$ and $\overline{I}_R$ is $(30 - \phi)$

$$\therefore \quad W_1 = V_{RB}\, I_R \cos(30° - \phi)$$

Switch in position 2

$$I_R = \text{Current through current coil}$$
$$V_{RY} = \text{Voltage across pressure coil}$$
$$\overline{V}_{RY} = \overline{V}_r - \overline{V}_y$$

$\angle$ between $\overline{V}_{RY}$ and $\overline{I}_R = (30° + \phi)$

$$W_2 = V_{RY}\, I_R \cos(30° + \phi)$$

For balanced load

$$V_{RY} = V_{RB} = V_L$$
$$I_R = I_Y = I_B = I_L$$
$$W_1 = V_L I_L \cos(30° - \phi)$$
$$W_2 = V_L I_L \cos(30° + \phi)$$
$$W_1 + W_2 = V_L I_L \cos(30° - \phi) + V_L I_L \cos(30° + \phi)$$
$$= \sqrt{3}\, V_L I_L \cos\phi$$

4.7 ONE WATTMETER METHOD FOR REACTIVE POWER MEASUREMENT

Fig. 4.7 (a) shows the connection diagram of one wattmeter method. Fig. 4.7 (b) shows phasor diagram.

(a) For star connected load

I_R = Current through current coil of the wattmeter.

V_{YB} = Voltage across pressure coil of wattmeter.

$V_{YB} = V_y - V_b$

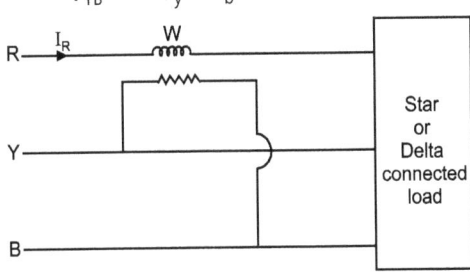

Fig. 4.7 (a)

$\angle$ between $\overline{V}_{YB}$ and $\overline{I}_R = (90° - \phi)$

Reading of wattmeter = $V_{YB} I_R \cos(90° - \phi)$

For balanced load, $W = V_L I_L \cos(90 - \phi)$

$= V_L I_L \sin\phi$

But, Total reactive power $= \sqrt{3} V_L I_L \sin\phi$

$= \sqrt{3} W$

$\therefore$ $\sqrt{3}$ times wattmeter reading gives the total reactive power of the circuit.

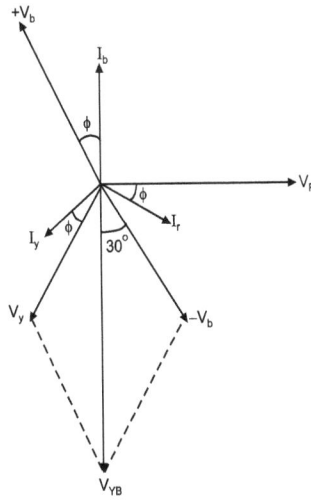

Fig. 4.7 (b)

4.8 TOD METER

Q. Explain TOD meter? [May 12, Dec. 12]

Time of day metering is a rate option that is offered by many utilities. When selected by the customer, a meter that records demand, time and energy usage is installed in place of the existing electrical meter. The metering option benefits utility companies by decreasing the required capacity. The metering option benefits the customers by providing reduced demand and usage rates during off peak times. This gives customers a change to reduce their utility bill. In many countries electricity have implemented TOD based energy meter to reduce the usage of electricity by increasing rates in peak hours and reducing rates in off peak periods. Time of day metering also known as time of usage or seasonal time of day. This metering involves dividing the day, month and year into tariff slots and with higher rates at peak load periods and low tariff rates at off peak load periods. This can be used to automatically control usage on the part of the customer resulting in automatic load control. This also allows the utilities to plan their transmission infrastructure appropriately. In Maharashtra there is provision for 6 times of day time zones for energy & demand. Timings of these TOD time zones are programmable in a meter.

4.9 WATTMETER ERRORS

Q. List the errors which occur in wattmeter.

Q. Which errors occur in wattmeter and how they are compensated?

In practice, the pressure coil current is not in phase with the voltage. One source of error is the phase angle by which current deviates from the voltage. Phase angle depends on the inductance of the pressure coil and the inter turn capacitance of the series resistance. The other sources of errors in wattmeters are the eddy current induced in the metal part and the method of connections of the current and pressure coils.

4.9.1 Error Due to Inductance of Pressure Coil

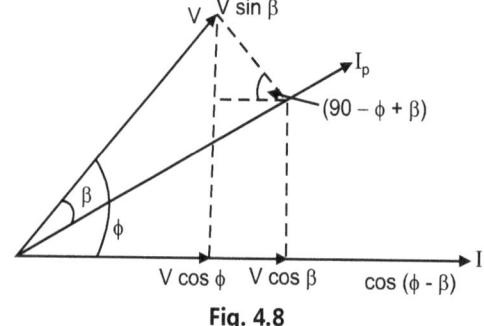

Fig. 4.8

Phasor diagram (4.8) shows the voltage vector V impressed across the pressure coil and current vector I of the current coil lagging the voltage by an angle ϕ.

Current through the pressure coil is

$$I_p = \frac{V}{\sqrt{R_p^2 + \omega^2 L_p^2}}$$

I_p lags the voltage by angle β given as

$$\beta = \tan^{-1}\left(\frac{\omega L_p}{R_p}\right)$$

$$\therefore \quad I_p = \frac{V \cos \beta}{R_p}$$

$$\text{Power} = W = VI \cos \phi$$

$$\text{Wattmeter reading} = VI \cos \beta \cos (\phi - \beta)$$

$$\therefore \quad \text{True reading} = \frac{\cos \phi}{\cos \beta \cos (\phi - \beta)} \times \text{Actual reading}$$

Correction factor by which the reading of wattmeter must be multiplied to give true reading is

$$\text{Correction factor} = \frac{\cos \phi}{\cos \beta \cos (\phi - \beta)}$$

$$\text{Error in reading} = W' - W$$
$$= I\,[V \cos \beta \cos (\phi - \beta) - V \cos \phi]$$

From the vector diagram

$$V \cos \beta \cos (\phi - \beta) - V \cos \phi = V \sin \beta \sin (\phi - \beta)$$

$$\text{Error} = VI \sin \beta \sin (\phi - \beta)$$

4.9.2 Error Due to the Capacitance of Pressure Coil

The non-inductive resistance connected in series with the pressure coil has some value of inter turn capacitance. The effect of this capacitance is to cancel the effect of inductance. Equivalent circuit of the pressure coil is shown in Fig. 4.9.

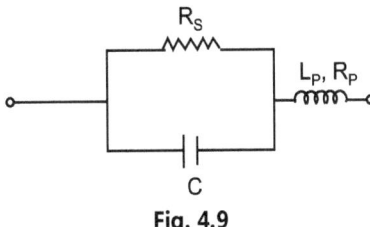

Fig. 4.9

Wattmeter reads low on lagging power factors. The effect of capacitance is exactly opposite to that of inductance.

Impedance of the Fig. 4.9 is

$$Z = R_P + j\omega L_P + \frac{R_S}{1 + j\omega C R_S}$$

$$= R_P + \frac{R_S}{1 + \omega^2 C^2 + R_S^2} + j\omega \left[L_P - \frac{C R_S^2}{1 + \omega^2 C^2 R_S^2} \right]$$

$$Z = R_P + R_S + j\omega [L_P - C R_S^2]$$

$$(\because \omega^2 C^2 R_S^2 \approx \text{Small. Hence, neglected})$$

$$\tan \beta = \frac{\omega [L_P - C R_S^2]}{R_P + R_S}$$

Ideally $\beta = 0$

$$\therefore L_P - C R_S^2 = 0$$

$$L_P = C R_S^2$$

If the capacitive reactance of the pressure coil is equal to its inductor reactance, there will be no error due to these effects since the two errors will neutralize each other.

4.9.3 Error Due to Eddy Current

The field of the current coil induces a voltage in any adjacent metal part and this in turn produces current lagging the induced voltage. Effect of eddy current is to increase the angle by which load current lags the voltage. The wattmeter reads low for lagging power factors and reads high for leading power factors. Hence if the eddy current is kept small by using metal of high resistivity then the effect of eddy current is to compensate for the pressure coil inductance error. In practice, a special type of wattmeter called low power factor wattmeter is used.

4.9.4 Error Due to Method of Connection

The connection of wattmeter is important for a low power factor instrument. There are two types of connections for a wattmeter as shown in Fig. 4.10 (a and b).

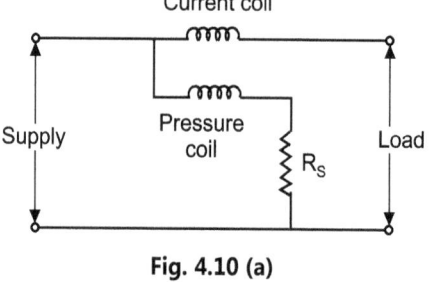

Fig. 4.10 (a)

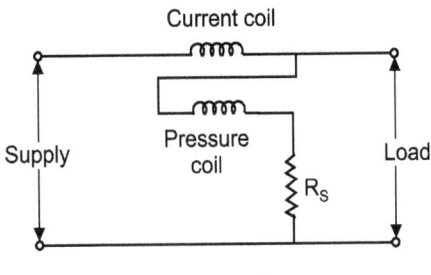

Fig. 4.10 (b)

In Fig. 4.10 (a), the voltage applied to the pressure coil is higher than that of the load on account of voltage drop in the current coil. Thus the instrument reads higher as it also measures I^2R_C loss in the current coil.

∴ Power indicated by wattmeter = Power consumed by load + Power loss in current coil

In Fig. 4.10 (b), the current coil carries, in addition of the load current the small current taken by the pressure coil. Wattmeter reads higher as it includes the power loss in pressure coil circuit.

∴ Power indicated by wattmeter = Power consumed by load + Power loss in pressure coil

$$= \text{Power consumed by load} + \frac{V^2}{R_p}$$

A compensating coil, in series with the pressure coil, is used to eliminate the error in Fig. (b). This coil is as nearly identical as possible and coincident with the current coil so that the magnetic field produced by this coil cancels the field produced by current coil when the load current is zero.

4.10 LOW POWER FACTOR DYNAMOMETER WATTMETER

Q. Write a short note on LPF type wattmeter. [Dec. 10, 11]

When an ordinary wattmeter is used for measurement of power in low power factor circuit (P.F. < 0.5) then the measurement would be inaccurate due to following reasons.
- The deflecting torque exerted on the moving system will be very small.
- Errors are introduced due to pressure coil inductance; which is large at low power factor.

In a low power factor dynamometer wattmeter special features are incorporated in a general electro dynamometer wattmeter circuit to make it suitable for use in low power factor circuit. They are given as follows.

- **Pressure coil current :** Resistance of the pressure coil circuit is designed to have low value so that current through pressure coil is increased to give an increased operating torque.

- **Compensation for pressure coil current :** Power is small and current is high on account of low power factor. Two types of connections of the pressure coil are shown below.

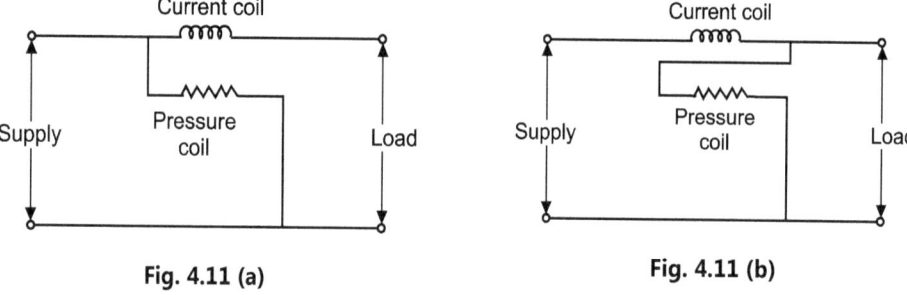

Fig. 4.11 (a)　　　　　　　　　　　Fig. 4.11 (b)

Connection 4.11 (a) cannot be used, due to high load current there would be high power loss in the current coil and hence wattmeter reading would be with large error. When connection 4.11 (b) is used then the power loss in the pressure coil circuit is also included in the meter readings. Therefore it is necessary to compensate for the pressure coil current in a low power factor wattmeter. For this a compensating coil is used in the instrument to compensate for the power loss in the pressure coil as shown in Fig. 4.12 below. This coil is as nearly identical as possible and coincident with the current coil so that the magnetic field produced by this coil cancels the field produced by current coil when the load current is zero.

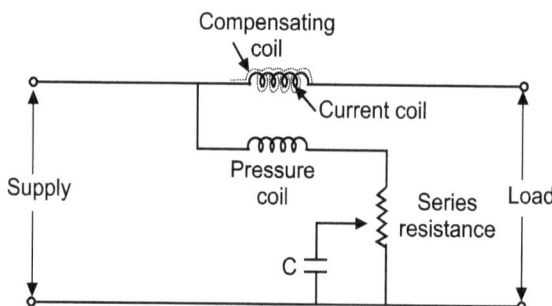

Fig. 4.12 : Low power factor wattmeter

- **Compensation for pressure coil inductance :** At low power factor, the error caused by the pressure coil inductance is very large. This is compensated by connecting a capacitor C across a portion of the series resistance in the pressure coil as shown in Fig. 4.12 above. Low power factor wattmeter are designed to have a very small control torque so that they can provide full scale deflection for power factor values as low as 10% Fig. 4.12 above is a low power factor wattmeter.

4.11 POLYPHASE WATTMETER

Q. Write a short note on Polyphase wattmeter. [Dec. 12]

Polyphase wattmeters have been developed for the measurement of power in polyphase circuits. This meter is a combination of two similar wattmeters with their moving systems mechanically coupled together and kept in same case. The pressure coils are mounted on the same spindle in case of dynamometer wattmeters. In one form of polyphase wattmeter the two similar single phase wattmeters are mounted one above the other, with their magnetic axes at right angle, so there is no magnetic coupling between them. The connection of wattmeter using two drysdale single phase wattmeters is shown in Fig. 4.13 below.

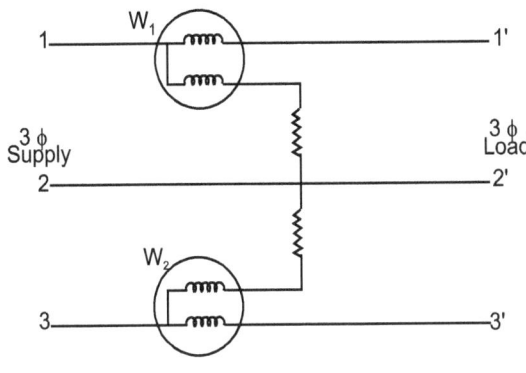

Fig. 4.13

The current is led into the pressure coils through the top and bottom suspension in addition two ligments. The reading of the polyphase wattmeter gives the total power supplied. Some of the commercial polyphase wattmeter consists of two systems placed one above the other with their axes not at right angle. The connections are shown below Fig. 4.14. An auxiliary resistance R is inserted between the junction of the two pressure coils and the third phase.

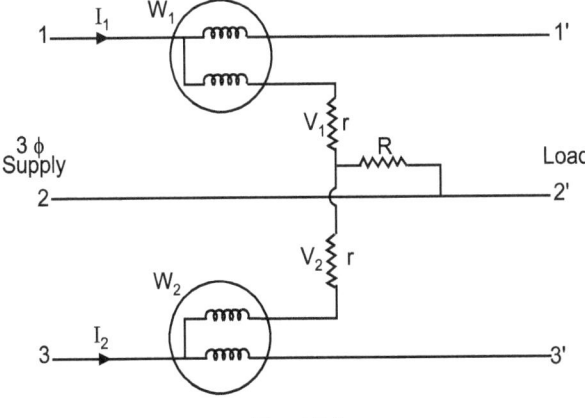

Fig. 4.14

4.12 ELECTRONIC MULTIMETER

Q. Explain in brief Electronic Multimeter

Multimeter is a measuring instrument. It can be used to measure voltage, current and resistance. Most modern multimeters are digital. Analog meter moves a needle along a scale. The function of the meter can be changed by switching the dial. Electronic multimeter is also known as voltage ohm meter. A multimeter consists of the following.

- A balanced bridge D.C. amplifier and an indicating meter.
- An input attenuator or range switches to limit the magnitude of the input voltage to the desired value.
- A rectifier section to convert an A.C. input to a proportional D.C. value.
- An internal battery and additional circuitry to measure resistance.
- A function switch to select various measurement functions of the instrument.

Fig. 4.15 shows the circuit diagram of a balanced bridge D.C. amplifier using JFETs.

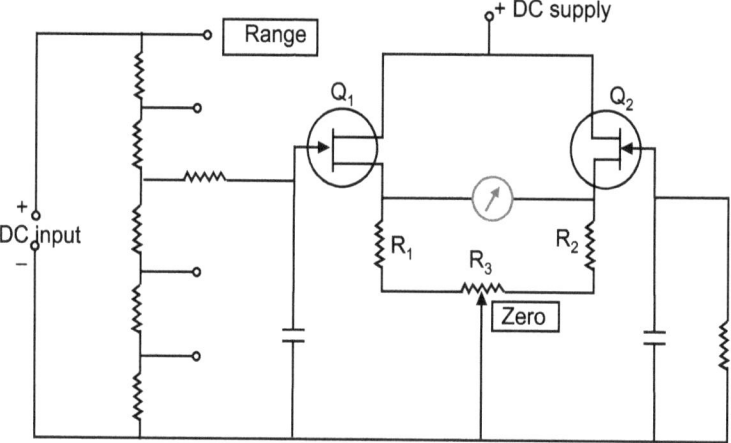

Fig. 4.15 : Balanced bridge D.C. amplifier with input attenuator and indicating meter

The two JFETs form the upper arms of a bridge circuit. Resistors R_1, R_2 together with zero adjust resistor R_3 form the lower bridge arms. The meter movement is connected between the source terminals of the FET, representing the two opposite corners of the bridge. The maximum voltage that can be applied to the gate of G, depends on the operating range of the JFET. It will usually be a few volts. The input is usually applied through a range switch.

Use of multimeter for resistance measurement

When the selector switch of the multimeter is put in the resistance range, the unknown resistor is connected in series with an internal battery. The voltage drop across the resistor is measured and it is proportional to the value of unknown resistor. The meter is calibrated in terms of resistance. The circuit diagram is shown below.

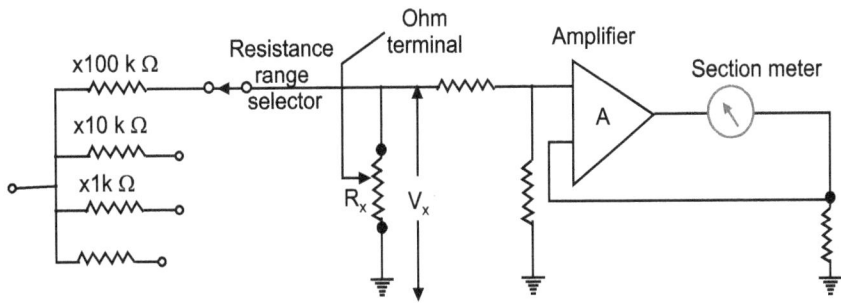

Fig. 4.16

The unknown resistor R_x is connected to the two terminals and the range switch is kept in the ohm position. The 1.5 V internal battery supplies current through one of the range resistors and the unknown resistor to the ground. A voltage drop V_x across R_x is applied to the input of the bridge amplifier and causes a deflection on the meter. The meter is calibrated in terms of resistance values. If the resistance value is more, the voltage drop will be more, therefore the meter deflection is also more. In electronic multimeter, the resistance values increases from left to right.

Advantages of electronic multimeter :

- Input impedance is high
- It is cheap
- The construction is rugged
- Frequency range is high
- It can measure D.C as well as A.C voltage and current

Disadvantages of electronic multimeter :

- Reliability is poor
- Accuracy is less
- Repeatability is poor
- Problem to interface the output with the external devices

NUMERICALS

Q.1 The readings of the wattmeter shown in figure are W_1 = 4600 W and W_2 = 2300 W. What is the total power flowing into and power factor of the load.

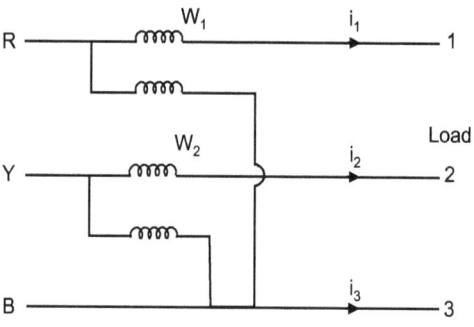

Fig. 4.17

Sol. Considering both readings are positive

$$\text{Power } P = W_1 + W_2$$
$$= 4600 + 2300$$
$$= 6900 \text{ W}$$

$$\tan \phi = \frac{\sqrt{3}(W_2 - W_1)}{(W_1 + W_2)}$$

$$= \frac{\sqrt{3}(2300 - 4600)}{4600 + 2300}$$

$$\phi = -30°$$

positive sign shows power factor is leading

$$\therefore \quad \cos \phi = \cos(-30°) = 0.866 \text{ leading}$$

Q.2 The sum of readings of the two wattmeters connected to measure the input to a three phase induction motor is 300 kW. The motor power factor is 0.8. Calculate the readings on both wattmeters.

Sol.
$$W = W_1 + W_2$$
$$\tan \phi = \frac{\sqrt{3}(W_2 - W_1)}{(W_1 + W_2)}$$

Given, W = 300 kW and $\cos \phi$ = 0.8

$$\tan \phi = \frac{\sin \phi}{\cos \phi} = \frac{0.6}{0.8} = 0.75$$

$$W_1 + W_2 = 300$$

$$W_2 - W_1 = \frac{(W_1 + W_2)}{\sqrt{3}} \tan \phi$$

$$= \frac{300 \times 0.75}{\sqrt{3}}$$

$$= 130$$

$$W_2 = 215 \text{ kW}$$
$$W_1 = 85 \text{ kW}$$

Q.3 A 400 V, 3 φ motor takes 50 kW. The ratio of the two wattmeter readings connected to measure the input power is 1 : 2. Find the power factor of the circuit and line current.

Sol. Let, $W_1 = x$, $W_2 = 2x$

$$\tan \phi = \frac{\sqrt{3}(W_2 - W_1)}{W_1 + W_2}$$

$$= \frac{\sqrt{3}(2x - x)}{x + 2x}$$

$$= \frac{1}{\sqrt{3}}$$

$$\phi = 30°$$

$$\cos \phi = \cos 30 = 0.8666$$

Power $W = \sqrt{3} \text{ VI} \cos \phi$

$$\therefore \quad I = \frac{W}{\sqrt{3} \text{ V} \cos \phi}$$

$$= \frac{500 \times 10^3}{\sqrt{3} \times 400 \times 0.866}$$

$$= 833 \text{ A}$$

Q.4 The readings of two wattmeter employed to measure power in a 3 φ balanced load system is $W_1 = -2000$ W and $W_2 = 4000$ W. Calculate (a) Power factor of the system and resistance of each phase.

Sol.
$$\tan \phi = \frac{\sqrt{3}(W_2 - W_1)}{(W_2 + W_1)}$$

$$= \frac{\sqrt{3}(4000 + 2000)}{4000 - 2000}$$

$$\cos \phi = 0.189$$

Total power absorbed in the load

$$W = W_1 + W_2$$
$$= 4000 - 2000$$
$$= 2000 \text{ W}$$

Let us consider load is star connected.

$$\text{Phase voltage} = \frac{400}{\sqrt{3}} = 231 \text{ V}$$

$$\text{Power per phase} = \frac{2000}{3}$$
$$= 666.7 \text{ W}$$
$$\text{Phase current} = \frac{666.7}{231 \times 0.189}$$
$$= 15.28 \text{ A}$$
$$\text{Phase impedance} = \frac{231}{15.28 \text{ A}}$$
$$= 15.12 \text{ }\Omega$$
$$\text{Resistance of each phase} = \sqrt{(15.12)^2 - (2.86)^2}$$
$$= 14.85 \text{ }\Omega$$

Q.5 A 3ϕ 10 kVA load has a power factor of 0.342. The power is measured by two wattmeter method. Find the reading of each wattmeter when (i) Power factor is lagging.

Sol.
$$\cos \phi = 0.342$$
$$10 \times 10^3 = \sqrt{3} \, V_L \, I_L$$
$$V_L \, I_L = 5773.5027 \text{ VA}$$
$$W_1 = V_L \, I_L \cos(30 - \phi)$$
$$\cos \phi = 0.342$$
$$\phi = 70°$$
$$W_1 = 5773.5027 \, [\cos(30 - 70)]$$
$$= 4422.7596 \text{ W}$$
$$W_2 = V_L \, I_L \cos(30 + \phi)$$
$$= 5773.5027 \cos(30 + 70)$$
$$= -1002.5582 \text{ W}$$

Q.6 A wattmeter has a current coil of 0.03 Ω resistance and a pressure coil of 6 kΩ resistance. Calculate the percentage error when the pressure coil is on load side and load takes 20 A at a voltage of 220 V and power factor = 0.6.

Sol.
$$\text{Power consumed} = VI \cos \phi$$
$$= 220 \times 20 \times 0.6$$
$$= 2.64 \text{ kW.}$$
$$R_C = 0.03 \text{ }\Omega$$
$$R_P = 6 \text{ k}\Omega$$

Power indicated by wattmeter = Power consumed by load + Power loss in pressure coil
$$= 2.64 + \frac{(220)^2}{6000}$$
$$= 2.648 \text{ kW}$$

$$\% \text{ Error} = \frac{2.64806 - 2.64}{2.64} \times 100$$

$$\% \text{ Error} = 0.3055\%$$

Q.7 A 440 V, 3φ motor has an output of 80 HP and an efficiency of 90% at power factor = 0.8 (lag). Calculate the readings on each of the two wattmeters connected to measure the input.

Sol.   Input on full load $= \dfrac{80 \times 735.5}{0.9}$

$= 65377.77$ watts

Power $= \sqrt{3}\ V_L I_L \cos \phi$

$I_L = \dfrac{65377.77}{\sqrt{3} \times 440 \times 0.8} = 107.2$ A

$\cos \phi = 0.8$

$\phi = 36.86°$

$W_1 = V_L I_L \cos(30 - \phi)$

$W_1 = 440 \times 107.2 \cos(30 - 36.86)$

$= 47168$ watt

$W_1 + W_2 = W$

$W_2 = 6577.77 - 47168$

$W_2 = 18209.77$ W

$W_2 = V_L I_L \cos(30 + \phi)$

$= 440 \times 107.2 \cos(30 + 36.86)$

$= 18536$ W

Q.8 A 3φ star connected load consists of 3φ similar coils. Each coil has a resistance of 12 Ω and reactance of 16 Ω. It is supplied from 440 V 3φ main. Find the readings on each of the two wattmeters connected to measure the input to the load.

Sol.   Impedance per phase $= \sqrt{R^2 + X_L^2}$

$= \sqrt{(12)^2 + (16)^2}$

$= 20$ Ω

Voltage/phase $= \dfrac{V_L}{\sqrt{3}} = \dfrac{440}{\sqrt{3}} = 254$ V

Current/phase $= \dfrac{V_P}{I_P} = \dfrac{254}{20} = 12.7$ A

Power factor of load $= \dfrac{R}{Z} = \dfrac{12}{20} = 0.6$ lag

$\phi = 53.13°$

Reading of $W_1 = V_L I_L \cos(30 - \phi)$

$$= 440 \times 12.7 \cos(30 - 53.13)$$
$$= 5138.81 \text{ W}$$
$$\text{Reading of } W_2 = V_L I_L \cos(30 + \phi)$$
$$= 440 \times 12.7 \times \cos(30 + 53.13)$$
$$= 668.41 \text{ W}$$

Q.9 The reading of two wattmeters connected to measure the total power in a 3ϕ, three wire circuit are 10 kW and 1 kW. 1 kW reading being obtained after reversal of the current coil connections. Find the total power and power factor of the load.

Sol.
$$W_1 = 10 \text{ kW}$$
$$W_2 = -1 \text{ kW}$$
(∵ reading is obtained after reversal of current coil connections)
$$W = W_1 + W_2$$
$$= 10 + (-1)$$
$$= 9 \text{ kW}$$
$$\tan \phi = \frac{\sqrt{3}(W_1 - W_2)}{W_1 + W_2} = \frac{\sqrt{3}(10 - (-1))}{10 + (-1)}$$
∴
$$\tan \phi = 2.117$$
$$\cos \phi = 0.4273$$

Q.10 A 3ϕ, 440 V, 50 Hz induction motor takes a line current of 30 A and delivers 10 kW output power under full load. Assuming its efficiency as 90%. Calculate
(a) P.F. of motor.
(b) Total reactive power.
(c) Readings on the two wattmeters connected to measure the input power to the motor.

Sol.
$$\text{Input power} = \frac{\text{O/P power}}{\eta} = \frac{10}{0.9} = 11.11 \text{ kW}$$
$$P = \sqrt{3} \, V_L I_L \cos \phi$$
$$11.11 \times 10^3 = \sqrt{3} \times 440 \times 30 \times \cos \phi$$
$$\cos \phi = 0.486$$
$$\phi = 60.92°$$

Reading of wattmeter
$$W_1 = V_L I_L \cos(30 - \phi)$$
$$= 440 \times 30 \times \cos(30 - 60.92)$$
$$= 11.324 \text{ kW}$$
$$W_2 = V_L I_L \cos(30 + \phi)$$
$$= 440 \times 30 \times \cos(30 + 60.92)$$

$$= -211.94 \text{ W}$$

$$\text{Total reactive power} = \sqrt{3} \, V_L \, I_L \sin \phi$$

$$= \sqrt{3} \times 440 \times 30 \sin(60.92)$$

$$= 19.981 \text{ kVAr}$$

Q.11 Input to a synchronous motor is measured using two wattmeter method, each wattmeter reading 20 kW. Determine the power factor of the motor.

Sol. $W_1 = W_2 = 20$ kW

$$\tan \phi = \sqrt{3} \left(\frac{W_1 - W_2}{W_1 + W_2} \right) = \sqrt{3} \left(\frac{20 - 20}{20 + 20} \right) = 0$$

$$\phi = 0°$$

$$\cos \phi = \cos 0° = 1$$

$$\text{Input power} = W_1 + W_2$$

$$= 20 + 20$$

$$= 40 \text{ kW}$$

UNIVERSITY QUESTIONS

Dec. 2010

Q.1 State and explain errors in dynamometer type wattmeter. Also state the compensation for each type of error. **(6 Marks)**

Q.2 With a block diagram explain working of digital frequency meter. **(6 Marks)**

Q.3 With a circuit diagram and phasor diagram explain one wattmeter method for measurement of reactive power in (R + L) load. **(6 Marks)**

Q.4 Write a short note on LPF type wattmeter. **(4 Marks)**

Q.5 Draw block diagram of multimeter. **(4 Marks)**

Q.6 Two wattmeter method is used to measure power of three phase star connected lamp bank at balanced load condition. The phase voltage is $\frac{200}{\sqrt{3}}$ volt and line current is 5.5 amp. What will be the reading of each wattmeter? If now load is connected in delta across same supply, what will be the reading of each wattmeter? **(6 Marks)**

May 2011

Q.7 Draw and explain the construction, working of dynamometer type wattmeter. Also derive its torque equation. **(10 Marks)**

Q.8 A wattmeter has current coil of 0.03 Ω resistance and n pressure coil of 6000 Ω resistance. Calculate the percentage error if the wattmeter is so connected that : **(8 Marks)**

(a) The current coil is on the load side.

(b) The pressure coil is on the load side :
   (i) If the load takes 20 A at a voltage of 220 V and 0.6 power factor in each case.
   (ii) What load current would give equal errors with the two connections?

Dec. 2011

Q.9 Explain two wattmeter methods for measuring power in a (R + L) load. Draw the phasor diagram. **(8 Marks)**

Q.10 Write a short note on digital multi-meter. **(8 Marks)**

Q.11 Write a short note on LPF type wattmeter. **(4 Marks)**

Q.12 What are the errors in dynamometer type wattmeter? How are these errors compensated? **(4 Marks)**

Q.13 A wattmeter reads 5 kW when its current coil is connected in red phase and its voltage coil is connected between neutral and red phase of symmetrical 3-phase system supplying a balanced three-phase inductive load of 25 A at 440 V. What will be the reading of the wattmeter if the connections of current coil remain unchanged and voltage coil be connected between blue and yellow phases? Hence determine the total reactive power in the circuit. Draw the diagram both the cases. **(8 Marks)**

May 2012

Q.14 Draw and explain working principle of dynamometer type wattmeter and derive its torque equation. **(9 Marks)**

Q.15 Draw and explain the three wattmeter method for measurement of power in three phase system for balanced and unbalanced load. **(9 Marks)**

Q.16 Write short notes on : **(18 Marks)**
   (i) Digital frequency meter
   (ii) TOD meter
   (iii) Tri-vector meter

Dec. 2012

Q.17 Draw the connection diagram and vector diagram for power measurement in a 3-phase capacitive load using two wattmeters, assume the load is star connected. Hence derive the expression for the power factor of load circuit. **(8 Marks)**

Q.18 Draw the connection diagram and vector diagram for reactive power measurement in 3-phase balanced circuit. Derive the expression for the reactive power of the load circuit. **(8 Marks)**

Q.19 Write notes on : **(8 Marks)**
   (i) Polyphase wattmeters
   (ii) TOD meter
   (iii) Extension of wattmeter range by instrument transformer

Chapter 5

MEASUREMENT OF ENERGY

5.1 INTRODUCTION

The total power consumed by a load during an interval of time is Energy.

$$\text{Energy (E)} = \text{Power (P)} \times \text{Time (t)}$$

If the voltages and currents are not constant and have 'n' values over the time 't', then

$$E = \sum_{i=1}^{n} P_i\, t_i$$

$$= \sum_{i=1}^{n} V_i\, I_i\, t_i$$

It can also be expressed as

$$E = \int_0^t P\, dt$$

$$= \int_0^t V \cdot I \cdot dt$$

The unit of energy is watt second or Joule. Commercial unit is kilowatt hours or kWh which is defined as the energy consumed by a load of 1000 watts over a period of one hour.

5.2 ENERGY METER

Q. Describe the construction of single phase induction type energy meter?[Dec. 10, 11, 12]
Q. Explain the working principle of energy meter?
Q. With neat diagram explain construction and working principle of single phase induction type energy meter.

Energy meter is an instrument which measures electrical energy. It is also known as watt hour meter. It is an integrating device. There are several types of energy meter but single phase induction type energy meter are very commonly used to measure electrical energy consumed in domestic and commercial installation.

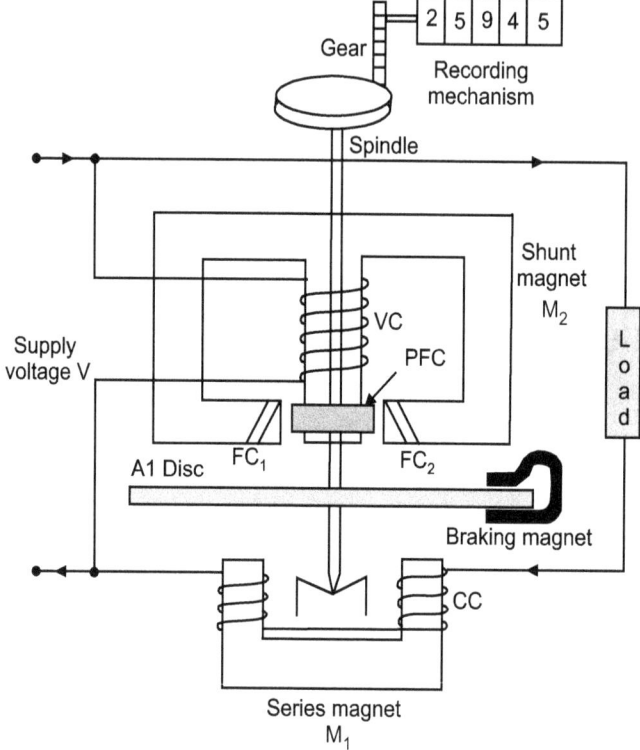

Fig. 5.1 : Energy meter

5.2.1 Working Principle

The basic principle of induction type energy meter is electromagnetic induction. When an alternating current flows through two suitably located coils i.e. current coil and potential coil, produces rotating magnetic field which is cut by the metallic disc suspended near to the coils. Thus, an e.m.f is induced in the thin aluminium disc which circulates eddy currents in it. Torque is developed by the interaction of rotating magnetic field and eddy currents and causes disc to rotate.

5.3 CONSTRUCTION

A single phase induction type energy meter has following main parts of the operating mechanism.
- Driving system
- Moving system
- Braking system
- Registering system
- **Driving System:** This system of energy meter consists of two silicon steel laminated electromagnets M_1 and M_2 as shown in Fig. 5.1. The electromagnet M_1 is called the series

magnet and the electromagnet M_2 is called shunt magnet. The series magnet M_1 carries a coil consisting of a few turns of thick wire. This coil is called the current coil (CC) and it is connected in series with the circuit. The load current flows through this coil. The shunt magnet M_2 carries a coil consisting of many turns of thin wire. This coil is called voltage coil or pressure coil (VC) and is connected across the supply. It carries of current proportional to supply voltage. Short circuited copper bands are provided on the lower part of the central limb of the shunt magnet. These copper bands are called power factor compensator (PFC). A copper shading band is provided on each outer limb of the shunt magnet (FC_1 and FC_2). These bands provide frictional compensation.

- **Moving System:** The moving system consists of a thin aluminium disc mounted on a spindle and is placed in the air gap between the series and the shunt magnets. Since control spring is not there, the disc makes continuous revolution under the action of deflecting torque.
- **Braking System:** The braking system consists of a permanent magnet called the brake magnet. It is placed near the edge of the disc. As the disc rotates in the field of brake magnet, eddy currents are induced in it. These currents react with the flux and exert a torque. This torque acts in a direction to oppose the motion of disc. The braking torque is proportional to the speed of the disc.
- **Registering System:** It keeps the record of energy consumed by load. The disc spindle is connected to a counting mechanism. This mechanism records a number which is proportional to the number of revolutions of the disc. The counter is calibrated to indicate the energy consumed directly in kilowatt-hour.

5.4 TORQUE EQUATION OF SINGLE PHASE INDUCTION TYPE ENERGY METER

Q. Derive the torque equation for single phase induction type energy meter.

[Dec. 10, 11, 12]

Fig. 5.2 shows the phasor diagram of a single phase induction type energy meter.

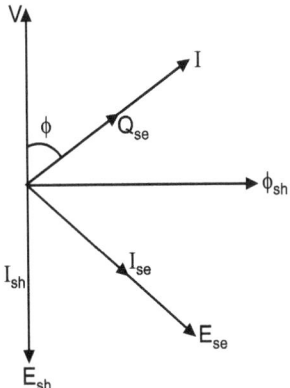

Fig. 5.2 : Phasor diagram of 1φ induction type energy meter

Let,
V = Supply voltage
I = Load current lagging behind V by ϕ.
$\cos \phi$ = Load power factor (lagging).
I_{sh} = Current set up by ϕ_{sh} in the disc
I_{se} = Current set up by ϕ_{se} in the disc.

Instantaneous deflecting torque,
$$T_d = (\psi_{sh} i_{se} - \psi_{se} i_{sh})$$
where ψ and i are instantaneous values.

Average deflecting torque.

$\therefore$
$$T_d \propto [\phi_{sh} I_{se} \cos \phi - \phi_{se} I_{sh} \cdot \cos(180 - \phi)]$$
$$T_d \propto [\phi_{sh} I_{se} \cos \phi + \phi_{se} I_{sh} \cos \phi]$$
$$T_d \propto [\phi_{sh} I_{se} + \phi_{se} I_{sh}] \cos \phi$$

Since,
$\phi_{sh} \propto V$
$I_{se} \propto I$
$\phi_{se} \propto I$
$I_{sh} \propto V$

$\therefore \quad T_d \propto [VI + VI] \cos \phi$
$\therefore \quad T_d \propto 2VI \cos \phi$
$$T_d = K_1 VI \cos \phi \quad \ldots (1)$$

The braking torque is due to eddy currents induced in the aluminium disc. The magnitude of eddy currents is proportional to the speed N of the disc. Hence braking torque is proportional to the speed N.

$$T_b \propto N$$
$$T_b = K_2 N \quad \ldots (2)$$

For steady speed of rotation
$$T_d = T_b$$

From (1) and (2),
$$K_1 VI \cos \phi = K_2 N$$
$\therefore \qquad N = K VI \cos \phi$

Total number of revolutions in t sec = $\int_0^t N \, dt$

$$= \int_0^t K(VI \cos \phi) \, dt$$

Total number of revolutions = K × Energy

$$\text{As energy} = \int_0^t VI \cos\phi \, dt$$

$$\therefore \quad K = \text{Meter constant} = \frac{N}{\text{Energy}}$$

$$= \frac{\text{No. of revolutions}}{\text{Energy in kWh}}$$

Thus, meter constant K is number of revolutions of the disc per kWh of energy consumed.

5.5 ERRORS OF SINGLE PHASE CONVENTIONAL ENERGY METER

Q. Explain various errors in energy meter?
Q. Explain compensation used in energy meter?
Q. Which are the possible errors in induction type single phase energy meter?
[Dec. 11]
Q. Explain calibration of 1φ energy meter. [Dec. 10, 11, 12]
Q. Describe electronic energy meter. [Dec. 10]
Q. Give the advantages of electronic energy meter? [May 12]
Q. Explain how the following adjustments are made in single-phase induction type of energy meter :
  (i) Lag adjustment
  (ii) Adjustment of friction
  (iii) Creep

Following are the common errors observed in the energy meters.
- Error due to friction
- Error due to variation of frequency
- Phase or low power factor error
- Speed error
- Error due to temperature variation
- Creeping error
- Change in resistance of disc

Above mentioned errors are required to be compensated to get correct reading. Compensation of errors is done to get accurate readings. Errors are explained in brief as given below.

- **Error due to Friction :** Error in the reading of energy meter may be caused due to friction at bearing of the spindle and in the registration system. This error depends on the speed of the spindle or on the load of the system.
- **Phase or Low Power Factor Error :** The flux produced by shunt coil does not have a phase difference of exact 90° due to its applied voltage. At zero power factor load the torque is not zero.
- **Error due to Variation of Frequency :** Normal frequency of operation is 50 Hz. The change in frequency will result in change of reactance of their coils which will change the magnitude of current and also the flux due to its cause error.
- **Creeping Error :** In creeping error the energy meter disc will rotate even at no load. This may be due to over voltage applied across the meter or stray magnetic field.
- **Speed Error :** The speed of the disc is proportional to current in ampere hours and to power in case of watt hour meters. The braking torque is produced by permanent magnets, if its strength is weaken then the braking torque will be less than deflecting torque and the disc will run fast.
- **Error due to Temperature Variation :** The effects of temperature changes on the driving and braking system tend to balance each other.
- **Overload Error :** This error is developed in the energy meter when it carries a current in excess of the rated current for the meter. This causes saturation of current coil magnet and the meter tends to be slow at high load currents.

5.6 COMPENSATION OF ERROR

- **Over Load Compensation :** Majority of the braking action is provided by the braking magnets, the voltage and current electromagnets also exert some amount of braking torque. Flux of the shunt magnet is constant as voltage and frequency are constant. Hence this will not affect the shape of the load curve. But the flux from the current electromagnet varies with the main current and so the braking action of this magnet varies with the load. The brake torque varies as the square of the flux and the variable braking action of the current electromagnet introduces the most serious error at full load and overload. Registration of the meter at overload is low. To minimize the self braking action of the speed of the disc at full load is kept as low as possible and the flux of the current electromagnet is made as small as possible as compared with the voltage electromagnet flux. An over load compensator is also provided. Fig. 5.3 shows a saturable magnetic shunt for the current magnet.

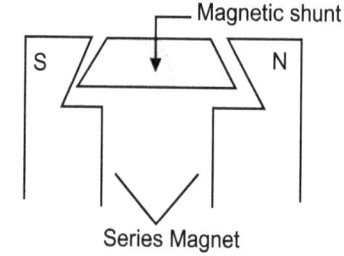

Fig. 5.3

- **Compensation for Creeping Action :** When the potential coil is excited then even at no load current, a slow and continuous rotation of the disc is obtained. This rotation of disc without any current through current coil and only due to excitation of pressure coil is called creeping. This may be due to vibration, stray magnetic fields or excess of supply voltage, over friction compensation. This creeping is prevented by cutting two holes or slots in disc on opposite sides of the spindle. When one of the holes comes under one of the poles of the shunt magnet, the disc tends to remain stationary. In some cases, a small piece of iron is attached to the edge of the disc. The force of attraction of the braking magnet on the iron piece is responsible to prevent rotation of disc on no loads.

3. **Phase Error and Inductive Load Compensation:** It is desirable for the shunt flux to lag behind the voltage by an angle of 90°. This is achieved by adjusting the position of the shading band in the central limb of shunt electromagnet. The effect of any error in phase will be more on a load of zero power factor, the method of correcting phase error is known as inductive load compensation. The adjustment of shading band is done after checking the revolutions of the meter on 0.5 power factor with full load current. As a check, with a rated current at zero power factor, the disc should remain stationary.

4. **Low Load or Friction Compensation :** It is necessary to overcome the friction at the bearings and register mechanism so that the meter can respond to very low loads. This is done by providing two shading bands embracing the flux in the two outer limbs of the shunt electromagnet. This is shown in Fig. 5.4. Thus eddy currents are induced in the bands which cause a phase displacement between the fluxes of outer limbs and central limb. A driving torque is exerted on the disc. This torque can be adjusted by adjusting the position of bonds to compensate for the friction torque. By testing the meter on light loads, the correctness of the friction compensation can be checked.

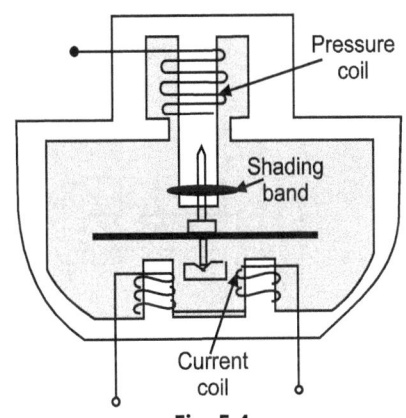

Fig. 5.4

5. **Temperature Compensation :** As the temperature increases then there increase in the resistance of the copper and aluminium parts. Error due to temperature variation includes increase in eddy current resistance path, reduction in shunt magnet flux decrease in angle of lag ∝ of the eddy currents. These errors are not serious. But at low lagging power factor loads, these error cause problems. These can be compensated by providing a temperature shunt on the brake magnet. A special magnetic material such as Mutemp is used to provide temperature compensation which does not allow the disc to rotate faster as temperature increases.

6. **Compensation for Error in Registration :** There is error in revolutions made by energy meter due to weakening of strength of permanent magnet or wrong adjustment of compensating mechanism. This error can be compensated by adjusting the braking magnet or by changing the registering system.

5.7 CALIBRATION OF ENERGY METER

Q. Write note on Electronic Energy Meter

Calibration of energy meter means its testing with the help of sub standard equipment or with the help of rotary sub standard energy meter to determine its % error. The graph of % error against the load current I can be obtained which is called calibration curve of the energy meter. Once the calibration curve is obtained by observing the curve, the range of load current where it is severe can be predicted. Percent Error is given as :

$$\% \text{ Error} = \frac{\text{Energy recorded} - \text{Energy consumed}}{\text{Energy consumed}} \times 100$$

Energy meters are tested under following conditions and if its registration system shows error in recording, then adjustments are done to minimize the errors.

- At rated current with 0.5 lagging power factor.
- At 100% or 125% of marked full load with unity power factor.
- At 5% of rated full load current with unity power factor load.

5.8 ELECTRONIC ENERGY METER

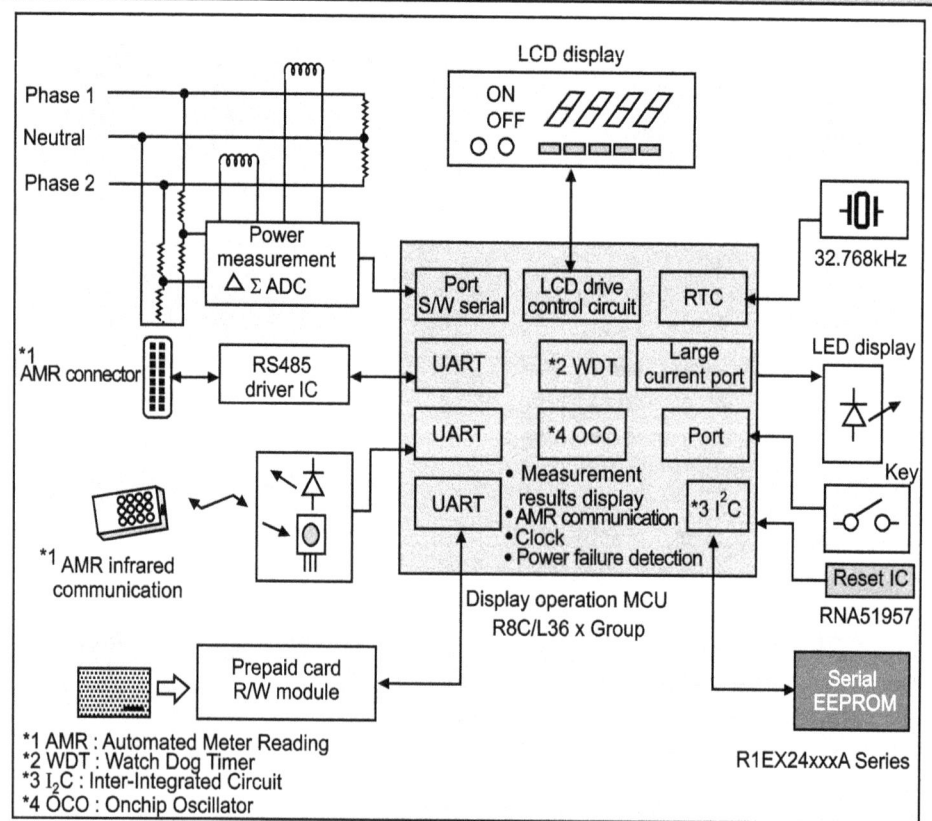

Fig. 5.5 : Block diagram of electronic energy meter

An electronic energy meter functionally outperforms the traditional Ferrari's wheel meter. Electronic energy meter (EEM) is based on digital micro technology and uses no moving parts. So, electronic energy meter is also known as "static energy meter". In electronic energy meter the accurate functioning is controlled by a specially designed IC called ASIC (Application Specified Integrated Circuit). ASIC is constructed only for specific applications using embedded system technology. In addition to ASIC, analog circuits, voltage transformer, current transformer etc are also present in electronic energy meter to "sample" current and voltage. The input voltage is compared with a programmed reference voltage and finally a "voltage rate" will be given to the output. This output is then converted into 'Digital Data' by the AD converters present in ASIC. Digital data is then converted into an "average value". Average value is the measuring unit of power. The output of ASIC is available as "Pulses" indicated by the LED placed on the front panel of EEM. These pulses are equal to average kilo watt hour (unit). Different ASIC with various are used in different makes of electronic energy meters. Usually 800 to 3600 pulses/kWh generating ASIC are used in electronic energy meter. The output of ASIC is sufficient to drive a stepper motor to give display through the rotation of digits embossed wheels. The output pulses are indicated through LED. ASIC are manufactured by Analogue Device Company. ADE 7757 IC is generally used in many countries to make electronic energy meter. Block diagram of electronic meter is shown in Fig. 5.5.

Advantages of electronic energy meter are :

- In non-linear loads, its metering is highly accurate and electronic measurement is more robust than that of conventional mechanical meters.
- Electronic energy meter improves the cost and quality of electricity distribution.
- Electronic energy meter measures current in both phase and neutral lines and calculate power consumption based on the larger of the two currents.
- It reduces the cost of theft and corruption on electricity distribution network with electronic designs and prepayment interfaces.

5.9 THREE PHASE ENERGY METER

Q. Explain three phase energy meter? [Dec. 11]

Following types of meters are commonly used for L.T. consumers.

- Three phase 4 wire meters.
- Three phase 3 wire meters.
- Three phase 4 wire meters with CT and MD (maximum demand)
- Three phase 3 wire meters with CT and MD (maximum demand)

- **Three Phase 4 Wire Meters :** In a 3φ, 4 wire meter 3 coils of each type i.e. potential coil and current coil are provided. A 3φ, 4 wire meter can be said to be 3 number of single phase parameter accommodated in one frame, potential and current coil element maintaining its own identity. A single common disc is there to record the consumption. It is necessary that operation of each element is checked separately when it is carrying load current to ensure that all elements are recordings in positive direction and no negative torque is exerted in any element. In practice, such wrong cases of connections have been noticed and detected. Each of the 3 elements of the meter produces equal torque i.e. 1/3 of the total torque under all conditions of varying power factor. 3φ, 4 wire meters are used for agricultural and industrial consumers. 3φ supply is availed by these category of consumers either at H.T. or L.T. The meters are directly connected to the supply if the load is upto 50 amp. If the load is more than 50 A it is preferable to provide C.T.S. They are rated for 415 V.

- **Three phase, 3 Wire Meters :** A 3φ, 3 wire meter has 2 elements of each type instead of 3 elements as in case of 3φ, 4 wire meter. The basic principle of operation is same as that for 4 wire meter. The torque produced by 2 elements is equal to each other only when the power factor is unity, otherwise at other power factors, the individual torques produced by 2 elements are not equal and are of varying proportion. Usually three phase 3 wire meters are not used in recording consumption of LT power consumers for the reason that lighting load e.g. pilot lamp in case of agricultural consumers has to be properly connected on one of the phases R or B, else it is connected on Y phase where no current coil is provided, the energy consumption would not get recorded. B element produces more torque at lagging power factor while R element produces more torque at leading power factor. This feature can be made use of to find out the power factor of load current of the consumer for the purpose of checking at site.

- **Three phase, 3 Wire Meter with CT and MD (maximum demand) :** It is same as 3φ, 4 wire meter and work on the same principle. However, while connecting, precaution has to be taken to connect it properly. It records maximum demand in kW.

- **Three phase, 4 Wire Meter with CT and MD :** For load more than 50A, CT operated meters are used. CT's are available in ratio of 50, 100, 150, 200, 300, 350, 400/5 Amp. CTs are to be properly selected for accurate recording. Usually rating of CT should fall within 50 to 80% of the maximum load current of the consumer. Sometimes, LT consumers opt for two part tariff and are required to be provided with metering having recording arrangement for maximum demand in kW as the tariff provides for kW demand charges, the polyphase meters are provided with maximum demand indicators, which is additional mechanism attached to the meters to record the rate of consumption over a fixed period (usually half an hour) each time and then get reset with the help of time switch. A pointer indicating the highest ever rate of consumption thus recorded by the MD indicator is left behind, which has to be manually reset taking down the reading every month.

ELECT. MEASURE. & INSTRUS (S.E. ELECTRICAL)   MEASUREMENT OF ENERGY

NUMERICALS

Q.1 A lamp load of 2000 W was connected for a period of 6 hours through an energy meter. It has a constant of 600 revolutions per kWh. Disc of energy meter rotate at 20.2 rpm. Calculate the % error of the meter and find whether the meter is fast or slow?

Sol. Actual energy supplied to the load = 2000 × 6 = 12000 Wh = 12 kWh

$$\text{Total energy recorded} = \frac{\text{Revolutions of disc per min} \times \text{Time}}{\text{Meter constant}} = \frac{20.2 \times 6 \times 60}{600}$$

$$= 12.12 \text{ kWh}$$

Since, the recorded energy is greater than actual energy supplied, the meter is fast.

$$\% \text{ Error} = \frac{\text{Energy recorded} - \text{Energy consumed}}{\text{Energy consumed}} \times 100$$

$$= \frac{12.12 - 12}{12} \times 100 = 1\%$$

Q.2 A 230 V 1ϕ energy meter has a constant load current of 4 A passing through it for 5 hours at unity p.f. If the meter disc makes 1104 revolutions during this time then calculate the meter constant. Calculate the number of revolutions of the disc if the load power factor changes to 0.8.

Sol. Energy consumed for p.f. = 1 = VI cos ϕ × t = 230 × 4 × 1 × 5 = 4.6 kWh

Total no. of revolutions of the disc for recording this energy = 1104

$$\text{Meter constant} = \frac{\text{No. of revolutions}}{\text{Energy consumed}} = \frac{1104}{4.6} = 240 \text{ rev/kWh}$$

For cos ϕ = 0.8, Energy consumed = 230 × 4 × 0.8 × 5 = 3.68 kWh

Total no. of revolutions = 3.68 × 240 = 883.2 ≈ 883

Q.3 A meter recorded 0.5 kWh, in a test of 30 min duration with a constant current of 5A. If now the same meter is used on 200 V supply, determine error.

Sol. Energy recorded = VI cos ϕ t

$$0.5 \times 1000 = V \times 5 \times 1 \times \frac{30}{60}$$

V = 200 V

Since, the applied voltage during test is 200 V, the same meter will be used on 200 V. It will not have error during reading.

Q.4 5A energy meter was run at full load for 30 min and had registered 0.56 kWh. If the meter was used at 220 V. Calculate the error.

Sol.
$$E = \int_0^{0.5} VI\,dt$$

$$0.56 = 2.5 \times 10^{-3}\,V$$

$$V = 224 \text{ Volts}$$

Actual energy consumed $= 220 \times 5 \times 0.5 \times 10^{-3} = 0.55$ kWh

$$\text{Error} = \frac{0.56 - 0.55}{0.55} \times 100 = 1.82\%$$

UNIVERSITY QUESTIONS

Dec. 2010

Q.1 Explain two element energy meter with neat diagram. **(8 Marks)**

Q.2 Explain construction and operation of single phase induction type energy meter with neat diagram. Derive torque equation. **(12 Marks)**

Q.3 An energy meter is designed to make 3200 impulses of LED for one unit of energy. Calculate the number of impulses made by it when connected to a load carrying 20 A, 230 V, 0.8 p.f. for an hour. If it actually makes 12000 impulses, find the % error.

(4 Marks)

Q.4 A 230 V, single phase energy meter is connected to a constant load of 6 A, unity power factor for 8 hours. **(6 Marks)**
  (i) If the impulses made during this are 35328, what is meter constant in imp/kWh.
  (ii) Calculate the power factor of load if number of impulses made by LED are 31795 when operating at 230 V, 9 A for 6 hours.

May 2011

Q.5 Explain with neat sketch, two elements, three-phase induction type energy-meter.

(8 Marks)

Q.6 What is meant by creeping in an energy-meter and how is it prevented? **(5 Marks)**

Q.7 An energy-meter is designed to make 100 revolutions of disc for 1 unit of energy. Calculate number of revolutions made by it, when connected to a load carrying 40 A at

230 V and 0.4 p.f. for an hour. If it actually makes 360 revolutions, find the percentage error. **(8 Marks)**

Dec. 2011

Q.8 Derive torque equation of single-phase induction type energy meter with the help of phasor diagram. **(8 Marks)**

Q.9 Show a neat connection diagram of a three-phase energy meter used for measurement of energy incorporating CT and PT. **(4 Marks)**

Q.10 Which are the possible errors in an induction type single phase energy meter, explain and give compensation for the errors? **(8 Marks)**

Q.11 What is creeping error in an induction type energy meter? How is it overcomed? **(4 Marks)**

Q.12 An energy meter has constant of 3200 imp/kWh rated for 220 V, 5 A. Calculate total numbers of impulses in one minute for full load at unity power factor. In a test run at half load, the meter takes 59.5 sec to complete 30 impulses. Calculate error of meter. **(6 Marks)**

Q.13 A 230 V single-phase energy meter has constant load of 5 A passing through it for 8 hours at 0.9 P.F. If the meter LED makes 26500 impulses during this period, find the metre constant in imp/kWh. Calculate the power factor of the load if the number of impulses are 11230 when operating at 230 V and 6 A for 5 hours. **(6 Marks)**

May 2012

Q.14 Define calibration of Energy meter. Give and explain the experimental set-up used in laboratory to calibrate the single phase energy meter. **(8 Marks)**

Q.15 An energy meter is designed to make 200 revolutions of the disc for 1 unit of energy. Calculate the number of revolutions made by it when connected to a load carrying 10 A at 230 V at 0.8 p.f. for an hour. If it actually makes 360 revolutions, find the % error. **(4 Marks)**

Q.16 State the advantages of electronic energymeter. **(8 Marks)**

Q.17 A 230 V, single-phase watt hour meter has a constant load of 5 A passing through it for 6 hours at 0.8 p.f. If the meter disc makes 4978 revolutions during this period find the meter constant in the revolutions/kWh. Calculate the power factor of the load if the number of revolutions made are 2000 when operating at 230 V and 8 A for 4 hours. **(4 Marks)**

Q.18 Draw the connection diagram of two-element energy meter with CT and PT for range extension. **(6 Marks)**

Dec. 2012

Q.19 Describe the construction and working of single-phase induction type energy meter with a neat diagram. Draw the phasor diagram of energy meter showing respective quantities? **(10 Marks)**

Q.20 A 5 A, 230 V meter on full load unity power factor test makes 60 revolutions in 360 sec. If the normal disc speed is 520 rev per kWh. What is percentage error? **(4 Marks)**

Q.21 Draw the connection diagram of two element energy meter with CT and PT for range extension. **(12 Marks)**

Q.22 Explain how the following adjustments are made in single-phase induction type of energy meter : **(12 Marks)**
  (i) Lag adjustment
  (ii) Adjustment of friction
  (iii) Creep

Chapter 6

OSCILLOSCOPE

6.1 INTRODUCTION

The device which allows, the amplitude of signals, to be displayed primarily as function of time, is called cathode ray oscilloscope, commonly known as C.R.O. It gives the visual representation of the time varying signals. The oscilloscope has become an universal instrument and integral part of electronic laboratories. Oscilloscopes also come in analog and digital types. An analog oscilloscope works by directly applying a voltage being measured to an electron beam moving across the oscilloscope screen. The voltage deflects the beam up and down proportionally, tracing the waveform on the screen. This gives an immediate picture of the waveform. In contrast, a digital oscilloscope samples the waveform and uses an analog-to-digital converter (or ADC) to convert the voltage being measured into digital information. It then uses this digital information to reconstruct the waveform on the screen.

6.1.1 Analog Oscilloscopes

Fig. 6.1 is a simple block diagram that shows how an analog oscilloscope displays a measured signal. An analog oscilloscope displays the voltage waveforms by deflecting an electron beam generated by an electron gun inside a cathode ray tube on to a fluorescent coating. Because of the use of the cathode ray tube, analog oscilloscopes are also known as cathode ray oscilloscopes. When you connect an oscilloscope probe to a circuit, the voltage signal travels through the probe to the vertical system of the oscilloscope.

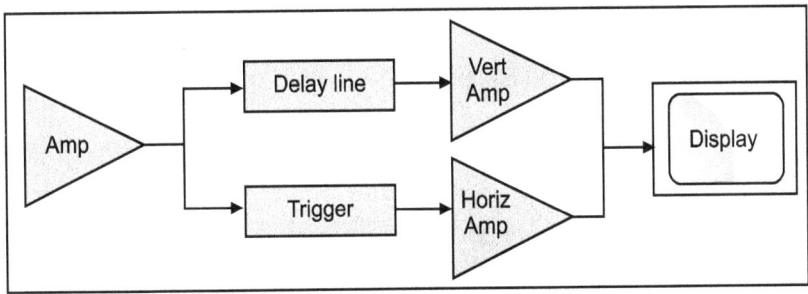

Fig. 6.1 : Analog oscilloscope block diagram

6.2 BASIC PRINCIPLE

The CRO operates on voltage. It is possible to convert current, pressure, strain, acceleration and other physical quantities into the voltage using transducers and obtain their visual representations on the CRO. The electron beam can be deflected in two directions that is in the horizontal or x-direction and the vertical or y-direction. Thus an electron beam producing a spot can be used to produce two dimensional displays, CRO which is similar to a fast x-y plotter. The x-axis and y-axis can be used to study the variation of one voltage as a function of another. Typically the x-axis of the oscilloscope represents the time while the y-axis represents variation of the input voltage signal. When the varying sinusoidal input voltage signal is applied to the y-axis of CRO and x-axis represents the time axis, then the spot moves and the sinusoidal waveform can be seen on the screen of the oscilloscope. The oscilloscope is so fast device that it can display the periodic signals having time period as small as microseconds and even nanoseconds.

6.3 BLOCK DIAGRAM OF CRO (CATHODE RAY OSCILLOSOPE)

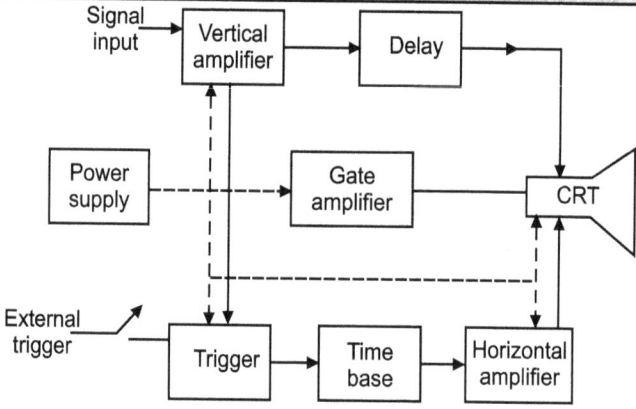

Fig. 6.2 : Block diagram of CRO

Oscilloscope refers to the total instrument including the Cathode Ray tube, amplifiers, controls and power supplies. Capture, display and analyze are the three functions of an oscilloscope.

Parts of an oscilloscope as shown in Fig. 6.2 are :
- Cathode ray tube
- Vertical amplifier including probe or transducer
- Time base circuit
- Horizontal amplifier circuit
- Trigger or sync circuit.
- Gate amplifier circuit
- Power supply

The input signal is applied to the diode sampling gate. At the start of each sampling cycle a trigger input pulse is generated which activates blocking oscillator. The oscillator output is given to the ramp generator which generates the linear ramp signal. Since the sampling must be synchronized with the input signal frequency, the signal is delayed in the vertical amplifier. The power supply block provides the voltages required by cathode ray tube to generate and accelerate the electron beam, as well as supply the required operating voltages for other circuit of oscilloscope. CRT (Cathode Ray Tube) is the heart of oscilloscope, which generates electron beam. It accelerates the beam to a high velocity and deflects the beam to create image. CRT contains the phosphor screen, where the electron beam eventually becomes visible. The oscilloscope has time base generator which generates the correct voltage to supply the cathode ray tube to deflect spot at a constant time depend rate. The horizontal amplifier amplifies the voltage generated by time base circuit before it is applied to horizontal deflection plates. After getting all the signal to the vertical and horizontal deflection plate in CRT, the signal is displayed on the screen.

6.3.1 Functions of Various Parts of CRO

> Q. Explain the block diagram of CRO.
> Q. State various constructional parts of general purpose CRO.   [May 12]

- **Cathode Ray Tube (CRT):** The electron gun consists of filament, cathode, control grid, accelerating anodes and focusing anode. CRT produces a sharply focused beam of electrons, accelerated to a very high velocity. This electron beam travels from electron gun to the screen. While traveling to the screen, electron beams passes between a set of vertical deflecting plates and a set of horizontal deflection plates. Voltages applied to these plates can move the beam in vertical and horizontal plane respectively. The electron beam then strikes the fluorescent material (phosphor) deposited on the screen with sufficient energy to cause the screen to light up in a small spot.

- **Vertical Amplifier:** The input signal is applied to vertical amplifier. The gain of this amplifier can be controlled by VOLT/DIV knob. Output of this amplifier is applied to the delay line.

- **Delay Line:** The delay Line retards the arrival of the input waveform at the vertical deflection plates until the trigger and time base circuits start the sweep of the beam. The delay line produces a delay of 0.25 microseconds so that the leading edge of the input waveform can be viewed even though it was used to trigger the sweep.

- **Trigger Circuit:** A sample of the input waveform is fed to a trigger circuit which produces a trigger pulse at some selected point on the input waveform. This trigger pulse is used to start the time base generator which then starts the horizontal sweep of CRT spot from left hand side of the screen.

- **Time Base Generator :** This produces a saw – tooth waveform that is used as horizontal deflection voltage of CRT. The rate of rise of positive going part of saw tooth waveform is controlled by TIME/DIV knob. The saw tooth voltage is fed to the horizontal amplifier if the switch is in INTERNAL position. The switch is in EXTERNAL. position then an external horizontal input can be applied to the horizontal amplifier.
- **Horizontal Amplifier:** This amplifies the saw – tooth voltage. As it includes a phase inverter two outputs are produced. Positive going saw tooth and negative going saw tooth are applied to right hand and left hand horizontal deflection plates of CRT.
- **Blanking Circuit :** The blanking circuit is necessary to eliminate the retrace that would occur when the spot on CRT screen moves from right side to left side. This retrace can cause confusion if it is not eliminate. The blanking voltage is produced by sweep generator. Hence a high negative voltage is applied to the control grid during retrace period or a high positive voltage is applied to cathode in CRT. When a saw tooth voltage is applied to horizontal plates and an input signal is applied to vertical plates, display of vertical input signal is obtained on the screen as a function of time.
8. **Power Supply :** A high voltage section is used to operate CRT and a low voltage section is used to supply electronic circuit of the oscilloscope.

6.4 PARTS OF CATHODE RAY OSCILLOSCOPE

Following are the main parts of Cathode Ray Oscilloscope :
1. **Cathode Ray Tube (CRT) :** The cathode ray tube (CRT) is the heart of the CRO. The main parts of the CRT are: (i) Electron gun, (ii) Deflection system, (iii) Fluorescent screen, (iv) Glass tube or envelope and, (v) Base Electron beam generated by the electron gun first deflected by the deflection plates, and then directed onto the fluorescent coating of the CRO screen, which produces a visible light spot on the face plane of the oscilloscope screen. Thus the CRT generates the electron beam, then accelerates the beam, deflects the

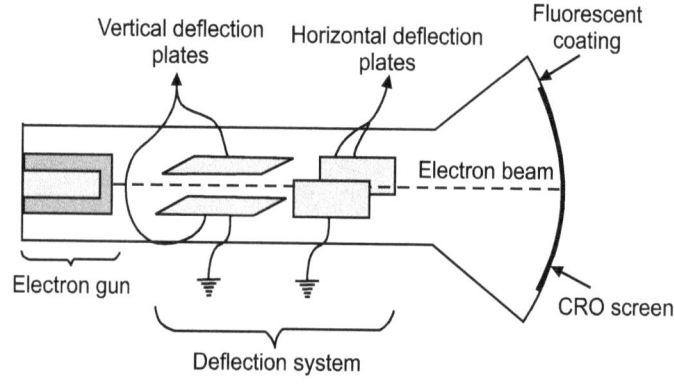

Fig. 6.3 : Cathode ray tube

beam and on the screen beam becomes visible, as a spot. A detailed representation of a CRT is given in Fig. 6.3 CRT is composed of two main parts:
- Electron Gun
- Deflection System

2. **Electron Gun:** Electron gun provides a sharply focused electron beam directed toward the fluorescent-coated screen. The beam tends to diverge because the electron beam consists of many electrons, this is due to the charges on the electrons repulse each other. Electrostatic field is created between two cylindrical anodes, called the focusing anodes, to compensate for these repulsion forces. The variable positive voltage on the second anode cylinder is used to adjust the focus or sharpness of the bright spot. The control grid provides an axial direction for the electron beam and controls the number and speed of electrons in the beam. The thermally heated cathode emits electrons in many directions. The momentum of the electrons determines the intensity, or brightness, of the light emitted from the fluorescent coating due to the electron bombardment. Electrons are negatively charged, so a repulsion force is created by applying a negative voltage to the control grid, which adjust their number and speed. A more negative voltage results in less number of electrons in the beam and hence decreased brightness of the beam spot.

3. **The Deflection System:** The deflection system consists of pairs of parallel plates: vertical and horizontal deflection plates. One of the plates in each set is permanently connected to the ground, and the other plate of each set is connected to input signal or triggering signal of the CRO. The electron beam passes through the deflection plates. A positive voltage applied to the X input terminal will cause the electron beam to deflect horizontally toward the right, while a negative voltage applied to the X input terminal will cause the electron beam to deflect horizontally toward the left of the screen. A positive voltage applied to the Y input terminal causes the electron beam to deflect vertically

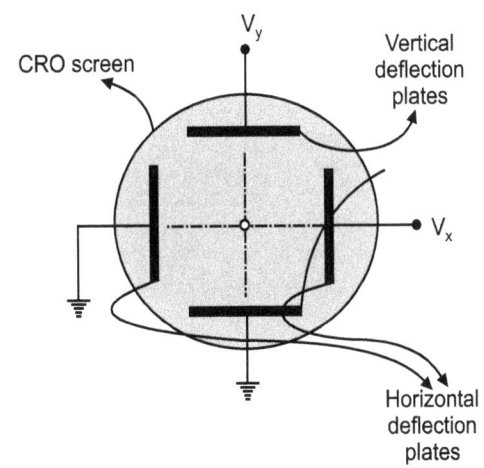

Fig. 6.4 : Deflection system

upward, due to attraction forces, while a negative voltage applied to the Y input terminal causes the electron beam to deflect vertically downward, due to repulsion forces. The amount of vertical or horizontal deflection is directly proportional to the corresponding applied voltage. When the electrons hit the screen, the phosphor emits light and a visible light spot is seen on the screen. Since the amount of deflection is proportional to the applied voltage, actually the voltages V_y and V_x determine the coordinates of the bright spot created by the electron beam.

4. **Fluorescent Screen:** The function of the fluorescent screen is to display where the electrons are hitting the CRT. The two commonly used materials for fluorescent screen are zinc sulphide or phosphorus. Phosphor Screen Characteristics are shown in fig 6.5. Many phosphor materials are available having different excitation times and colors. Medical oscilloscopes require longer phosphor decay and hence phosphors like P7 and P39 are preferred for such applications. Very slow displays like radar require long persistence phosphors to maintain sufficient flicker free picture. Phosphors used are P19, P26 and, P33.

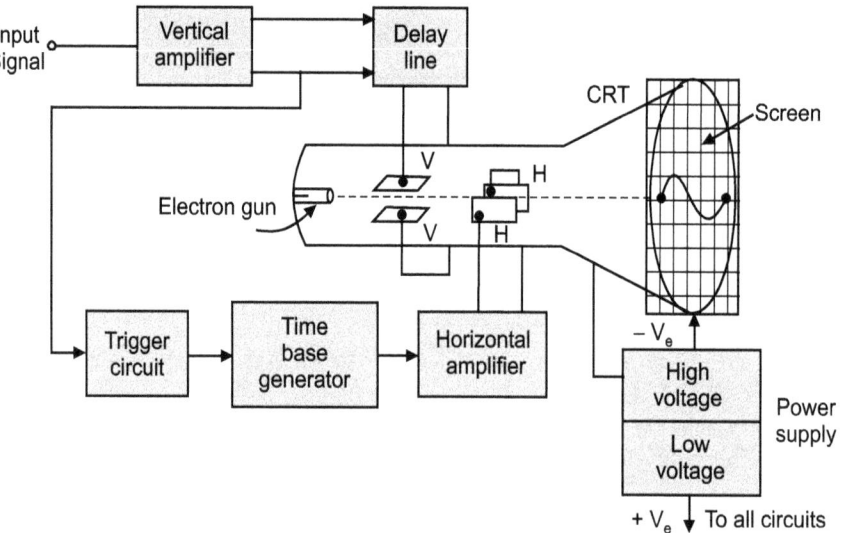

Fig. 6.5 : Phosphor screen characteristics

5. **Vertical Amplifier :** The input signals are not strong enough to provide the measurable deflection on the screen. Vertical amplifier is used to amplify the input signals. Wide band amplifiers are used to pass the entire band of frequencies to be measured. The attenuators are used to bring the signals within the proper range of operation. It consists of several stages with fixed sensitivity. The input stage consists of an attenuator followed

by FET source follower. It has high input impedance required to isolate the amplifier from the attenuator. It is followed by BJT emitter follower to match the output impedance of FET output with input of phase inverter. The phase inverter provides two anti phase output signals which are required to operate the push pull output amplifier.

6. **Delay Line:** The input signal is not applied directly to the vertical plates but is delayed by some time using a delay line circuit. The delay line is used to delay the signal for some time in the vertical sections. When the delay line is not used, the part of the signal gets lost.

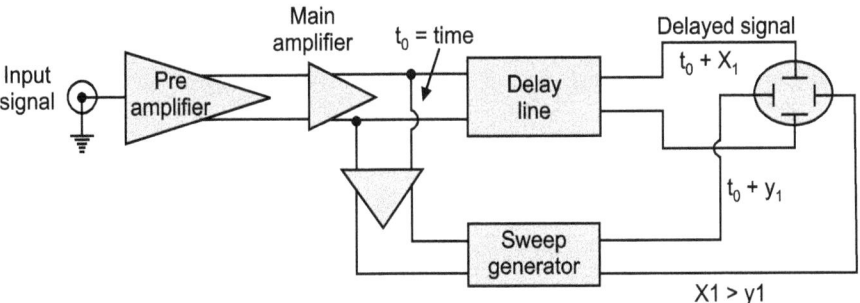

Fig. 6.6 : Delay line

The design of delay line is such that the delay time X_I is higher than the time Y_1. Two types of delay lines used in CRO are:
- Lumped parameter delay line.
- Distributed parameter delay line.

7. **Trigger Circuit:** To synchronize horizontal deflection with vertical deflection, a synchronizing or triggering circuit is used. It is necessary that horizontal deflection starts at the same point of the input vertical signal, each time it sweeps. Hence triggering circuit converts the incoming signal into the triggering pulses, which are used for the synchronization.

8. **Time Base Generator:** The time base generator is used to generate the saw tooth voltage, required to deflect the beam in the horizontal section.

6.5 FRONT PANEL CONTROLS OF A CRO

Q. Explain the functions of various controls on the front panel of a dual trace CRO with the help of the front panel diagram.

Fig. 6.7 shows the controls on the front panel of a CRO.

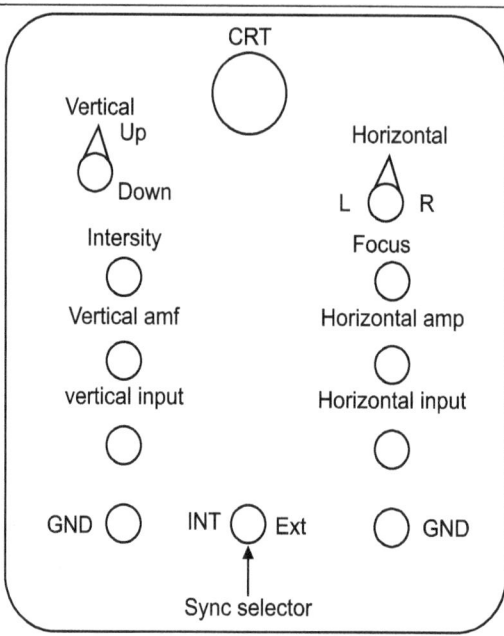

Fig. 6.7 : Front Panel Control of CRO

Various front panel controls of a CRO are :

- **On-Off switch :** It is used to turn on or turn off the CRO.
- **Vertical Up/Down :** It moves the spot up or down for centering.
- **Horizontal L/R :** This control moves the display left or right for centering.
- **Focus:** This control is used to increase sharpness of the spot. This is anode potential adjustment. It makes the image sharper if it is blurred. Focusing of the spot is obtained by varying voltage applied to the focusing anodes of the cathode ray tube.
5. **Vertical Amplifier :** It is used to amplify the input signal to the vertical plates.
6. **Horizontal Amplifier :** It is used to amplify the input signal to the horizontal plates.
7. **Synchronizing Voltage :** There will be an internal synchronizing oscillator for horizontal deflection or sweep or it may be fed externally also.
8. **Synchronization :** Synchronization is used to obtain stationary pattern on the screen. There are various signals which can be applied to the trigger circuit. Internal and external signals can be selected. In internal signal, the trigger is obtained from signal being measured through the vertical amplifier.

Vertical Controls : Vertical controls are used to position and scale the waveform vertically. Fig. 6.8 shows vertical control of oscilloscope.

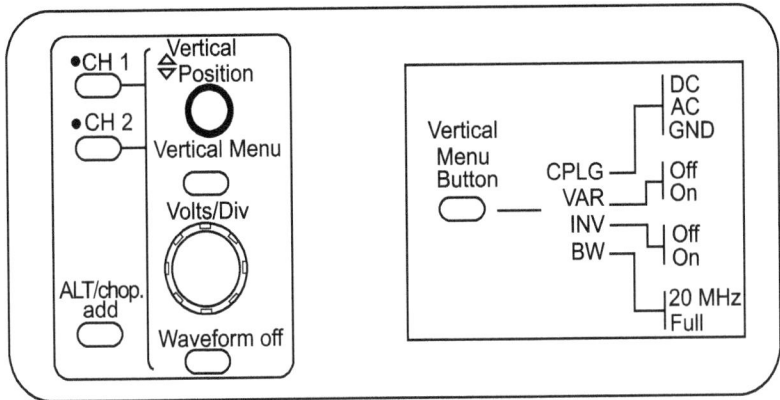

Fig. 6.8 : Typical vertical controls

Position and Volts per Division Settings: The scale knob varies volts per division, which determines the voltage value corresponding to each vertical division on the oscilloscope's screen. The position knob moves the waveform vertically. As the volt/division value is altered, the size of the waveform on the screen changes. The volt/division setting is a scale factor. For example, when 10 vertical divisions are there on the oscilloscope screen and if volts/division setting is 5 volts, the each of the vertical division represents 5 volts and entire screen can show 50 volts from bottom to top.

Horizontal Controls: Horizontal controls are used to position and scale the waveform horizontally. The horizontal position control (x position) is used to move the waveform from left and right to the required position on the screen.

Time/div setting allows to select the rate at which waveform is drawn across the screen also known as the sweep speed or time base setting. This setting is a scale factor. For example, if the setting is 1 ms, each horizontal division represents 1 ms and the total screen width represents 10 ms (ten divisions). By changing the time/division setting allows to look at longer or shorter time intervals of the input signal.

Time/division knob actually controls the trace time of saw tooth waveform in the sweep generator. When saw tooth waveform is zero volt, the bright spot is at the extreme left hand position and when it is maximum, the bright spot is at the extreme right position. For the time equal to trace time, the bright spot travels from extreme left to extreme right. For example, CRO screen is divided into N equal horizontal divisions. The bright spot travels the N divisions in T_r seconds. Each division corresponds to (T_r/N) seconds.

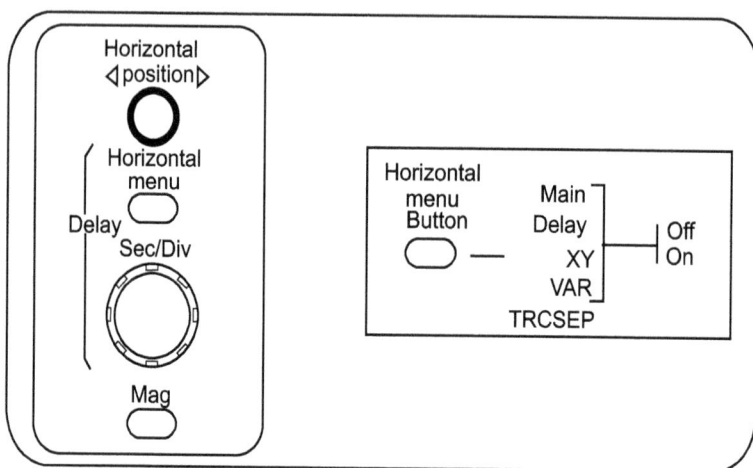

Fig. 6.9 : Typical horizontal controls

Input Coupling : Coupling means the method used to connect an electrical signal from one circuit to another. The input coupling is the connection from your circuit to the oscilloscope. The coupling can be set to A.C., D.C. or ground. When the coupling control is set to A.C., the D.C. offset voltage is removed from the input waveform so the resultant waveform is centered at zero volts. When D.C. coupling is selected, both D.C. and A.C. components of the input waveform are passed to the oscilloscope. The ground setting disconnects the input signal from the vertical system which allows to see where zero volts are on the screen. With grounded input coupling and auto trigger mode, a horizontal line on the screen can be seen which represents zero volts.

X-Y Button : Most oscilloscopes have a capability of displaying a second channel signal along X-axis instead of time. This is called XY mode. By pressing the XY button the oscilloscope is used in XY mode. The phase difference between the signals can also be determined in XY mode of the oscilloscope. In the XY mode, the X-axis data is taken from one channel, Y-axis data is taken from other. In this way, channel I versus Channel II graph can be obtained so that the variation of a signal with respect to another can be observed. In XY mode, the leading or lagging signal can not be determined. One has to switch to dual mode in order to specify the leading signal.

Invert Button : When the INVERT button of a channel is depressed, negative of the signal is displayed on the CRO screen.

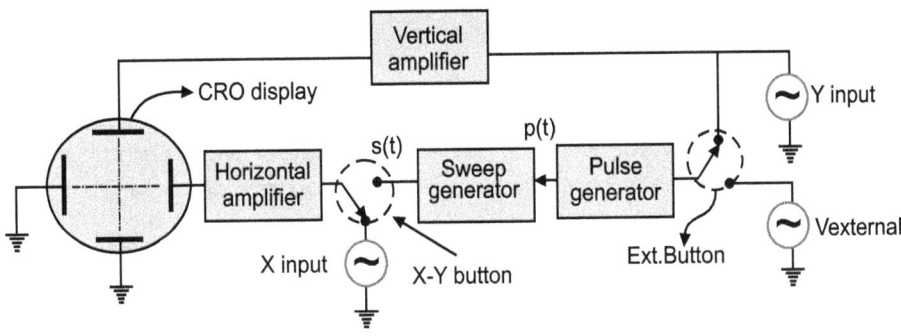

Fig. : 6.10

EXT Button : When the EXT button is depressed, the oscilloscope is used in external triggering mode. Fig. 6.11 shows typical graphs in XY mode corresponding to different values of phase difference.

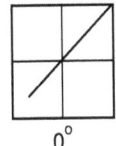 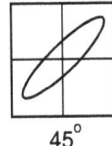 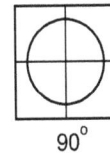 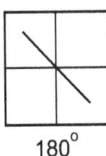

    0°   45°   90°   180°

Fig. 6.11

6.6 SYNCHRONIZATION

Whatever type of sweep is used, it must be synchronized with the signal being measured. Synchronization is done to obtain stationary pattern. If synchronization is not done pattern appears to drift across the screen in random fashion.

Following sources of synchronization can be selected by synchronizing selector :

- **Interval :** In this synchronization, trigger is obtained from the signal being measured through vertical amplifier.
- **External :** In this synchronization, the external trigger source is used to trigger the signal being measured.
- **Blanking Circuit :** If retrace or fly back time is large then the movement of the spot appears as thin and dim line. If fly back time is small then the spot remain invisible. Ideally it should be zero, but practically it is not zero. So traces should be eliminated by applying a high negative voltage to grid during fly back period.
4. **Intensity Control :** The intensity of the beam can be varied by using the intensity control potentiometer which changes the grid potential with respect to the cathode. The grid potential determines the amount of electrons leaving the cathode and thus controls the intensity of beam.

5. **Focus Control :** The focusing electrodes acts like a lens whose focal length can be changed. This change can be brought about by changing the potential of focusing anode.
6. **Horizontal and Vertical Positioning Control :** It is necessary to provide some means of positioning the trace on the screen. The positioning of trace is done by applying internal D.C. voltages to the horizontal and vertical deflecting plates. Control can be obtained by varying the voltage with the help of potentiometer.

6.7 DEFLECTION SENSITIVITY OF CRO

Deflection sensitivity of CRO is defined as the deflection of screen per unit deflection voltage. Deflection sensitivity,

$$S = \frac{D}{E_d}$$

$$= \frac{L\, l_d}{2dE_a}$$

where,

D = Deflection of electron beam on screen in Y direction.

E_d = Potential between deflecting plates (in volts)

Unit of deflection sensitivity is m/V.

6.8 APPLICATIONS OF CATHODE RAY OSCILLOSCOPE

- Measurement of current and voltage simultaneously. Double beam CRO is used for measurement of current and voltage simultaneously.
- It can be employed for measurement of direct or alternating voltage.
- In television receiver, use of cathode ray tube along with associated sweep circuits is made for the projection of the images. Magnetic deflection is generally used.
- It is used in radar; information about a detected object within the range of the radar is displayed on a cathode ray tube.
- Determination of characteristics of thermionic values.
- Tracing of hysterisis loop for magnetic material.
- Measurement of degree of modulation.
- It is used to measure capacitance, inductance.
- It can be used to check the faulty components in the various circuits.
- It is used to display the cardiograms which are useful for the diagnosis of heart of the patient.
- Study of transistor characteristics.

- Measurement of checking of switching time.
- Measurement of phase difference and frequency.
- Study of Lissajous figures.

6.9 CRO MEASUREMENT

Q. Explain measurement of voltage, current phase angle and frequency using CRO.
Q. Give the applications of CRO?

The major concern in observing a signal on the oscilloscope screen is to make voltage and time measurements. These measurements may be helpful in understanding the behaviour of a circuit component of the circuit itself, depending on what you measure. Except for the S-Y mode of operation, the oscilloscope displays the voltage value of the waveform as a function time. The oscilloscope screen is partitioned into grids, which divide both the horizontal axis (voltage) and vertical axis (time) into divisions which will be helpful in making the measurements. The values are determined by two variables namely time/division and volt/division both of which can be adjusted from the relevant buttons available on the front panel of the oscilloscope. The time/division button controls the trace time of the sweep generator whereas volt/div. button controls the "gain" in the vertical amplifiers in the vertical deflection system. Fig. 6.12 shows the typical quantities when observing a signal with scope.

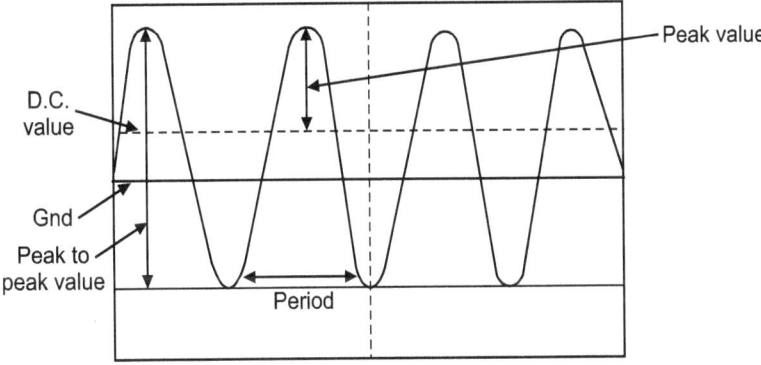

Fig. 6.12 : CRO Measurement

6.9.1 Measurement of Voltage and Currents

Voltage Measurement :
- The expression for electrostatic deflection of CRO shows that deflection is proportional to the deflection plate voltage.
- It is usual to calibrate the tube under given operating conditions by observing the deflection produced by a known voltage.

- Direct voltage may be obtained from static deflection of the spot. Alternating voltages from the length of the line produced, when the voltage is applied to Y plate while no voltage is applied to X plate.
- For sinusoidal voltages, the RMS value is given by dividing the peak to peak voltage by $2\sqrt{2}$.
- Waveform can be adjusted on the screen by using shift controls. To reduce errors, peak to peak value of the signal is measured and its amplitude and r.m.s. value is calculated.

Following Steps are done to Measure Amplitude :
- Note down the selection in volt/division from front panel selected for measurement.
- Adjust shift control to adjust signal on screen so it becomes easy to count number of divisions corresponding to peak to peak value of the signal.
- Note peak to peak value in terms of number of divisions.
- Then,

V_{pp} [Peak to peak value in volts] = (No. of divisions) × (Volts/div.)

$$\text{Amplitude} = \frac{V_{pp}}{2}$$

RMS value of sinusoidal signal

$$V_{RMS} = \frac{V_m}{\sqrt{2}} = \frac{V_{pp}}{2\sqrt{2}} \qquad \text{[For sinusoidal signal]}$$

Current measurement :

The value of a current can be obtained by measuring the voltage drop across a known resistance connected in circuit. The voltage across resistance is displayed on CRO and is measured. This measured voltage divided by known resistance gives the value of the unknown current.

$$I = \frac{V \text{ measured on CRO}}{R}$$

6.9.2 Measurement of Frequency

- Lissajous pattern may be used for accurate measurement of frequency.
- The signal whose frequency to be measured is applied to Y plate.
- Accurate calibrated standard frequency source is used to supply voltage to the X plates with the internal sweep generator switched off.
- The standard frequency is adjusted until pattern appears indicating that both signal are of same frequency.
- When it is not possible to adjust a standard signal frequency to the exact frequency of the unknown signal, the standard is adjusted to a multiple or a submultiples of frequency of the unknown source so that pattern appear stationary.

Steps involved are :

(a) Note the time/division selected on the front panel. Then period of the waveform can be obtained as :

$$T = (\text{No. of divisions occupied by 1 cycle}) \times \left(\frac{\text{Time}}{\text{Division}}\right)$$

(b) $$\text{Frequency} = \frac{1}{\text{Time period}}$$

Lissajous pattern for integral frequencies.

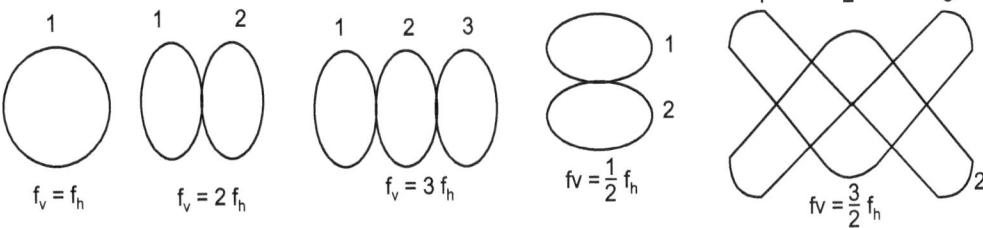

Fig. 6.13

where,

f_v = Vertical signal.
f_h = Horizontal signal.

Lissajous pattern for non-integral frequencies

NUMERICALS

Q.1 A Lissajous pattern on the oscilloscope is stationary and has 6 vertical maximum values and 5 horizontal maximum values. The frequency of horizontal input is 1500 Hz. Determine the frequency of vertical input.

Sol.
$$\frac{\text{Points of tangency to a vertical side}}{\text{Points of tangency to a horizontal side}}$$

$$= \frac{W_x}{W_y} = \frac{f_x}{f_y}$$

$$\frac{f_x}{f_y} = \frac{5}{6}$$

$$F_y = \frac{6}{5} \times 1500$$

$$= 1800 \text{ Hz}$$

[Note : Lissajous pattern has 6 vertical maximum values and thus a horizontal line will be tangent to it 6 times. The pattern has 5 horizontal maximum values and thus a vertical line will be tangent to it 5 times.**]**

Q.2 A CRO is calibrated for 20 volts per inch and its sweep circuit set for 6 m sec. Three complete sine curves with a distance of 2.25 in between their upper and lower extremities appear on the screen. Find the frequency and r.m.s. voltage.

Sol.
$$F = \frac{1}{T} = \frac{1}{6 \times 10^{-3}} = 166.7 \text{ Hz}$$

Frequency of sine wave is = $166.7 \times 3 = 500$ Hz

Voltage = $20 \times 2.25 = 45$ V

$$\therefore \quad \text{RMS} = \frac{E_m}{2\sqrt{2}} = \frac{45}{3\sqrt{2}} = 15.9 \text{ V}$$

Q.3 Two nearly equal frequencies are to be compared. The Lissajous figure is an ellipse which is not stationary but makes one complete rotation in 4 sec of the known frequency of 50 Hz. What is the frequency of the unknown?

Sol. The frequency of rotation of ellipse is $\frac{1}{4} = 0.25$, so unknown frequency is 50 ± 0.25 Hz.

Q.4 Calculate the BW in Hz required of an oscilloscope vertical amplifier if the rise time of the pulse is 20 ns.

Sol.
$$BW = \frac{0.35}{T_r} = \frac{0.35}{20 \times 10^{-9}} = 17.5 \text{ MHz}$$

Q.5 A square wave signal is observed on the oscilloscope to have one cycle measured as 6 cm at a horizontal sweep rate of 30 µs/cm. Find the signal frequency.

Sol.
Sweep rate = 30 µs/cm

For 6 cm = 180 µs/cm

180 µs = 1 cycle

$$1 \text{ sec} = \frac{1}{180 \times 10^{-6}} = 5.55 \text{ kHz}$$

Q.6 The Lissajous pattern obtained on the screen by applying horizontal signal of frequency 1 kHz has 2 vertical tangencies and 5 horizontal tangencies. Calculate the unknown frequency of vertical signal.

Sol. No. of vertical tangencies = 2

No. of horizontal tangencies = 5

$$\frac{f_v}{f_h} = \frac{5}{2}$$

∴ Unknown frequency of vertical signal is $f_v = \frac{5}{2} \times 1 = 2.5$ kHz

Q.7 The Lissajous pattern obtained on the screen is shown in Fig. 6.18 below. Calculate the unknown frequency of vertical signal when horizontal signal of frequency 2 kHz is applied to it.

ELECT. MEASURE. & INSTRUS (S.E. ELECTRICAL)   OSCILLOSCOPE

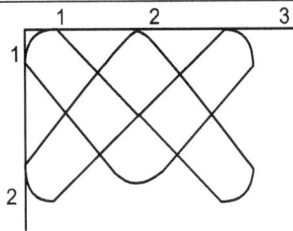

Fig. 6.14

Sol. No. of horizontal tangencies = 3
No. of vertical tangencies = 2

$$\therefore \quad \frac{f_v}{f_h} = \frac{3}{2}$$

$$f_v = \frac{3}{2} \times f_h$$

$$= \frac{3}{2} \times 2$$

$$\therefore \quad f_v = 3 \text{ kHz}$$

Q.8 The deflection sensitivity of an oscilloscope is 35 cm/V. If the distance from the deflection plates to the CRT screen is 16 cm, length of the deflection plates is 2.5 cm and the distance between the deflection plates is 1.2 cm. Find the accelerating anode voltage?

Sol.
$$S = 35 \text{ cm/V}$$
$$L = 16 \text{ cm}$$
$$l_d = 2.5 \text{ cm}$$
$$d = 1.2 \text{ cm}$$

$$S = \frac{L l_d}{2d\, E_a}$$

$$E_a = \frac{L l_d}{2d_s}$$

$$= \frac{16 \times 10^{-2} \times 2.5 \times 10^{-2}}{2 \times 1.2 \times 10^{-2} \times 35 \times 10^{-2}}$$

$$= 0.47 \text{ V}$$

Q.9 Voltage E_1 is applied to horizontal input and voltage E_2 is applied to vertical input of CRO. E_1 and E_2 have same frequency. Trace is ellipse. Slope of the major axis is +ve. The maximum vertical value is 3 div and the point where the ellipse crosses the vertical axis 2.6 div. Ellipse is symmetrical about vertical and horizontal axis. Find the possible phase angles of E_2 with respect to E_1 when slope of the major axis is –ve.

Sol. Max. vertical value = Y_2 = 3 div
Point where ellipse crosses vertical axis = Y_1 = 2.6

Ch 6 | 6.17

$$\sin \phi = \frac{Y_1}{Y_2}$$

$$\phi = \sin^{-1}\left(\frac{2.6}{3}\right) \quad \phi = 60°$$

As major axis is –ve,

$$\phi = 180° - 60° = 120°$$

Possible phases are 120° or 240°

UNIVERSITY QUESTIONS

Dec. 2010

Q.1 Explain the following terms associated with CRO : **(6 Marks)**
(i) Volts/division (ii) X10 (iii) Invert

Q.2 In an experiment, the voltage across 5 kΩ resistor is applied to CRO. The screen shows a sinusoidal signal of total vertical occupancy 4 cm and total horizontal occupancy of 2 cm. The front panel controls volts/div and time/div are on 5 V/div and 5 ms/div respectively. Calculate the maximum rms values of voltage across resistance and current through resistance. Also find its frequency. **(6 Marks)**

Q.3 Explain the functions of various controls on the front panel of a dual trace CRO with the help of the front panel diagram. **(8 Marks)**

Q.4 State various constructional parts of general purpose CRO. **(4 Marks)**

Q.5 Explain front panel controls of CRO : **(8 Marks)**
(a) Time/div (c) Dual ch. (e) x-position (g) xy mode
(b) Volt/div (d) Invert   (f) y-position (h) CH1 CH2

Q.6 In an experiment, the voltage across a 10 kΩ resistor is applied to CRO. The screen shows s sinusoidal signal of total vertical occupancy 3 cm and total horizontal occupancy of 2 cm. The front panel controls of V/div and time/div are on 2 V/div and 2 ms/div respectively. Calculate the r.m.s. value of the voltage across the resistor and its frequency. Also find r.m.s. value of current. **(6 Marks)**

May 2012

Q.7 Explain the functions of the following blocks of CRO : **(4 Marks)**
(i) Trigger circuit   (ii) Time-base generator
(iii) Delay line   (iv) Horizontal amplifier

Dec. 2012

Q.8 Explain measurement of voltage, current phase angle and frequency using CRO.
(8 Marks)

Chapter 7

TRANSDUCERS

7.1 INTRODUCTION

Transducer is a device which converts a physical quantity into the proportional electrical signal. The electrical signal produced may be a voltage, current or frequency. The process of transforming signal from one form to other is called transduction. The transduction element transforms the output of the sensor to an electrical output as shown in Fig. 7.1.

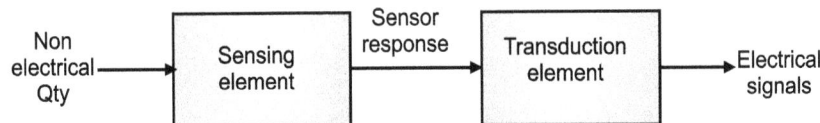

Fig. 7.1

The common range of an electrical signal used to represent analog signal in the industrial environment is 0 to 5 V or 4 to 20 mA. 4 to 20 mA range is most commonly used in industrial applications to represent analog signal. The zero current condition represents open circuit in the signal transmission line. Thus the standard range is offset from zero. The transducer is a part of a circuit and works with other elements of that circuit to produce the required output. This circuit is called signal conditioning circuit.

7.1.1 Block Diagram of Transducers

Transducer contains two parts that are closely related to each other

- Sensing element: The sensing element is called as the sensor. It is device producing measurable response to change in physical conditions.

- Transduction element: The transduction element converts the sensor output to suitable electrical form.

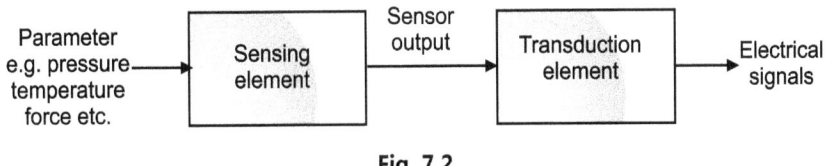

Fig. 7.2

7.2 CHARACTERISTICS OF TRANSDUCERS

Q. Explain different characteristics of transducer.

1. **Ruggedness :** Transducer should be rugged to withstand overload.
2. **Linearity :** Transducer should have linear I/P -O/P characteristics.
3. **Sensitivity :** It should be high for Transducer. The transducer must be sensitive enough to produce detectable output.
4. **Repeatability :** Under same environment conditions, the output of transducer should be same with same input applied repeatedly.
5. **Accuracy :** Transducer should have high accuracy.
6. **Reliability :** To have minimum error in measurement the output of transducer should be reliable.
7. **Speed of Response :** It should be high.
8. **Size of Transducer :** Size of the transducer should be small with minimum weight.

7.3 TRANSDUCERS SELECTION FACTORS

Q. Explain selection factors while selecting Transducer.

1. **Operating Principle :** The transducers are many times selected on the basis of operating principle used by them. The operating principle used may be resistive, inductive, capacitive, optoelectronic, piezo electric etc.
2. **Operating Range :** The transducer should maintain the range requirement and have a good resolution over the entire range.
3. **Selection of Transducer :** The selection of transducer depends on the nature of the quantity to be measured. Selection of transducer also depend on cost of transducer and availability of transducer
4. **Cross Sensitivity :** It has to be taken into account when measuring mechanical quantities. There are situation where the actual quantity is being measured is in one plane and the transducer is subjected to variation in another plan.
5. **Errors :** The transducer should maintain the expected input-output relationship as described by the transfer function so as to avoid errors.
6. **Transient and Frequency Response :** The transducer should meet the desired time domain specification like peak overshoot, rise time, setting time and small dynamic error.
7. **Loading Effects :** The transducer should have a high input impedance and low output impedance to avoid loading effects.
8. **Environmental Compatibility :** It should be assured that the transducer selected to work under specified environmental conditions maintains its input-output relationship and does not break down.

9. **Insensitivity to Unwanted Signals :** The transducer should be minimally sensitive to unwanted signals and highly sensitive to desired signals.
10. **Good Dynamic Response :** Output is faithful to input when taken as a function of time. This effect is analyzed as the frequency response.
11. **Excellent Mechanical Characteristics :** This can affect the performance in static, quasi-static, and dynamic states. The major effects are :
    (a) **Mechanical Hysteresis :** The dependence of the strain not only on the instantaneous value of the stress but also on the previous history of stress. Effect depends on the raw material used, aging, etc.
    (b) **Viscous Flow or Creep :** Effect due to viscous flow in the material of the sensing element. Magnitude increases with increasing load and temperature. Materials with low melting point show larger creep values.
    (c) **Elastic after Effect :** A continued deformation when the load is applied and kept constant. This effect decreases with time. Like creep, there is a similar relaxation towards the original position when the load is removed. Virtually no deformation is observed.

7.4 CLASSIFICATION OF TRANSDUCERS

Q. Give detailed classification of transducers.
Q. What are the advantages of electric transducer?
Q. State the difference between active and passive transducer?

The transducers can be classified as:
1. Active and passive transducers.
2. Analog and digital transducers.

On the basis of transduction principle used:
1. Primary and secondary transducer.
2. Transducers and inverse transducers.

7.4.1 Active Transducers

These transducers do not need any external source of power for their operation. They are also called as self generating type transducers. The active transducer operates under the energy conversion principle. Active transducers are again sub divided as shown below:

Classification of Active Transducers :

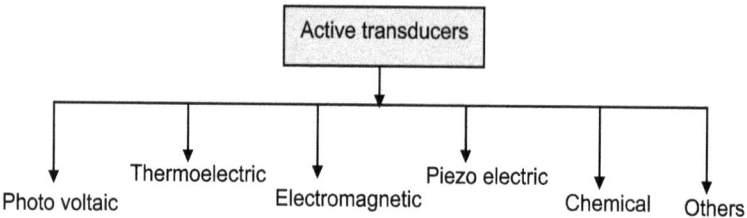

Fig. 7.3

7.4.2 Passive Transducers

These transducers produce the output signal in the form of variation in resistance, capacitance, inductance or some other electrical parameter in response to the quantity to be measured .These transducers need external source of power for their operation. So they are not self generating type transducers. A DC power supply or an audio frequency generator is used as an external power source. In electrical circuits, there are combinations of three passive elements: resistor, inductor and capacitor. These three passive elements are described with the help of the primary parameters such as resistance, self or mutual inductance and capacitance respectively. Any change in these parameters can be observed y if they are externally powered. The transducers based on variation of parameters such as resistance, self or mutual inductance capacitance, due to an external power are known as passive transducers. Passive transducers are again sub divided as shown below:

Classification of Passive Transducers :

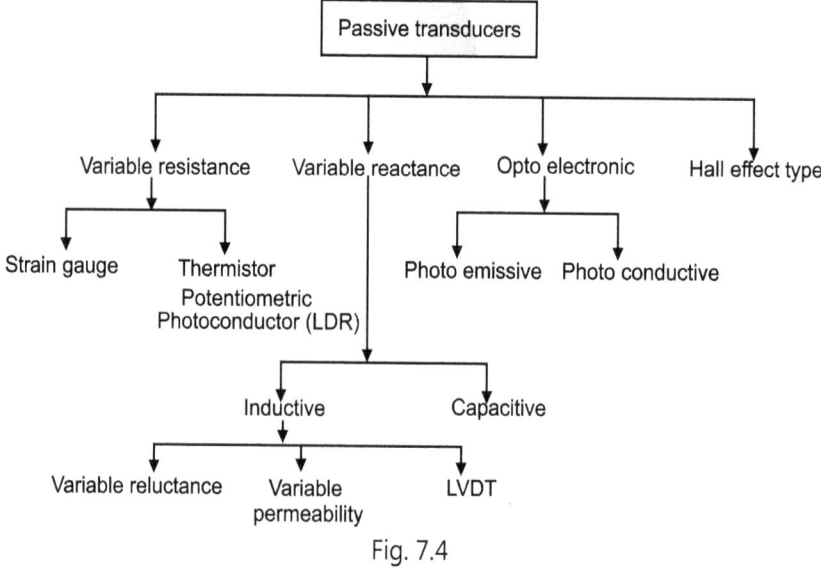

Fig. 7.4

7.4.3 Primary and Secondary Transducers

The mechanical device converts the physical quantity to be measured into a mechanical signal. Such mechanical devices are called as the primary transducers, because they deal with the physical quantity to be measured. Some transducers contain the mechanical as well as electrical device. The electrical device convert mechanical signal into a corresponding electrical signal. Such electrical devices are known as secondary transducers.

7.4.4 Classification according to Transduction Principle

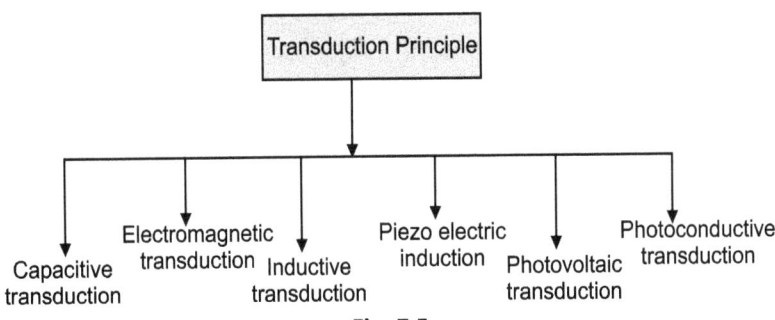

Fig. 7.5

1. Capacitive Transducer: A typical capacitor is comprised of two parallel plates of conducting material separated by an electrical insulating material called a dielectric. The plates and the dielectric may be either flattened or rolled. The purpose of the dielectric is to help the two parallel plates maintain their stored electrical charges. The relationship between the capacitance and the size of capacitor plate, amount of plate separation, and the dielectric is given by $C = \varepsilon_0 \varepsilon_r A/d$.

Where,

d is the separation distance of plates (m)

C is the capacitance (F)

ε_0 : absolute permittivity of vacuum

ε_r : relative permittivity

A is the area of capacitor plates (m²)

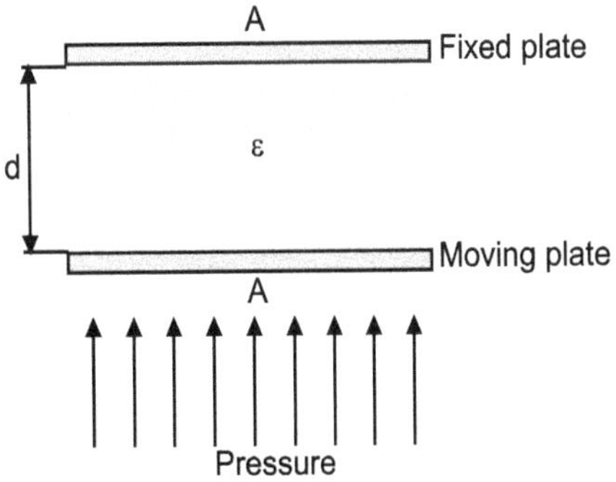

For examples :

(a) Variable Capacitance Pressure Gauge : The change in capacitance is due to the change of distance between two parallel plates caused by an external force is known by its corresponding displacement or pressure.

Fig. 7.6

(b) Capacitor Microphone : The change in capacitance due to the variation in sound pressure on a movable diagram is known by its corresponding sound.

(c) Dielectric Gauge : The change in capacitance due to a change in the dielectric is known by its corresponding liquid level or thickness.

2. **Electromagnetic Transduction :** The electromagnetic transducers are self generating active transducers. The measurand is converted to voltage induced in conductor by change in the magnetic flux, in absence of excitation. The motion between a piece of magnet and an electromagnet is responsible for the change in flux.

3. **Inductive Transducer:** The measurand is converted into a change in the self inductance of a single coil. It is achieved by displacing the core of the coil that is attached to a mechanical sensing element.

4. **Piezo Electric Induction :** In piezoelectric induction the measurand is converted into a change in electrostatic charge q or voltage V generated by crystals when mechanically it is stressed as shown in Fig. 7.7.

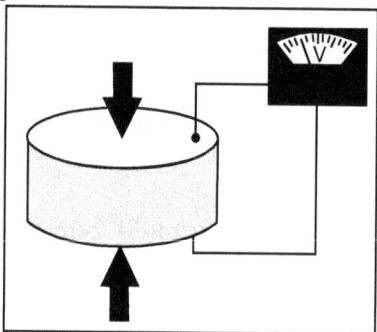

Fig. 7.7

5. **Photovoltaic Transduction :** The measurand is converted to voltage generated when the junction between dissimilar materials is illuminated as shown in Fig. 7.8.

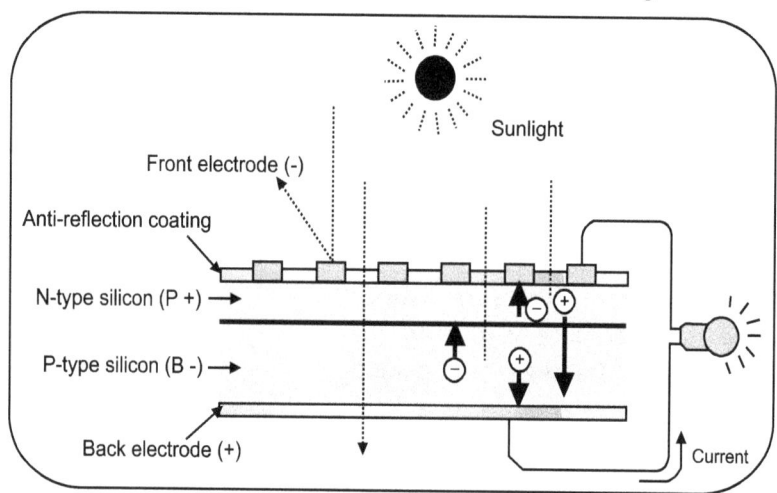

Fig. 7.8

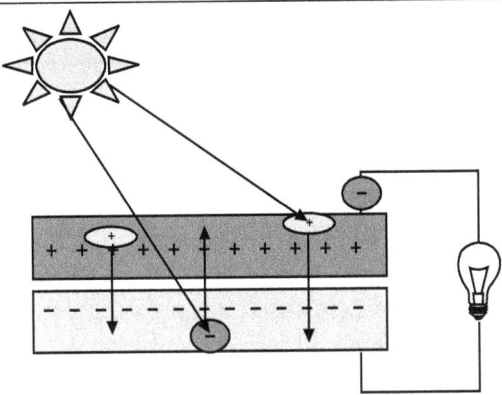

Fig. 7.9

7.4.5 Analog and Digital Transducer

Analog transducer: Analog transducer converts the input quantity into an analog output which is continuous function of time. Analog transducers converts input signal into output signal, which is a continuous function of time such as THERMOSTAT, strain gauge, LVDT, thermocouple etc.

Digital Transducer : Digital transducers produce an electrical output in the form of pulses. Output may be in discrete steps. Digital transducers converts input signal into the output signal in the form of pulses e.g. it gives discrete output. These transducers are becoming popular due to advantages associated with digital measuring instruments. Also digital signals can be transmitted over a long distance without causing much distortion due to amplitude variation and phase shift.

7.4.6 Primary and Secondary Transducers

Primary Transducer : When the input signal is directly sensed by the transducers and physical phenomenon is converted into the electrical form directly then such a transducer is called the primary transducer. For example, thermistor used for the measurement of temperature fall I this category. The thermistor senses the temperature directly and causes the change in resistor with the change in temperature.

Secondary Transducers : When the input signal is sensed first by sensor and its output being of other form than input signal then it is given as input to a transducer for conversion into electrical form, them such as transducer falls in the category of secondary transducers. For example, in case of pressure measurement, bourdon tube is a primary sensor which converts pressure first into displacement, and then the displacement is converted into an output voltage by an LVDT. In this case LVDT is a secondary transducer.

7.5 PRESSURE MEASUREMENT

Pressure is the action of one force against another force. Pressure is force applied to, or distributed over, a surface. Everyday pressure measurements, such as for tire pressure, are usually made relative to ambient air pressure. In other cases measurements are made relative to a vacuum or to some other specific reference. When distinguishing between these zero references, the following terms are used :

Absolute Pressure : It is zero-referenced against a perfect vacuum, so it is equal to gauge pressure plus atmospheric pressure. Zero absolute represents total lack of pressure.

Gauge Pressure : It is zero-referenced against ambient air pressure, so it is equal to absolute pressure minus atmospheric pressure. Negative signs are usually omitted. To distinguish a negative pressure, the value may be appended with the word "vacuum" or the gauge may be labeled a "vacuum gauge".

Differential pressure is the difference in pressure between two points.

Vacuum :

Pressure below atmospheric.

Static and Dynamic Pressure : Static pressure is uniform in all directions, pressure measurements are independent of direction in an static fluid. Flow applies additional pressure on surfaces perpendicular to the flow direction, while having little impact on surfaces parallel to the flow direction. This directional component of pressure in a moving fluid is called dynamic pressure. An instrument facing the flow direction, measures the sum of the static and dynamic pressures. This measurement is called the total pressure. Since dynamic pressure is referenced to static pressure; it is a differential pressure.

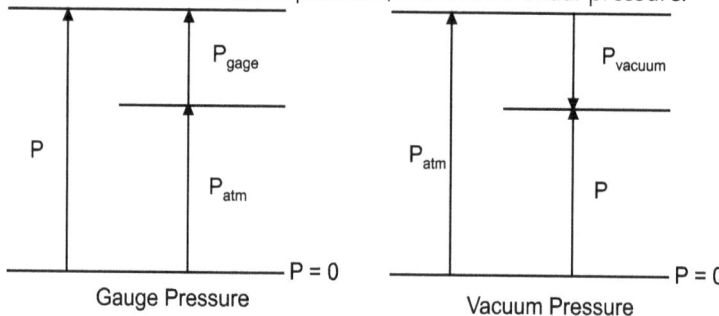

Fig. 7.10

Atmospheric Pressure :

The pressure exerted by the earth's atmosphere. Atmospheric pressure at sea level is 14.696 psia. The value of atmospheric pressure decreases with increasing altitude.

Barometric Pressure : Same as atmospheric pressure.

$$P = F/A$$

Hydrostatic Pressure :

The pressure below a liquid surface exerted by the liquid above.

Line Pressure :

Force per unit area exerted on a surface by a fluid flowing parallel to a pipe wall.

Working Pressure :

Same as line pressure

The SI unit for pressure is the pascal (Pa), equal to one newton per square metre (Nm^{-2} or $kg\ m^{-1}\ s^{-2}$). This special name for the unit was added in 1971.

7.6 U-TUBE MANOMETER

Technically a manometer is any device used to measure pressure. However, the word manometer is commonly used to mean a pressure sensor which detects pressure change by means of liquid in a tube. Manometers are differential pressure sensors. A differential pressure sensor measures the difference between a pressure being applied to it and a reference pressure (often atmospheric pressure).

U-tube manometer :

The U-tube manometer consists of a clear glass or plastic tube shaped into the form of a 'U'. The tube is partially filled with a liquid, such as water, alcohol, or mercury. For safety reasons mercury is no longer commonly used. The diagram shows a basic U-tube manometer. Both ends of the tube are open, and atmospheric pressure acts equally on the liquid through each end. Therefore, the height of the liquid on each side of the U (in each limb) is equal.

In Fig. 7.12 U-tube manometer with an unknown pressure $P_{unknown}$ applied to one limb. The other limb of the tube is left as it was, that is, atmospheric pressure P_{atm} is maintained at its open end. The unknown pressure acts on the liquid in the tube, forcing it down the limb. Because the liquid is incompressible, it rises up the other limb. Hence, the height of the liquid on either side of the tube is no longer equal. The difference between the heights of the liquid in each limb, 'h' is proportional to the difference between the unknown pressure and atmospheric pressure. In a U-tube manometer, the difference between the unknown pressure and atmospheric pressure is the gauge pressure. In a U-tube manometer,

$$P_{gauge} = P_{unknown} - P_{atm} = \rho g h$$

where,

ρ is the density of the liquid in the tube($kg\ m^{-3}$)

h is difference between the heights of the liquid in each limb(m)

g is the acceleration due to gravity,

If atmospheric pressure is known, then $P_{unknown}$ is given as,

$$P_{unknown} = P_{atm} + \rho g h$$

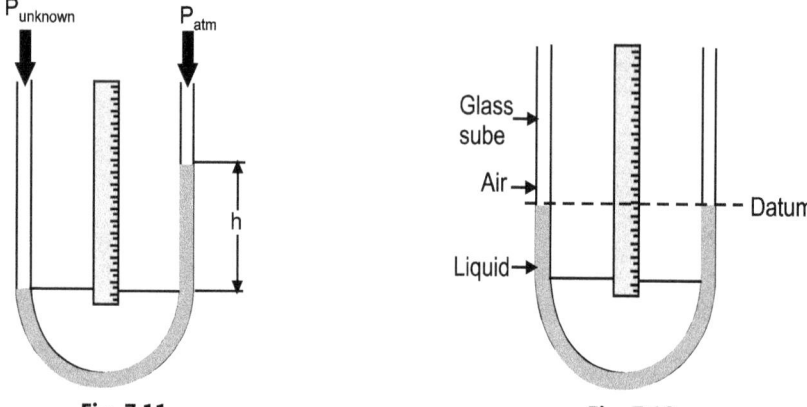

Fig. 7.11   Fig. 7.12

The U-tube manometer is not in wide use in industry, it is sometimes used to calibrate other instruments. It is mainly used in laboratories for experimental work and demonstration purposes. It can be used to measure the pressure of flowing liquids as well as gases, but cannot be used remotely. If pressures fluctuate rapidly its response may be poor and reading will be difficult.

7.6.1 Inclined Tube Manometer

The inclined tube manometer is a differential pressure sensor more sensitive than the U-tube manometer. Hence it is more suitable for use with smaller pressure measurements or where greater accuracy is required. One limb of the inclined tube manometer forms into a reservoir. The other limb of the manometer is inclined at a known angle "θ". The inclined limb is made from a transparent material such as glass or plastic. The reservoir is usually made of plastic, but need not be transparent. The surface area of the fluid in the reservoir A_1 is much larger than the surface area of the fluid in the inclined limb A_2. Both limbs are open ended and so subject to atmospheric pressure. If an unknown pressure $P_{unknown}$ is applied to the reservoir limb, the change in height h_1 will be relatively small compared to the change in height in the inclined limb h_2.

The gauge pressure is given by the equation

$$P_{gauge} = P_{unknown} - P_{atm} = \rho g d (A_2/A_1 + \sin\theta)$$

where,

r is the density of the liquid in the tube(kg m$^{-3)}$
g is the acceleration due to gravity, (9.81 ms$^{-2)}$
d is the distance the liquid has moved along the inclined limb (m)
A_2 is the cross-sectional area of the reservoir (m^2)
A_1 is the cross-sectional area of the liquid in the inclined limb
θ is the angle of the inclined limb from the horizontal.

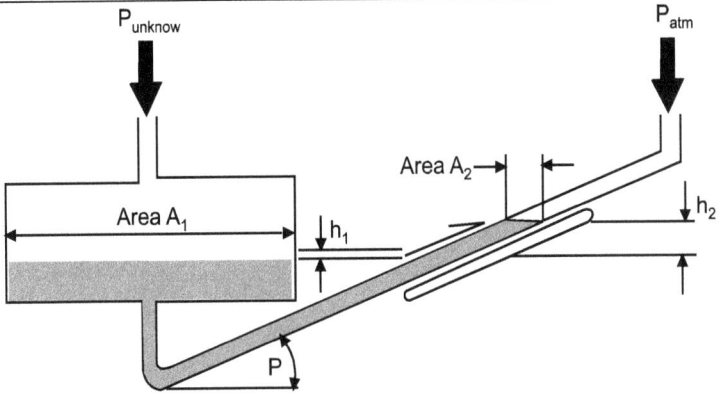

Fig. 7.13

$$P_{gauge} = P_{unknown} - P_{atm} = \rho g d \sin\theta$$

If we know the atmospheric pressure, or can accept the errors which occur using the standard value, then we can find $P_{unknown}$ by rearranging the equation,

$$P_{unknown} = P_{atm} + \rho g d \sin\theta$$

7.7 BOURDON TUBE PRESSURE GAUGE

The Bourdon tube pressure gauge, is the most popular pressure sensor named after Eugene Bourdon. The Bourdon tube pressure gauge consists of a Bourdon tube connected to a pointer. The pointer moves over a calibrated scale. When pressure is applied, the movement of the tube is fairly small, so to increase the movement of the pointer it is mechanically amplified. This is usually by a connecting mechanism consisting of a lever, quadrant and pinion arrangement. The Bourdon pressure gauge uses the principle that a flattened tube tends to straighten or regain its circular form in cross-section when pressurized.

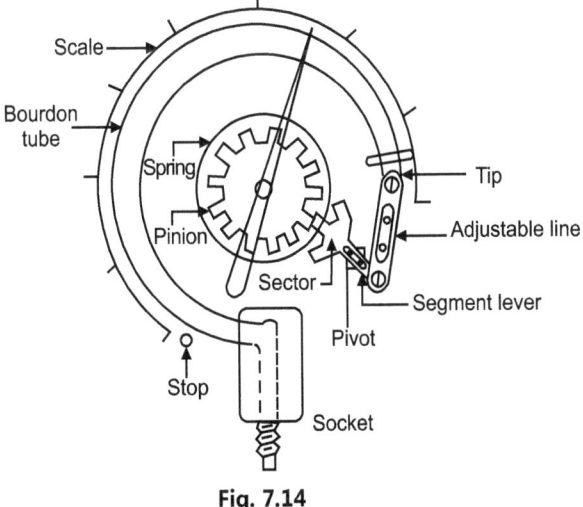

Fig. 7.14

Although this change in cross-section may be hardly noticeable, and thus involving moderate stresses within the elastic range of easily workable materials, the strain of the material of the tube is magnified by forming the tube into a C-shape or even a helix, such that the entire tube tends to straighten out or uncoil, elastically, as it is pressurized. Basic Bourdon tubes are made from metal alloys such as stainless steel or brass. They consist of a tube of elliptical or oval cross-section, sealed at one end. Various shapes of Bourdon tube include helical, spiral and twisted. A common design is the C-shape, is shown in Fig 7.14. Here the tube is at atmospheric pressure. When increased pressure is applied to the open end, it deflects outwards in proportion to the pressure inside the tube where the outside of the tube remains at atmospheric pressure. As the pressure is decreased, the tube starts to return to its atmospheric pressure position. The amount by which the tube moves in relation to the pressure applied to it depends on factors including its material, shape, thickness, and length.

7.8 BELLOWS

Bellows are differential pressure sensing devices mainly used in low pressure ranges of about 0 to 1000 pascals. The bellows are made of a thin copper alloy tube pressed into a corrugated shape. This is sealed at one end, with a small hole at the other end. When pressure is applied via the hole, the bellows expand a distance d. This displacement can be calibrated in terms of pressure.

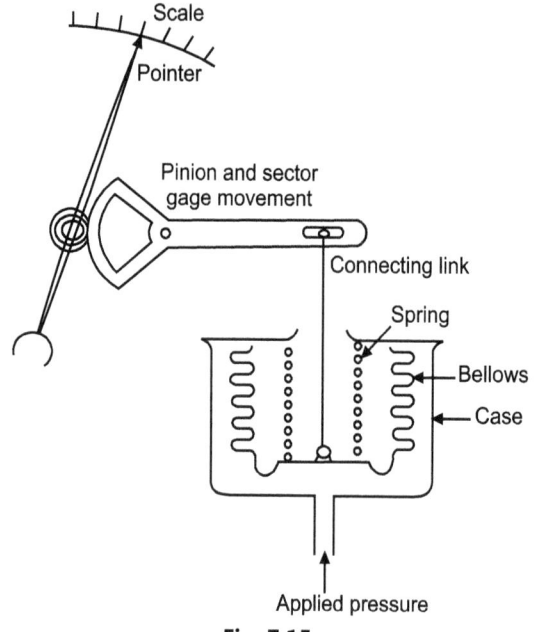

Fig. 7.15

The pressure applied to the bellows $P_{unknown}$ is given by the equation $P_{unknown} = (d/A) \lambda$.
where,

d is the distance moved by the bellows in m

A is the cross sectional area of the bellows in m²

λ is the stiffness of the bellows in Nm⁻¹

Elastic element used in pressure transducers takes the form of a bellows.

In one arrangement, pressure is applied to one side of a bellows, and the resulting deflection is partly counterbalanced by a spring. In other differential arrangement, one pressure is applied to the inside of one scaled bellows while the other pressure is led to the inside of another sealed bellows. By suitable linkages, the pressure difference is indicated by a pointer.

7.9 PRESSURE SENSOR TYPES

There are a variety of pressure sensor designs due to different measurement conditions, ranges, and materials used in construction of the sensor. Common pressure sensor types are bridge-based, amplified, and piezoelectric sensors. Pressure is measured by converting the physical phenomenon to an intermediate form, such as displacement, which can be measured by a transducer.

1. **Bridge-Based Sensors:** Wheatstone bridge or strain-based transducers are a common way of measuring displacement. Bridge sensors are used for high and low pressure applications, and can measure absolute, gauge, or differential pressure. Bridge-based sensors use a strain gauge to detect the deformity of a diaphragm subjected to the applied pressure Sensors using this type of design fulfill a variety of requirements such as accuracy, size, cost, and ruggedness.

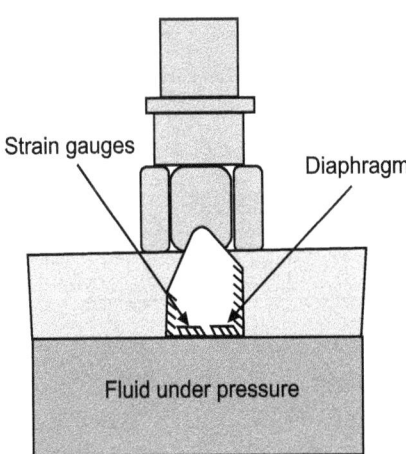

Fig. 7.16 : Cross Section of a Typical Bridge-Based Pressure Sensor

A change in pressure causes the diaphragm to deflect, corresponding to a resistance change of the strain gauge which can be measured by a conditioned DAQ system. Foil strain gauges can be bonded directly to a diaphragm or bonded to an element that is connected mechanically to the diaphragm. Silicon strain gauges are also used.

2. Capacitive Pressure Sensors :

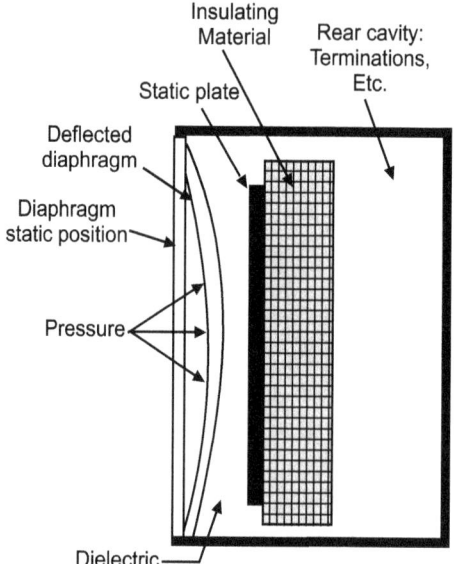

Fig. 7.17 : Capacitance Pressure Transducer

A variable capacitance pressure transducer measures the change in capacitance between a metal diaphragm and a fixed metal plate. The capacitance between two metals plates changes if the distance between these two plates changes due to applied pressure.

3. Piezoelectric Pressure Sensors :

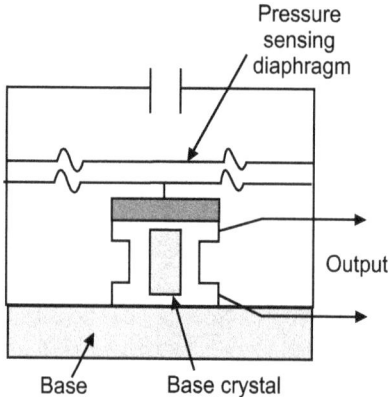

Fig. 7.18 : Piezoelectric Pressure Transducer

Piezoelectric pressure sensors do not require an external excitation source and are very rugged. The sensors require charge amplification circuitry and are very susceptible to shock and vibration. Piezoelectric sensors rely on quartz crystals rather than a resistive bridge transducer. Electrodes transfer charge from the crystals to an amplifier built into the sensor. These crystals generate an electrical charge when they are subjected to strain.

4. Amplified Pressure Sensors :

Sensors that include amplifiers are referred to as amplified sensors. These types of sensors may be constructed using bridge-based, capacitive, or piezoelectric transducers. In the case of a bridge-based amplified sensor, the unit itself provides resistors and amplification necessary to measure the pressure directly with a DAQ device. While excitation will be provided but the accuracy of the excitation is less important.

7.10 LOW PRESSURE MEASUREMENT

To measure very low gas pressures approaching vacuum, many instruments have been developed. These instruments are called as vacuum gauge. A convenient unit for expressing such as low pressure is a column of mercury 1 µm in height and is simply called a micron. Instruments used for measuring pressures as low as 10^{-7} micron are thermocouple vacuum gauge, Pirani gauge, Mcleod gauge etc.

7.10.1 Pirani gauge

Q. Explain with neat sketch Pirani-Gauge for low pressure measurements.

The "Pirani gauge" is a robust thermal conductivity gauge used for the measurement of the pressures in vacuum systems. It was invented in 1906 by Marcello Pirani.

Structure

Pirani gauge consists of a metal filament usually platinum suspended in a tube which is connected to the system whose vacuum is to be measured. Connection is usually made either by a round glass joint or flanged metal connector, sealed with an 'O' ring. The filament is connected to an electrical circuit from which, after calibration, a pressure reading can be taken.

Principle of Operation

The Pirani gauge head is based around a heated wire placed in a vacuum system, the electrical resistance of the wire being proportional to its temperature. At atmospheric pressure, gas molecules collide with the wire and remove heat energy from it. As gas molecules are removed there are less molecules and hence less collisions. Fewer collisions mean that less heat is removed from the wire and so it heats up. As it heats up, its electrical resistance increases. A simple block diagram shown below utilizing the wire detects the change in resistance and once calibrated it can directly correlate the relationship between pressure and resistance. This effect works in pressure range of approximate 0.5 torr to

10^{-4} torr. The electrical resistance of wire varies with its temperature, so the resistance indicates the temperature of wire. In many systems, the wire is maintained at a constant resistance R by controlling the current through the wire. The resistance can be set using a bridge circuit. The power delivered to the wire is I^2R, and the same power is transferred to the gas. The current required to achieve this balance is therefore a measure of the vacuum.

7.10.2 McLeod Gauge

Q. Describe low pressure measurement by McLeod gauge.
Q. Explain measurement of pressure using McLeod gauge.
Q. Explain with neat sketch, the working of McLeod Gauge for vacuum measurement.

Mcleod gauge is a modification of monometer that can measure absolute pressure of gases quite accurately and is used to calibrate other gauges.

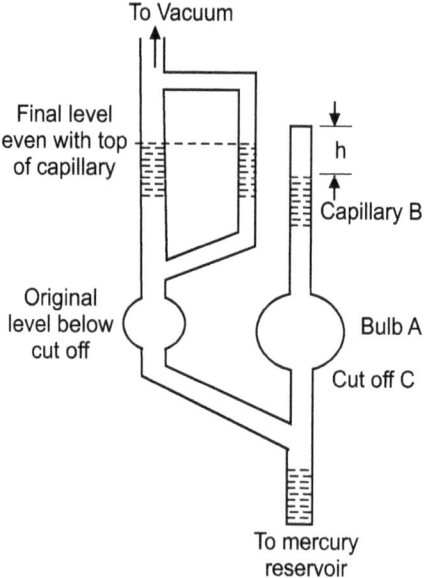

Fig. 7.19 : McLeod gauge

As shown in Fig. 7.19 above it traps a fixed volume of gas from the vacuum and then compresses its volume, raising the pressure to a point where it can be easily read. Mcleod gauge measures pressure intermittently rather than continuously.

A vacuum is established with the mercury level at original level as shown in figure 7.19. To measure the pressure, the mercury level is raised trapping a volume V_o of gas at the vacuum pressure P_v. The volume V_o is the combined volume of the bulb 'A' and the capillary 'B'. The mercury is then raised until the level in the tube connected to vacuum and equal to the top of the sealed capillary indicated by dashed line. The compressed gas trapped in the capillary is at a high pressure and keeps the mercury at a lower level. The height difference between two final mercury levels is 'h' and cross sectional area of capillary is A.

$\therefore$ Final volume = $V_f = hA$

By Boyle's law

Final pressure $P_f = P_o \left(\dfrac{V_o}{V_f} \right)$

Assuming vacuum is at low pressure, $P_f - P_v \approx P_f = h$ torr.

$$P_v = \left(\dfrac{A}{V_o} \right) h^2$$

Disadvantages :
1. At higher pressures in the capillary some vapors present in the system may be condensed leading to an incorrect reading.
2. The gauge is bulky and breakable and contains mercury which is hazardous material.
3. It is not a continuous reading gauge and it involves considerable operator intervention to make reading.

UNIVERSITY QUESTIONS

Dec. 2010

Q.1 What are different selection factors for selecting transducers ? (4 Marks)

Q.2 Explain Pirani gauge for measurement of low pressure. Also state advantages and disadvantages. (6 Marks)

Q.3 What are the advantages of electric transducer? (8 Marks)

Q.4 Explain different characteristics of transducer. (6 Marks)

May 2011

Q.5 State advantages of electrical transducers over other types of transducers. (8 Marks)

Q.6 State difference between active and passive transducer. (2 Marks)

Q.7 Explain with neat sketch Pirani-Gauge for low pressure measurements. (7 Marks)

Dec. 2011

Q.8 Describe low pressure measurement by McLeod gauge. (8 Marks)

Q.9 Explain vacuum pressure. (2 Marks)

Q.10 Explain pressure capacitance transducer with a neat diagram. Write advantages and disadvantages of capacitive transducer. (8 Marks)

May 2010

Q.11 Explain with neat sketch, the working of McLeod Gauge for vacuum measurement. (6 Marks)

Q.12 With suitable diagram, explain how capacitive transducers are used to measure pressure. (6 Marks)

Q.13 Explain the working of Pirani Gauge for measurement of pressure. State its limitations. (6 Marks)

Dec. 2012

Q.14 Explain measurement of pressure using McLeod gauge. (8 Marks)

Q.15 Give detailed classification of transducers. (6 Marks)

Q.16 Explain vacuum pressure. (2 Marks)

UNIT VI

Chapter 8

LEVEL & DISPLACEMENT MEASUREMENT

(A) LEVEL *MEASUREMENT*

8.1 INTRODUCTION

Measurement of level is defined as "determination of position of an existing surface interface between two media". These media are usually fluids, but they may be solids or a combination of solid and a fluid. The interface can exist between a liquid and its vapour, two liquids or a granular or fluidized solid and gas.

Units of level : mm, cm, m, inches, feet.

8.2 METHODS OF LEVEL MEASUREMENT

Two methods used to measure level :

(1) **Direct or Mechanical Method:** Direct level measurement is simple, almost straight forward and economical. It uses direct measurement of the distance which is usually height from the datum line and used for local indication.

(2) **Indirect or Inferential Method :** Indirect or inferred methods of level measurement depend on the material having a physical property which can be measured and related to level. Many physical electrical properties have been used for this purpose and are well suited to produce proportional output signals for remote transmission.

1. **Mechanical Methods for Level Measurement :**

    (a) **Dipsticks and lead lines :** This is the simple and cheap device used for liquid measurement. It consists of metal bar on which scale is marked. Such a metal bar is positioned properly in a vessel containing liquid. Limitation of this device is the inability to successfully and conveniently measure level values in pressurized vessels. Flexible lines fitted with end weights called chains or lead lines have been used

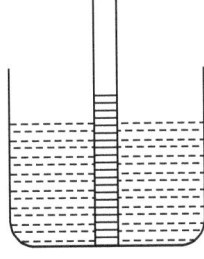

Fig. 8.1

for centuries by seafaring men to gauge the depth of water under the ships.

(b) Sight Glass Method : This method also called as level glass. In this method, a graduated glass tube is mounted near the tank containing liquid. It provides a continuous visual indication of liquid level in a process vessel or a small tank and are more convenient than dip stick, dip rod and manual gauging tapes. This method is not useful if the liquid in the tank is at high temperature which changes the density of liquid. Glass elements can also get dirty and are susceptible to breakage.

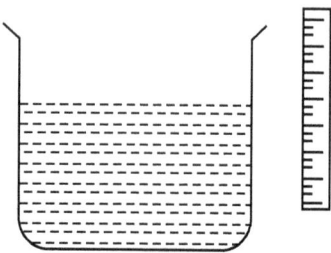

Fig. 8.2

(c) Chain or Float Gauge : Float type instrument uses the principle of a buoyant element that floats on the surface of liquid and changes position as the liquid level varies. Many methods have been used to give an indication of level from a float position with most common being a float and cable arrangement. Fig. 8.3 shows a float and cable diagram. The float is connected to weight through pulley. The floats used may be of cylindrical, disc or spherical shape. Hollow metallic spherical float or cylindrical or disc shaped ceramic floats are used. Nickel plated copper floats can also be used. Due to buoyant force, the float rests on the surface of a liquid. The counter weight attached to the float attached keeps the tape under tension and takes up slack when float rises.

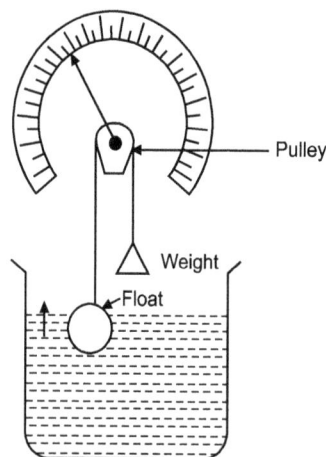

Fig. 8.3

Two types of the floats used for level measurement are :

(i) **Constant displacement type float :** The float is partially submerged in the liquid. When it moves up and down, the distance is same as the actual level change in the liquid. Position of float directly indicates the level.

(ii) **Variable displacement type float :** The weight of the displace is always kept greater than that of the liquid displaced at full immersion of it. The vertical displacement is restricted here. It is most suitable for the measurement of small level changes.

(d) Indirect Methods or Inferential Method : These methods of level measurement depend on the material having a physical property which can be measured and related to level. Many physical and electrical properties have been used for this purpose and are well suited to produce proportional output signals for remote transmission. These methods include :

- **Buoyancy :** The force produced by a submerged body which is equal to the weight of the fluid it displaces.
- **Hydrostatic Head :** The force or weight produced by the height of the liquid.
- **Weight :** The force due to weight can be related very closely to level when its density is constant.
- **Resistance :** Pressure of the measured material squeezes two narrowly separated conductor together, reducing overall circuit resistance in an amount proportional to level.
- **Radiation :** The material measured absorbs radiated energy. As in the capacitance method, vapour space above the measured material also has an absorbing characteristic, but the difference in absorption between two is great enough that the measurement can be related quite accurately to measured material.
- **Capacitance :** The material to be measured serves as a variable dielectric between two fixed capacitor plates. In reality, there are two substances which form the dielectric the material whose measurement is desired and vapour space above it. The total dielectric value change as the amount of one material increases while other decreases.
- **Conductance :** At desired points of level detection, the material to be measured conducts electricity between two fixed probe locations or between a probe vessel wall.

8.3 HYDROSTATIC PRESSURE METHOD OF LEVEL MEASUREMENT

Oldest and simplest method of level measurement is called the air bubbler, air purge or dip tube. Fig. 8.4 shows air bubblers.

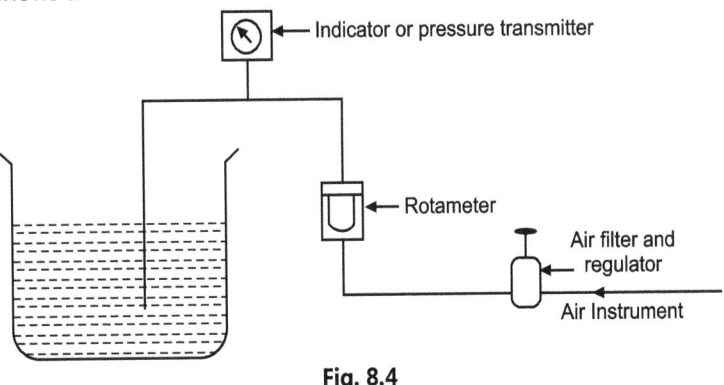

Fig. 8.4

With the supply air blocked, the water level in the tube will be equal to the tank. When air pressure is increased from the regulator till the water in the tube is displaced by air. Air pressure in the tube is equal to the hydrostatic head of the liquid in the tube. The pressure set in the regulator must overcome the liquid head and bubble up through the measured liquid. This will be indicated by a continuous flow, which contributes to the formation of bubbles rising to the level of the liquid in the tank.

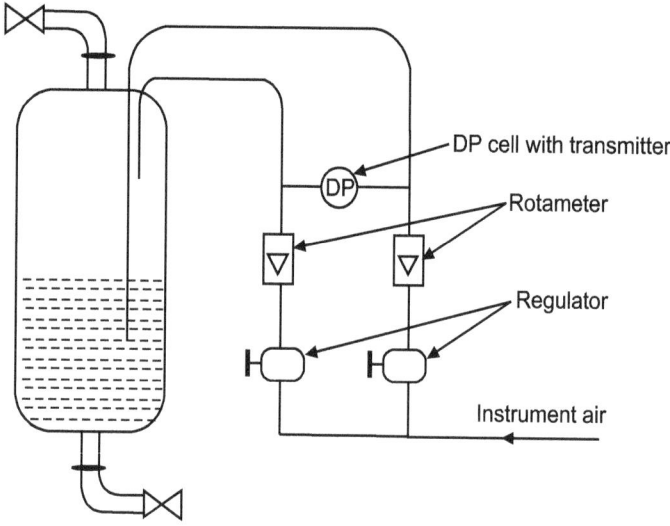

Fig. 8.5

It is simple to visually inspect the tank for the presence of the bubbles. An air flow indicator will usually be installed in the air line running into the tank. Rotameter is used for this. Maintaining a flow through the tube lies in the fact that the liquid in the tube must be displaced by air and back pressure on the air line provides the measurement which is related to level. The level is measured by an indicator or DP cells. Readout is from local or remote place. When transmission distance is greater than 20 m then differential pressure transmitters are usually used to transmit standard signals to remote locations.

For the closed tank application, the following bubbler system can be used. Two dips are installed with the shorter one dipped for maximum level of liquid to be measured and a longer dip has its tip at minimum level. Instrument air which is usually adjusted to 4 bar, is supplied to the system at both dips. DP cell transmitter is placed to sense and measure level and produce a proportional signal according to the level.

Advantages of Bubbler System :
- Measuring instrument can be mounted at any location and elevation with respect to tank.
- It is useful for level measuring applications.
- Accuracy of bubbler system is as good. Its accuracy is independent on the constancy of the density of the material whose level is measured.

8.4 ULTRASONIC TYPE DETECTOR OR ULTRASONIC METHOD OF LEVEL MEASUREMENT

Q. Write note on Ultrasonic Type Detector? [May 11, 12]

Q. Explain Ultrasonic Method of level measurement? [Dec. 12]

Frequency range of ultrasonic instruments is around 20 kHz and that of sonic level instruments is around 10 kHz and below. Sonic electronic level measurement is based on a sound wave emission source i.e. transmitter and reflection of a sound wave pulse. Measurement of the transit time of this pulse provides a means for level detection and measurement. The equipment includes a transmitter that sends a sound pulse to the surface from the transducer, a receiver that amplifies the returning pulse and a time interval counter that measures the time elapsing between transmission of a pulse and receipt of the corresponding pulse echo. Echo pulses are reflected back from the surface of the liquid. Sonic or ultrasonic devices are used in level measuring applications where contact of the measuring instrument with the liquid in process is not desirable. This level measurement method measure the distance from one point in the vessel, which is reference point to the level interface with another liquid.

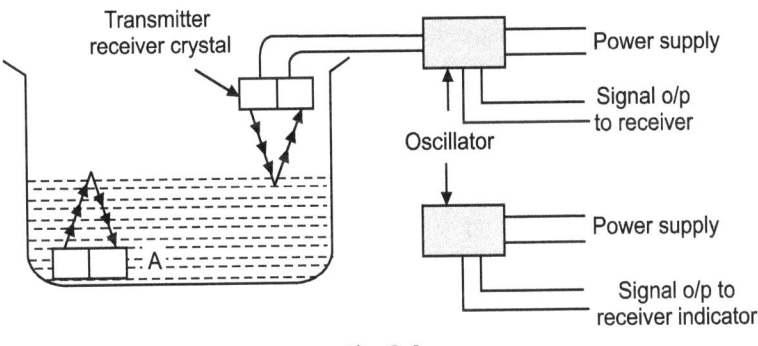

Fig. 8.6

8.5 ELECTRICAL METHODS FOR LIQUID LEVEL MEASUREMENT

Following are the methods for liquid level measurements.
1. Resistive method.
2. Inductive method.
3. Capacitive method.

8.5.1 Resistive Method for Liquid Level Measurement

Fig. 8.7 shows measurement of level of liquid by resistive method. This method uses mercury as a conductor. Numbers of contact rods are placed at various liquid levels. Ammeter is calibrated to read 'h'. As the head level increases, it shorts successive resistors 'F' and increases the value of 'h'. Resistance type level detectors use the electrical relationship between resistance and current flow to accurately measure level. Upper end of the resistance strip is connected to a low voltage power supply.

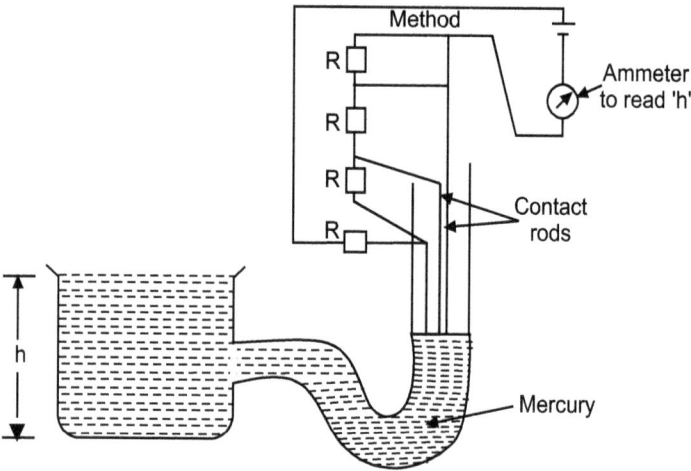

Fig. 8.7

The uniform separation on the resistance windings and known resistance per unit length is useful to determine the height of the interface. This is accomplished by measuring changes in current flow resulting from changes in circuit resistance. Resistance type level detectors require little maintenance. These devices can be used for liquid gas interfaces and for slurries or solids.

8.5.2 Inductive method for liquid level measurement

Fig. 8.8 (a) shows the measurement of liquid level with a variable permeability method. Fig. 8.8 (b) shows liquid level determination by loading of secondary winding.

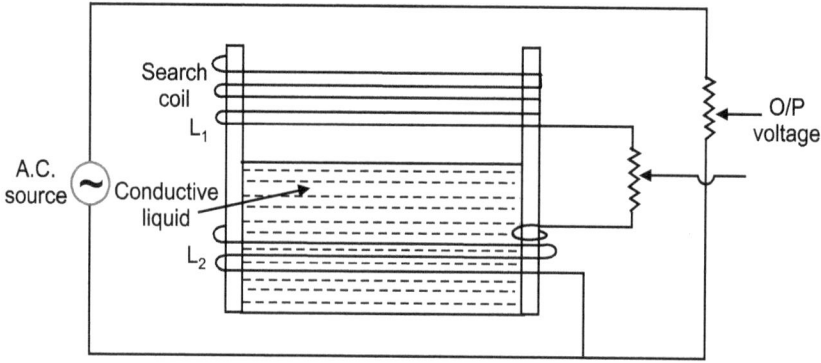

Fig. 8.8 (a)

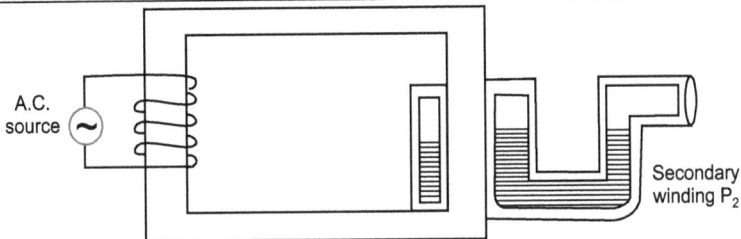

Fig. 8.8 (b)

Fig. 8.8 (a) consists of two coils L_1 and L_2 wound around a steel tube containing liquid. Coils are connected in series through a resistance and circuit is excited using A.C. excitation. L_1 coil acts as search coil. Inductance of each coil is initially equal. The inductance of search coil changes rapidly when the level of liquid increases in the plane of search coil as the permeability of medium changes. This method works properly as the tape material is weakly magnetic and liquid metal is a conductor which allows eddy currents to flow in it. Output voltage varies non linearly with the liquid level.

Fig. 8.8 (b) shows the level measurement using loading of secondary winding of a transformer. This method gives good results for conductive material like mercury. Primary coil is wound on a two limbed iron core transformer. Secondary winding has mercury column surrounding iron core. Resistance of secondary winding changes depending on level of mercury. Hence power consumption is indicative of the level of liquid. This method is based on variable permeability method. It is mainly used for the measurement of level of conductive liquids

8.5.3 Capacitive Method for Liquid Level Measurement

Q. Explain Capacitive method for liquid measurement?

This method has three types :
1. Variable dielectric constant method
2. Capacitive voltage divider method
3. Variable area method

1. **Variable dielectric constant method :** This method is best suitable for the measurement of liquid level of non conducting liquids. Fig. 8.9 shows the arrangement of measurement of liquid level using capacitive transducers. When the liquid is non conductive the electrode and tank wall forms the parallel plate capacitor and the insulation between them acts like a dielectric. Capacitance is proportional to the height of the liquid. More the height then value of capacitance is more and vice-versa.

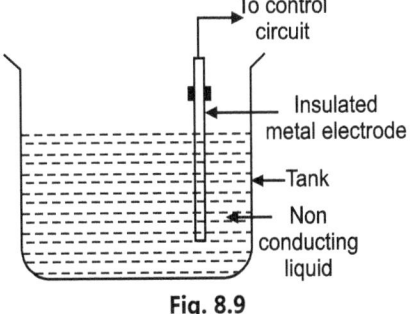

Fig. 8.9

2. **Variable area method :** This method is applicable for measurement of both solids and liquids. Electrical conducting tank containing material is one point of transducer and the metal rod covered by insulating material is another point of transducer. Insulating material acts like a dielectric medium. Capacitance of the capacitor is directly proportional to height of the material.

$$C = \frac{2\pi \varepsilon h}{\log_e \left(\frac{d_2}{d_1}\right)}$$

where,
d_2 = External diameter of insulator.
d_1 = Diameter of metal rod.
h = Height of material.

Advantages of capacitive level measurement :
- Reliable
- Relatively inexpensive
- Contains no moving parts
- Rugged in construction.
- Simple to use
- Easy to install and can be adapted easily for different size of vessels

Applications :

Capacitance level probes are used for measuring level of :
- Liquids
- Powered and granular solids
- Very high pressure industrial processes
- Corrosive materials like hydrofluoric acid

8.6 NUCLEONIC METHOD OF LEVEL MEASUREMENT

Q. Explain the Nucleonic method for level measurement with suitable diagram.   [May 11]
Q. Write note on Nucleonic method for level measurement ?   [May 12]

Nucleonic (Radiation) level measurement device generally consists of a radioactive source on one side of the tank and a suitable detector on the other. As the radiation passes through the tank, its intensity varies with the amount of material in the tank and can be related to level. It has advantage over other methods as nothing comes in contact with liquid. But it is very costly and difficulties are associated with radioactive materials. Radioactive techniques do have the ability to solve difficult level measuring problems.

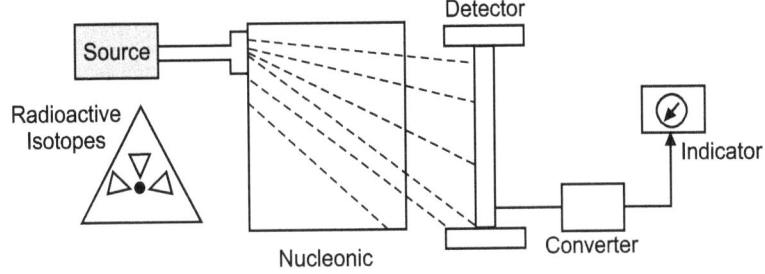

Fig. 8.10

The basic principle used in this measurement method is the absorption of beta or gamma rays varies with the amount of thickness of liquid between source and detector and hence is a function of liquid level. Commonly used radioactive sources are strontium 90 and cobalt 60 for beta and gamma radiations. As the components, source and detector are not in contact with liquid inside the tank, the measurement is not affected due to high and low temperatures or pressures or corrosion.

(B) DISPLACEMENT MEASUREMENT

8.7 INTRODUCTION

Displacement measurement can be of different types. The displacement may be in the range of few μm to few cm. Moreover, the measurement may be of contact type or noncontact type. Besides the measurement principles can be classified into two categories: electrical sensing and optical sensing. In electrical sensing, passive electrical sensors are used variation of either inductance or capacitance with displacement is measured. On the other hand the optical method mainly works on the principle of intensity variation of light with distance. Interferometric technique is also used for measurement of very small displacement in order of nanometers. But this technique is more suitable for laboratory purpose, not very useful for industrial applications.

8.8 POTENTIOMETER

Potentiometers are simplest type of displacement sensors. They can be used for linear as well as angular displacement measurement, as shown in Fig. 8.11. They are the resistive type of transducers and the output voltage is proportional to the displacement and is given by :

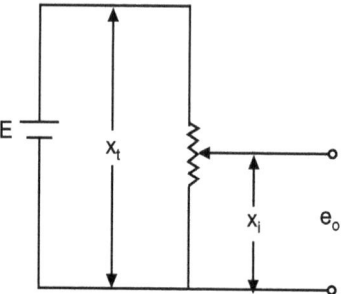

Fig. 8.11 : Potentiometer – Linear

$$e_o = \frac{x_i}{x_t} E,$$

where,

x_i is the input displacement, x_t is the total displacement and E is the supply voltage.

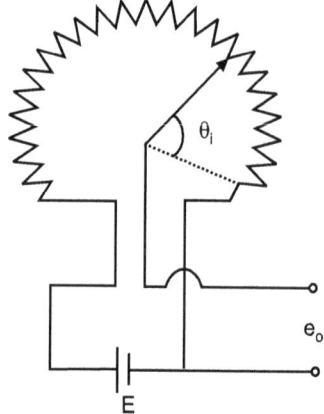

Fig. 8.12 : Potentiometer – Rotary

The major problem with potentiometers is the contact problem resulting out of wear and tear between the moving and the fixed parts. As a result, though simple, application of potentiometers is limited.

8.9 LINEAR VARIABLE DIFFERENTIAL TRANSFORMER (LVDT)

Q. Explain construction and working of LVDT with neat diagram. [Dec. 10, 11]

LVDT works on the principle of variation of mutual inductance. It is one of the most popular types of displacement sensor. It has good linearity over a wide range of displacement.

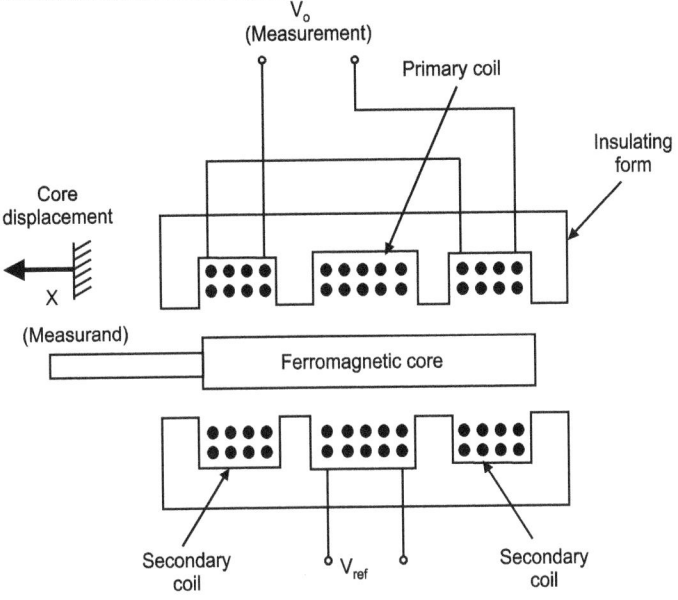

Fig. 8.13 (a) : Construction of LVDT

Due to the low inertia of the core; the LVDT has a good dynamic characteristic and can be used for time varying displacement measurement range. The construction and principle of operation of LVDT can be explained with Fig. 8.13 (a) and Fig. 8.13 (b). It works on the principle of variation of the mutual inductance between two coils with displacement. It consists of a primary winding and two identical secondary windings of a transformer, wound over a tubular former, and a ferromagnetic core of annealed nickel-iron alloy moves through the former.

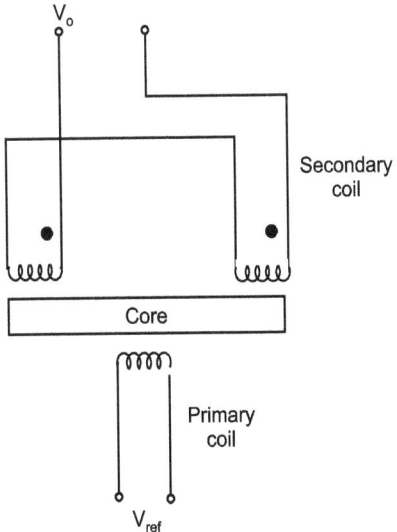

Fig. 8.13 (b) : Series opposition connection secondary windings

The two secondary windings are connected in series opposition, so that the net output voltage is the difference between the two.

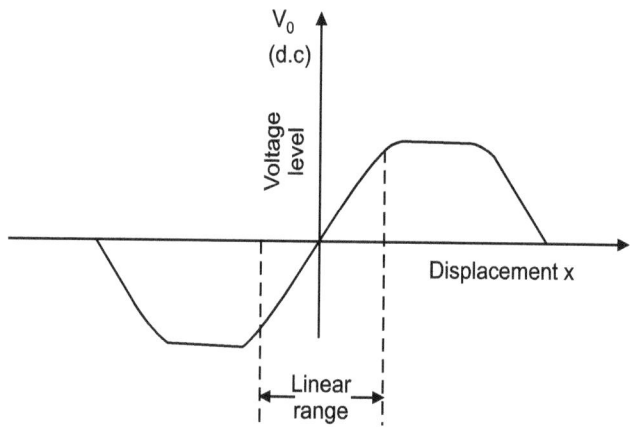

Fig. 8.13 (c) : Output voltage Vs. displacement characteristics of LVDT after phase sensitive detection

The primary winding is excited by 1-10 V r.m.s. A.C. voltage source, the frequency of excitation may be anywhere in the range of 50 Hz to 50 kHz. The output voltage is zero when the core is at central position (voltage induced in both the secondary windings are same, so the difference is zero), but increasing as the core moves away from the central position, in either direction.

Advantages of LVDTs are :
- Cost is less.
- Can operate in variety of environments
- No friction resistance, since the iron core does not contact the transformer coils.
- High signal to noise ratio and low output impedance.
- Displacement resolution is only limited by the resolution of the amplifiers and voltage meters used.
- Short response time, only limited by the inertia of the iron core and the rise time of the amplifiers.
- No permanent damage to the LVDT if measurements exceed the designed range.

8.9.1 Inductive Type Sensors

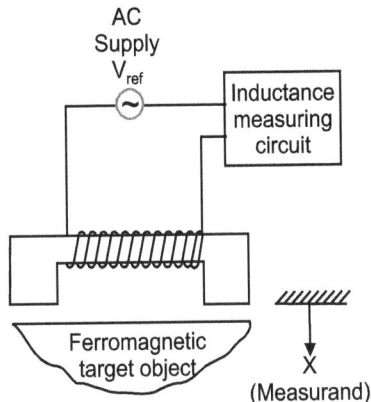

Fig. 8.14 : Schematic diagram of a self inductance type proximity sensor

LVDT works on the principle of variation of mutual inductance. There are inductive sensors for measurement of displacement those are based on the principle of variation of self inductance. These sensors can be used for proximity detection also. Such a typical scheme is shown in Fig. 8.14. In this case the inductance of a coil changes as a ferromagnetic object moves close to the magnetic former, thus change the reluctance of the magnetic path. The measuring circuit is usually an A.C. bridge.

8.10 ROTARY VARIABLE DIFFERENTIAL TRANSFORMER (RVDT)

Q. Describe RVDT ? [May 11]

Its construction is similar to that of LVDT, except the core is designed in such a way that when it rotates the mutual inductance between the primary and each of the secondary coils changes linearly with the angular displacement. Schematic diagram of a typical RVDT is shown in Fig. 8.24.

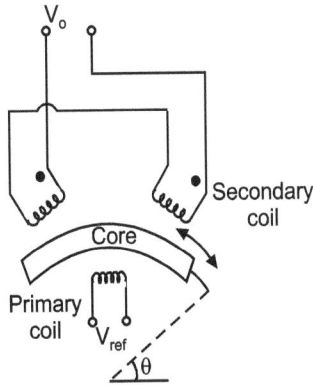

Fig. 8.15 : Rotary variable differential transformer (RVDT)

8.11 CAPACITANCE SENSORS

The capacitance type sensor is available in different size and shape. It can also measure very small displacement in micrometer range. Often the whole sensor is fabricated in a silicon base and is integrated with the processing circuit to form a small chip.

Consider the capacitance formed by two parallel plates separated by a dielectric. The capacitance between the plates is given by:

$$C = \frac{\varepsilon_r \varepsilon_0 A}{d}$$

Where,
- A = area of the plates
- d = separation between the plates
- ε_r = relative permittivity of the dielectric
- ε_0 = absolute permittivity in free space = 8.854×10^{-12} F/m

A capacitance sensor can be formed by either varying (i) the separation between the plates, or, (ii) the area of the plates (iii) the permittivity. A displacement type sensor is normally based on the variable distance and variable area principles, while the variable permittivity principle is used for measurement of humidity, level, etc.

Fig. 8.16 (a) shows a variable distance type sensor, where the gap between the fixed and moving plates changes. On the other hand, the area of overlap between the fixed plate and moving plate changes in Fig. 8.16 (b), maintaining the gap constant. The variable area type sensor gives rise to linear variations of capacitance with the input variable, while a variable separation type sensor follows inverse relationship.

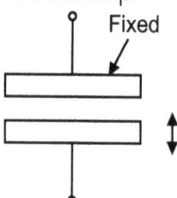

Fig. 8.16 (a) : Capacitive type displacement sensor – Variable separation type

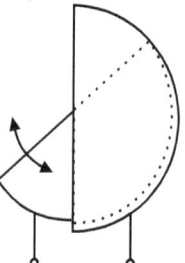

Fig. 8.16 (b) : Capacitive type displacement sensor – Variable area type

Capacitance sensors are used for proximity detection. Such a typical scheme is shown in Fig. 8.16 (b). Capacitive proximity detectors are small in size, non contact type and can detect presence of metallic or insulating objects in the range of approximately 0-5 cm. For detection of insulating objects, the dielectric constant of the insulating object should be much larger than unity. Fig. 8.17 shows the construction of a proximity detector. Its measuring head consists of two electrodes, one circular B and the other annular shaped one A; separated by a small dielectrical spacing. When the target comes in the closed vicinity of the sensor head, the capacitance between the plates A and B would change, which can be measured by comparing with a fixed reference capacitor. The measuring circuits for capacitance sensors are normally capacitive bridge type. The variation of capacitance in a capacitance type sensor is generally very small. These small changes in capacitor, in presence of large stray capacitance existing in different parts of the circuit are difficult. The output voltage is noisy, unless the sensor is designed and shielded carefully, the measuring circuit should be capable of reducing the effects of stray fields.

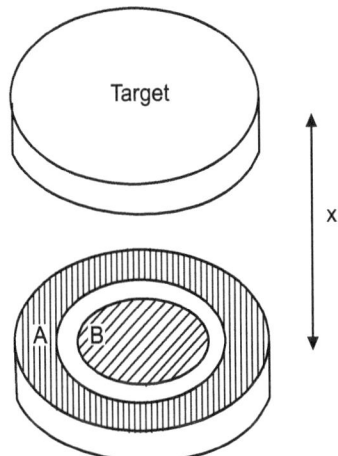

Fig. 8.17 : Capacitance proximity detector

8.12 RESISTIVE TRANSDUCERS

The resistance of a device is given by $R = \rho L / a$ where ρ is the resistivity, and L and a are the length and area of the conductor. Changes in resistance can be made by changing the length, area or resistivity. The strain gauge is based upon changing the dimensions of the resistor, while the thermistor and photoconductive transducer rely on changing the concentration of charge carriers. Resistive transducers are those transducers in which the resistance change due to the change in some physical phenomenon. The resistance of a metal conductor is expressed by a simple equation $R = \rho L/A$

Where,

- R = resistance of conductor in Ω
- L = length of conductor in m
- A = cross sectional area of conductor in m^2
- ρ = resistivity of conductor material in Ω-m

There are four types of resistive transducers :
- Potentiometers (POT)
- Strain gauge
- Thermistors
- Resistance thermometer

8.13 STRAIN

Q. Explain Strain?

Strain is the amount of deformation of a body due to an applied force. Strain (ε) is defined as the fractional change in length, as shown in Fig. 8.18.

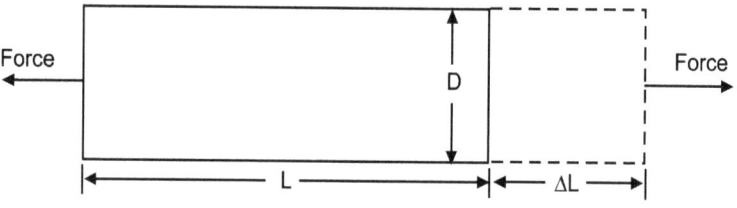

Fig. 8.18

Strain can be positive or negative. While dimensionless, strain is sometimes expressed in units such as in/in or mm/mm. In practice, the magnitude of measured strain is very small. Strain is often expressed as microstrain ($\mu\varepsilon$), which is $\varepsilon \times 10^{-6}$. When a bar is strained with a uniaxial force, a phenomenon known as Poisson Strain causes the girth of the bar, D, to contract in the transverse, or perpendicular, direction. The magnitude of this transverse contraction is a material property indicated by its Poisson's Ratio. The Poisson's Ratio v of a material is defined as the negative ratio of the strain in the transverse direction to the strain in the axial direction (parallel to the force), or $v = -\varepsilon T/\varepsilon$. Poisson's Ratio for steel, for example, ranges from 0.25 to 0.3.

8.14 THE STRAIN GAUGE

There are several methods of measuring strain, the most common is with a strain gauge, a device whose electrical resistance varies in proportion to the amount of strain in the device. The most widely used gauge is the bonded metallic strain gauge.

Bonded Metallic Strain Gauge : The metallic strain gauge consists of a very fine wire or, metallic foil arranged in a grid pattern. The grid pattern maximizes the amount of metallic wire or foil subject to strain in the parallel direction Fig. 8.28. The cross sectional area of the grid is minimized to reduce the effect of shear strain and Poisson Strain. The grid is bonded to a thin backing, called the carrier, which is attached directly to the test specimen. The strain experienced by the test specimen is transferred directly to the strain gauge, which responds with a linear change in electrical resistance. Strain gauges are available commercially with nominal resistance values from 30 to 3000 Ω, with 120, 350, and 1000 Ω being the most common values.

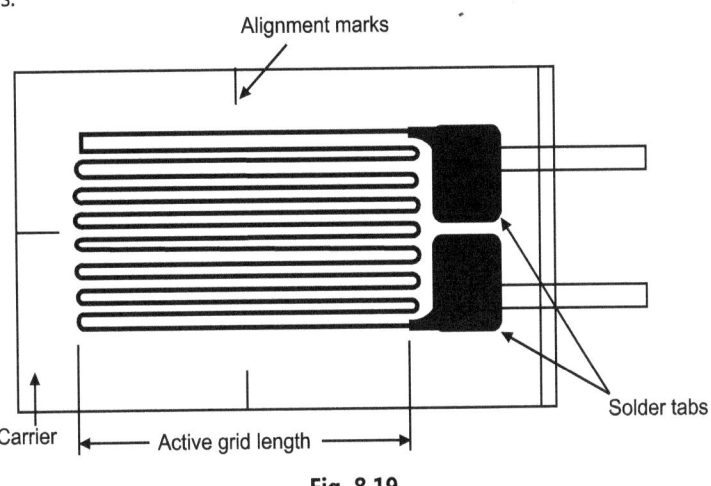

Fig. 8.19

8.15 GAUGE FACTOR

Q. State and explain Gauge factor?
Q. Derive the expression for Gauge factor?

A fundamental parameter of the strain gauge is its sensitivity to strain, expressed quantitatively as the gauge factor (GF). Gauge factor is defined as the ratio of fractional change in electrical resistance to the fractional change in length (strain):

$$GF = \frac{\Delta R/R}{\Delta L/L} = \frac{\Delta R/R}{\varepsilon}$$

The Gauge Factor for metallic strain gauges is typically around 2. The resistance of the strain gauge to change only in response to applied strain. Strain gauge material and the specimen material to which the gauge is applied, will respond to changes in temperature. Strain gauge manufacturers attempt to minimize sensitivity to temperature by processing the gauge material to compensate for the thermal expansion of the specimen material for which the gauge is intended. While compensated gauges reduce the thermal sensitivity, they do not totally remove it. For example, consider a gauge compensated for aluminium that has a temperature coefficient of 23 ppm/°C. With a nominal resistance of 1000 Ω, GF = 2, the equivalent strain error is still 11.5 με/°C. Therefore, additional temperature compensation is important.

8.16 DERIVATION OF GAUGE FACTOR

Gauge factor is defined as the unit change in resistance per unit change in length.
It is given as :

$$S = \frac{\Delta R/R}{\Delta L/L}$$

S = Gauge factor or sensitivity
R = Gauge wire resistance
ΔR = Change in wire resistance
L = Length of the gauge wire in unstressed condition
ΔR = Change in length in stressed condition

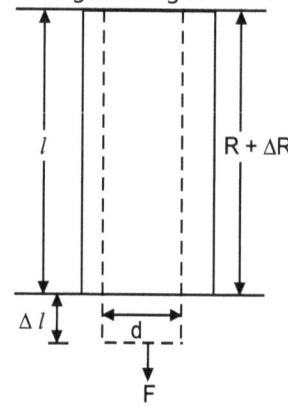

Fig. 8.20 : Deformed resistance wire

Fig. 8.20 shows deformed resistance wire. Let the resistance wire is under tensile stress and it is deformed by ΔL.

where
- L = Length of wire in m.
- A = Cross section area of wire in m².
- ρ = Specific resistance of wire in Ω-m.

When uniform stress is applied to this wire along the length, Resistance 'R' changes to (R + ΔR)

$$\sigma = \text{Stress} = \frac{\Delta L}{L}$$

$$\frac{\Delta L}{L} = \text{Per unit change in length.}$$

$\dfrac{\Delta A}{A}$ = Per unit change in area.

$\dfrac{\Delta \rho}{\rho}$ = Per unit change in specific resistance.

$$R = \dfrac{\rho L}{A}$$

$$\dfrac{dR}{d\sigma} = \dfrac{d\left(\dfrac{\rho L}{A}\right)}{d\sigma}$$

$$= \dfrac{\rho}{A}\dfrac{\delta L}{\delta \sigma} - \dfrac{\rho L}{A^2}\dfrac{\delta A}{\delta \sigma} + \dfrac{\delta \rho}{\delta \sigma}$$

$$\dfrac{\delta\left(\dfrac{1}{A}\right)}{\delta \sigma} = \dfrac{-1}{A^2}\dfrac{\delta A}{\delta \sigma}$$

Multiplying both sides by $\dfrac{1}{R}$,

$$\dfrac{1}{R}\dfrac{dR}{d\sigma} = \dfrac{\rho}{RA}\dfrac{\delta L}{\delta \sigma} - \dfrac{1}{R}\dfrac{\rho L}{A^2}\dfrac{\delta A}{\delta \sigma} + \dfrac{1}{RA}\dfrac{\delta \rho}{\delta \sigma}$$

$$\dfrac{1}{R}\dfrac{dR}{d\sigma} = \dfrac{1}{L}\dfrac{\delta L}{\delta \sigma} - \dfrac{1}{A}\dfrac{\delta A}{\delta \sigma} + \dfrac{L}{\rho}\dfrac{\delta \rho}{\delta \sigma}$$

$$\dfrac{dR}{R} = \dfrac{dL}{L} - \dfrac{dA}{A} + \dfrac{\delta \rho}{\rho}$$

$$\therefore \dfrac{\Delta R}{R} = \dfrac{\Delta L}{L} - \dfrac{\Delta A}{A} + \dfrac{\Delta \rho}{\rho} \qquad \ldots (a)$$

For a circular wire,

$$A = \dfrac{\pi}{4}d^2$$

$$\dfrac{\delta A}{\delta S} = \dfrac{\pi}{4}(2d)\dfrac{\delta d}{\delta S}$$

$$\dfrac{1}{A}\dfrac{\delta A}{\delta S} = \dfrac{1}{A}\dfrac{\pi}{4}(2d)\dfrac{\delta d}{\delta S}$$

$$\dfrac{1}{A}\dfrac{\delta A}{\delta S} = \dfrac{1}{d^2}(2d)\dfrac{\delta d}{\delta S}$$

$$\therefore \dfrac{\delta A}{A} = \dfrac{2}{d}\delta d$$

$$\therefore \dfrac{\Delta A}{A} = \dfrac{2\Delta d}{d} \qquad \ldots (b)$$

Poisson's ratio μ is the ratio of strain in lateral direction to strain in the axial direction.

$$\mu = -\frac{\Delta d/d}{\Delta l/l}$$

$$\frac{\Delta d}{d} = -\mu\left(\frac{\Delta l}{l}\right) \quad \ldots(c)$$

$$\therefore \frac{\Delta R}{R} = \frac{\Delta L}{L} - \frac{2\Delta d}{d} + \frac{\Delta \rho}{\rho} \quad \text{[From a, b, c]}$$

$$= \frac{\Delta L}{L} - 2\left(-\mu \frac{\Delta L}{L}\right) + \frac{\Delta \rho}{\rho}$$

$$\therefore \frac{\Delta R}{R} = \frac{\Delta L}{L}[1 + 2\mu] + \frac{\Delta \rho}{\rho} \quad \left[\text{Neglecting } \frac{\Delta \rho}{\rho}\right]$$

$$\frac{\Delta R}{R} = \frac{\Delta L}{L}[1 + 2\mu]$$

$$S = \text{Gauge factor} = \frac{\Delta R/R}{\Delta L/L} = 1 + 2\mu$$

$$\therefore S = 1 + 2\mu + \frac{\Delta \rho/\rho}{\Delta L/L}$$

8.17 TYPES OF STRAIN GAUGE BASED ON MOUNTING

1. **Bonded strain gauge** : A bonded strain gauge element, consisting of a metallic wire, etched foil, vacuum deposited film or semiconductor bar is connected to the strained surface.

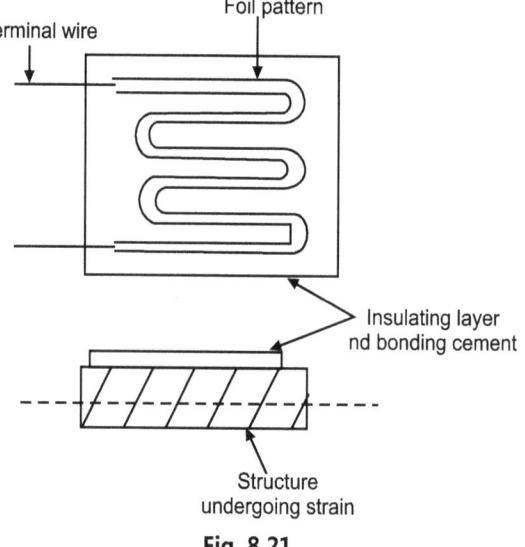

Fig. 8.21

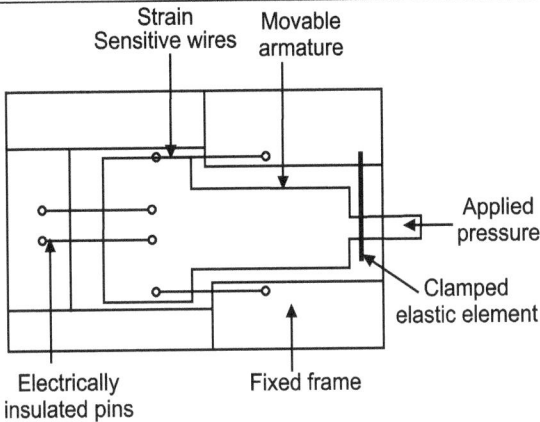

Fig. 8.22

2. **Unbonded strain gauge :** The unbonded strain gauge consists of a wire stretched between two points in an insulating medium such as air. One end of the wire is fixed and the other end is attached to a movable element. Armature can move in one direction only. It travel in the direction is limited by four filaments of strain sensitive wires.

8.18 TYPES OF STRAIN GAUGE BASED ON CONSTRUCTION

- **Optical Sensors :** They use interference fringes produced by optical flats to measure strain. They are delicate and operate best under laboratory conditions. They are sensitive and accurate.

- **Photoelectric Gauge :** It uses light beam, two fire gratings and a photocell detector to generate an electric current which is proportional to strain. They are costly and delicate. Their gauge length is as short as 1/16 inch.

- **Semiconductor Strain Gauge :** Basic principle of operation of semiconductor strain gauge is the piezo resistive effect which is the change in value of resistance due to change in resistivity of the semiconductor because of strain applied. Silicon and Germanium are used as resistive material for semiconductor gauges.

    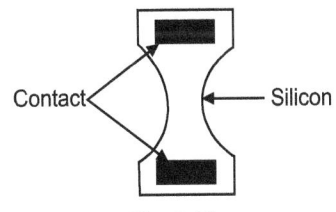

    Fig. 8.23

    They are also called as piezo resistors and are used for the measurements of small strain. The semiconductor bonded strain gauge is a wafer with the resistance element diffused into a substrate of silicon. The bonding of wafer element to the strained surface requires great care as only thin layer of epoxy is used to attach it. The cost is lower than for a metallic foil sensor. Disadvantage of semiconductor strain gauge is that resistance to strain relationship is non linear. The gauge factor is about $130 \pm 10\%$ for a unit of 350 Ω at room temperature. This strain gauge is sensitive to changes in temperature.

- **Diffused Semiconductor Strain Gauge :** This strain gauge uses photolithography masking technique and solid state diffusion of boron to molecularly bond the resistance elements. Electrical leads are directly attached to patter. They have improved in technology as they eliminate the need of bonding agents. They are used as sensing elements in pressure transducers.

Advantages :
- They are small and inexpensive.
- . They are accurate.
- They provide wide pressure range and generate strong output signal.

8.19 TYPES OF STRAIN GAUGES BASED ON PRINCIPLE OF WORKING

Q. Give detail types of strain gauge. Explain foil strain gauge. [May 11, Dec. 12]
Q. Explain foil strain gauge.

1. **Mechanical :** It consists of two separate plastic layers. One layer is glued to one side of the crack and one layer to other. The bottom layer has a ruled scale on it and top layer has a red arrow or pointer. As the crack opens, the layers slide very slowly and the pointer moves over the scale. The red cross hairs move on the scale as the crack widens.

2. **Electrical :** They are thin, rectangular shaped strips of foil with maze like wiring patterns on them. when the material is strained, the foil strip is very slightly bent out of shape and the maze like wires are either pulled apart or pushed together. by changing the width of metal wire its electrical resistance also changes. This change in resistance is proportional to the stress applies. The change in resistance is due to variation in length and cross sectional area of gauge wire.

8.19.1 Effect of Temperature

Resistive strain gauges are sensitive to temperature variation and it becomes necessary to account for variations in strain gauge resistance due to temperature changes. By using dummy gauge in opposite arm of the active gauge compensates the temperature variation.

Depending on the number of gauges used in the bridge, the circuit configurations are :

   (a) Quarter bridge

   (b) Half bridge

   (c) Full bridge

(a) **Quarter bridge :** In quarter bridge, the strain gauge is connected in one arm as shown in Fig. 8.24.

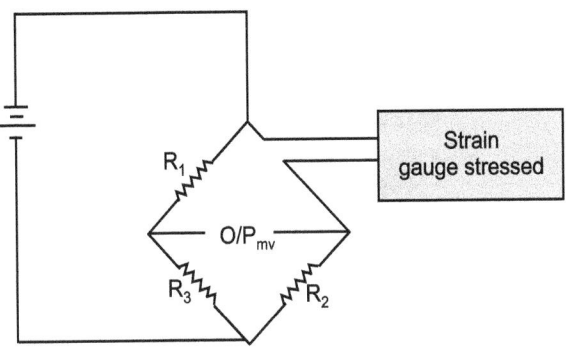

Fig. 8.24 : Quarter bridge

(b) **Half bridge :** Quarter bridge and half bridge circuits provide an output signal that is approximately proportional to applied strain gauge force. Linearity of these bridge circuits is best when the amount of resistance change due to applied force is very small compared to the nominal resistance of the gauge.

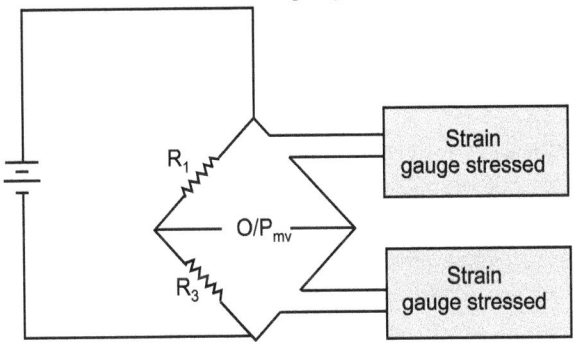

Fig. 8.25 : Half bridge

8.20 FOIL STRAIN-GAUGE

Most strain gages are of foil construction as shown in Fig. 8.26. Fine-wire strain gauges are used for special purposes, such as at high temperatures. Foil strain gages are usually made by a printed-circuit process. Since the foil used in a strain gauge must be very fine or thin to have a sufficiently high electrical resistance between 60 and 350 ohms, it is difficult to handle. For example, the foil used in gauges is often about 0.1 mm in thickness. In order to handle this foil, it must be provided with a carrier medium or backing material, usually a piece of paper, plastic, or epoxy. The backing material performs another very important function in addition to providing ease of handling and simplicity of application.

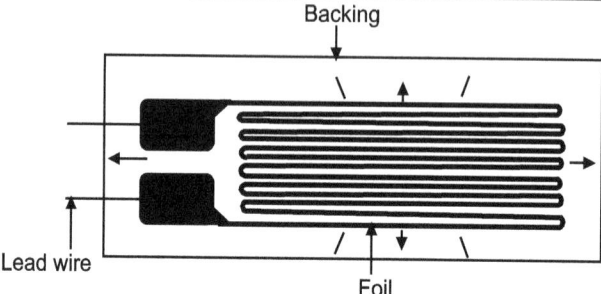

Fig. 8.26 : Foil strain gauge

The cement provides so much lateral resistance to the foil that it can be shortened significantly without buckling; then compressive as well as tensile strains can be measured. Lead wires or connection terminals are often provided on foil gauges, as illustrated in the typical foil gage shown in Fig. 8.26. A protective coating, recommended or supplied by the manufacturer, is usually applied over the strain gage, especially where the lead wires are attached.

8.21 ROSETTE STRAIN GAUGE

Q. Explain Rosette Strain gauge?

A wire strain gauge can effectively measure strain in only one direction. To determine the three independent components of plane strain, three linearly independent strain measures are needed i.e. three strain gauges positioned in a rosette like layout. When the direction of strain is unknown, it is necessary to use a multiple array of gauges which permit the calculation of the direction as well as the magnitude of the two principal strains. Three or four arm rosette gauges are most commonly used.

Consider a strain rosette attached on the surface with an angle 'α' from the X-axis. Suppose that strain measured from these three strain gauges are ε_a, ε_b and ε_c respectively.

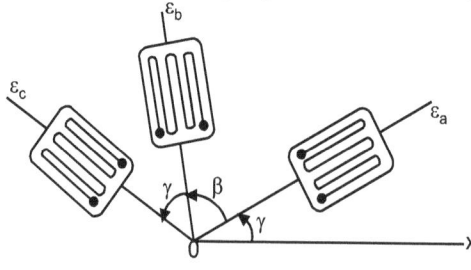

Fig. 8.27

The following coordinate transformation equation is used to convert the longitudinal strain from each strain gauge into strain expressed in X – Y coordinates.

$$\varepsilon_{x'} = \frac{\varepsilon_x + \varepsilon_y}{2} + \frac{\varepsilon_x - \varepsilon_y}{2} \cos 2\theta + \varepsilon_{xy} \sin 2\theta$$

$$\varepsilon_a = \frac{\varepsilon_x + \varepsilon_y}{2} + \frac{\varepsilon_x - \varepsilon_y}{2} \cos 2\alpha + \varepsilon_{xy} \sin 2\alpha$$

$$\varepsilon_b = \frac{\varepsilon_x + \varepsilon_y}{2} + \frac{\varepsilon_x - \varepsilon_y}{2} \cos 2(\alpha + \beta) + \varepsilon_{xy} \sin 2(\alpha + \beta)$$

$$\varepsilon_c = \frac{\varepsilon_x + \varepsilon_y}{2} + \frac{\varepsilon_x - \varepsilon_y}{2} \cos 2(\alpha + \beta + \gamma) + \varepsilon_{xy} \sin 2(\alpha + \beta + r)$$

These equations are then used to solve the three unknowns ε_x, ε_y and ε_{xy}.

Cases of Strain Rosette layout

Case I : 45° strain rosette aligned with the X-Y axis i.e. $\alpha = 0$, $\beta = \gamma = 45°$

$$\varepsilon_x = \varepsilon_a$$

$$\varepsilon_y = \varepsilon_c$$

$$\varepsilon_{xy} = \varepsilon_b - \frac{\varepsilon_a + \varepsilon_c}{2}$$

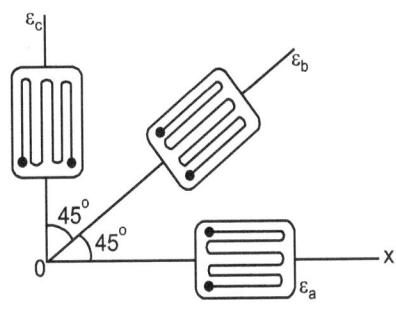

Fig. 8.28

Case 2 : 60° strain rosette, the middle of which is aligned with Y-axis i.e. $\alpha = 30°$, $\beta = r = 60°$

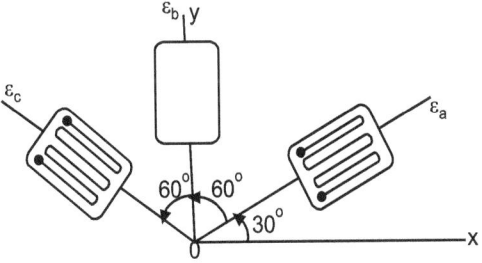

Fig. 8.29

$$\varepsilon_x = \frac{2}{3}\left[\varepsilon_a - \frac{1}{2}\varepsilon_b + \varepsilon_c\right]$$

$$\varepsilon_y = \varepsilon_b$$

$$\varepsilon_{xy} = \frac{1}{\sqrt{3}}[\varepsilon_a - \varepsilon_c]$$

UNIVERSITY QUESTIONS

Dec. 2010

Q.1 Explain construction and working of LVDT with neat diagram. **(8 Marks)**
Q.2 Explain hydraulic method for measurement of level. **(8 Marks)**
Q.3 Explain foil strain gauge. **(8 Marks)**

May 2011

Q.4 Explain construction, working and applications of RVDT. **(8 Marks)**
Q.5 Explain hydraulic method for measurement of level. **(8 Marks)**
Q.6 Explain foil strain gauge. **(8 Marks)**
Q.7 With a neat sketch write a short note on Load Cell. **(8 Marks)**
Q.8 Draw and explain ultrasonic method for level measurement. **(4 Marks)**
Q.9 Define strain. Explain the working principle of an electrical strain gauge. **(4 Marks)**

Dec. 2011

Q.10 Describe displacement measurement by LVDT in detail. **(8 Marks)**
Q.11 Explain level measurement by mechanical method. **(8 Marks)**
Q.12 Explain construction, working and application of load cell with a neat diagram. **(8 Marks)**

May 2012

Q.13 Define ultrasonic transducers. **(2 Marks)**
Q.14 Explain the Nucleonic method for level measurement with suitable diagram. **(6 Marks)**
Q.15 Explain the construction and working of semiconductor strain gauge. **(6 Marks)**
Q.16 State the importance of level measurement. List the different level measurement methods. **(4 Marks)**
Q.17 Explain the construction and working of load cells. **(6 Marks)**

Dec. 2012

Q.18 Define ultrasonic transducers. **(2 Marks)**
Q.19 Explain the construction and working of load cell. **(4 Marks)**
Q.20 Give detail types of strain gauge. Explain foil strain gauge. **(8 Marks)**

Notes

Notes

CPSIA information can be obtained
at www.ICGtesting.com
Printed in the USA
LVHW021317050323
740960LV00005B/431

9 789351 643623